DANGER'S
FATE

A HOLLY DANGER NOVEL:
BOOK SIX

AMANDA CARLSON

DANGER'S FATE
A HOLLY DANGER NOVEL: BOOK SIX

Copyright © 2019 Amanda Carlson, Inc.

ISBN-13: 978-1-795354-26-4
ISBN-10: 1-7953-5426-7

This book is a work of fiction. The characters, events, and places portrayed in this book are products of the author's imagination and are either fictitious or are used fictitiously. Any similarity to real persons, living or dead, is purely coincidental and not intended by the author.

OTHER BOOKS BY AMANDA CARLSON

·HOLLY·

Prologue

"Is anyone out there? We desperately need your help. This is Alaria. Things are about to get dangerous. We're trying, but we can't stop the tide. We're talking full annihilation if the bastard gets his way. People are going to die. Do you hear me? It's a scheduled extermination of our people. Please help us."

"It's been a week since we've heard from her," I said. We were all assembled in the Pleasure Emporium discussing what to do about the SOS that had come in from the Flotilla seven days ago from a girl named Alaria, or Ari as she'd been called. "We can't wait much longer to act, or there's a risk they'll all be dead." We had no idea how many lives were at stake. We'd tried hailing them, but nobody from the Flotilla had answered our calls.

Case stood against the wall, Bender straddled a chair, Lockland perched at the edge of a couch across from me,

1

and Daze and Darby were on the ground, Daze's shoulder pressed against my leg. Knox would've been with us, but he was due back in a few hours from down South, where he'd been facilitating the distribution of the resources we'd uncovered. Tillman's stash had been huge. The LiveBots were almost finished moving the goods from the mag-lev trains to the warehouse. The robots, retail bots programmed to provide cheerful service to customers, had done the work in much less time than any human could've, because sleeping and eating and normal human constraints were nonexistent. Once it was finished, and the inventory was complete, we would continue to transfer items up to the city based on order of importance. Thank goodness we had access to the mover drone. Lockland had set up an exchange with Port Station, allowing them to share in some of our goods while we borrowed their craft. Without it, we wouldn't have been able to haul the larger items, such as the pristine-condition bio-printers, back up to the city.

"Claire doesn't want us to leave unless we have a definitive location," Bender argued. Claire was in Government Square, along with Maisie, figuring out her new role as president. She'd been the over-whelming choice to serve once we'd arrived home and was doing a hell of a job. She'd reopened the Housing Division, was overseeing the Seeker Rehabilitation Program (SRP), which had already saved twenty-nine individuals who'd been infected by Plush, and was working on a new Food Dispensary system, headed by Walt. The improvements to the city were happening quickly, and the population had reacted with energy and enthusiasm. It was the most hope any of us had experienced since our births.

"It makes sense why Claire wants us to stay put," Bender continued, "since none of us have any experience piloting a craft over the sea for an extended period of time. We'd be flying blind, no place to land. It would be a dumbass move to head out without knowing where they are." He gave me an *I told you so* look, and I gave it right back, followed by a *so what?* eyebrow raise.

"Based on data from the militia members down South, who've had contact with the Flotilla in the past," I said, "we should be able to pinpoint a sixty-kilometer range. They're in an area called the Caribbean Colonies. Maisie has a detailed map in her database, and she's already cross-checked a likely location. With the seas rising in the aftermath of the meteor, there's only a few areas that would work as a sheltered spot between two larger islands. We haven't consulted the tech table at the barracks, but Case and I are heading there tomorrow. I think waiting too much longer is a mistake. You heard that girl. People are dying. If we don't act, who knows how many lives will be gone before we arrive?"

Lockland stood and began to pace. "We understand the necessity of acting quickly and so does Claire. But she's right. It's too dangerous to go in without knowing what lies ahead. The ocean is unpredictable. If something goes wrong with the craft, you're stranded out there." *Stranded* was another word for *dead*, because if we ended up in the sea, we weren't making a comeback.

"We have Maisie," I countered. "Tillman's X class dronecraft"—which I'd commandeered as my own and had rechristened Tilly in a bout of morbid irony—"is loaded with tech. The dash has a visual flight recorder and a superb distance radar. That, coupled with Maisie's NeuDAR and lidar, and we have very little to worry about. If we run into trouble, we can turn around and fly back. Tilly's top speed is almost four hundred kilometers per hour, almost twice as fast as Luce."

"We give it one more week," Lockland stated firmly. Before I could protest, he lifted a hand. "Complete as much research as you can, consult the maps, talk to the militia folks again, and get back to us. I give you my word you can move by then, even if we don't hear from the Flotilla. One week."

"By *us*, I assume you're referring to you and Claire, right?" I got to my feet, settling my hands on my hips. Claire had pretty much installed Lockland as her second-in-command without officially announcing it. It was a good choice, but it was beginning to interfere with our group dynamic. "I shouldn't have to remind you, but this group and the government are *separate* entities. We work on our own. I'm all for involving them when needed, and I love Claire like a mother, but what we decide to do here isn't up to them. It's up to us." I made a sweeping gesture to encompass everyone in the room. "*We* make the decisions about this mission, not the government." I left out several expletives hovering on the tip of my tongue, because I was becoming polite like that. Not that Lockland really deserved the courtesy.

"Things have changed." There was a hint of weariness in his voice. "Now that Claire's in charge, and we're all playing a prominent role in the restructuring of the city, we have a larger body to contend with."

I began to shake my head slowly, my expression set, hands still gripping my sides. At the moment, they were keeping me rooted so I wouldn't walk up to Lockland and swing my foot around like I wanted to.

Case pushed off the wall, sensing the crisis that was quickly taking shape. "We have time. We don't have to decide anything yet." His eyes flashed to mine. "Waiting a week is doable. We can handle it. More research needs to be done. We can't fly in blind."

I was about to tell Lockland exactly where he could put his one-man vote, ignoring Case's reasonable counter, when Daze scrambled up from his position next to me. "Can I go, too?" he pleaded, grabbing on to the bottom of my vest. "Maisie showed me pictures of the habitats. They look like spaceships with a big bubble on top and another bubble on the bottom." He mimicked the shape of a globe with his hands. Maisie had shown us varying styles of aquatic farming that were popular right before the meteor struck, as well as illustrations of how our ancestors had achieved space travel. The two had been remarkably similar. Although we had no idea what Case and Daze's grandfather, Martin Bancroft, aka Brock Shannon, had actually planned when he'd acquired a ten-thousand-hectare aquatic-farming community, we had a pretty good idea.

The main globelike structure was made of thick plexi and was watertight and buoyant, designed to flex while partially submerged. A segmented walkway encircled the exterior, floating outward in three pieces like ripples on a pond. Each path was two meters wide, containing a half-meter gap that allowed for the farming of seaweed. Outside the last ring sat enough docking stations for twelve homes, referred to as aquatic tenements located at sea, or atlases. These smaller spheres were designed to be either single-family or multifamily. The entire thing, biosphere plus the atlases, was referred to as a habitat or a farm. Together, they formed a functioning, self-sufficient microcosm.

I smiled at Daze, momentarily forgetting my irritation with Lockland. "You can't come on the first run," I told him. "Everything's unknown, which makes it too dangerous. But once things stabilize, we'll send for the rest of you."

"You're not scared of danger, though," Daze said. "Because it's your name."

I chuckled, settling a cool gaze on Lockland. "It is my name, but that doesn't mean I'm not scared. Helping Ari and her people is the right thing to do."

Bender grunted, knowing what was coming next. He rose from his chair, relocating it with a loud scrape. "One week," he announced, throwing in his vote. "Whatever Holly finds, we go with it." He'd directed his words at Lockland. We all knew falling into step with our government was an iron-soaked slope, one that we were going to have to navigate whether we liked it or not.

Lockland seemed as if he was going to say something, but changed his mind. Instead, he bowed his head. "One week."

·ARI·

Chapter 1

"Help! Help me!" a familiar voice cried from inside a small room in the only working biosphere they had left.

Alaria Bancroft didn't hesitate to raise her foot and smash it through the flimsy barrier. The door bounced open, the latch completely destroyed. "Don't move," she ordered the intruder, who had the barrel of his weapon pressed against the farmer's chest. He wore an aged militia uniform, more tan than its original brown. Uncertainty flashed over his face, even though she knew her father had given him explicit orders to destroy everything of value, including the precious few UV lights still in operation. Ari moved forward, sensing the militia guard's unease, using it in her favor as she raised her Blaster and leveled it at his face, where it would hurt the most. "Step back and let him go."

Her Blaster was technically a baby Blaster, almost too small to fit in her hand. It did nothing but spray a few pieces of whatever scrap metal she could find, but she'd gotten good at aiming it at sensitive places.

This biosphere, even at half capacity, with most of its vegetation wilting and dying, was their only chance of continued survival. She'd be damned if she'd let her unhinged, paranoid father destroy it like he'd been methodically doing with everything else over the past few months.

"Ari, *please*," the guard pleaded. "I'm here on your father's orders. I have to do what he says." The militiaman's name was Claude. He was no more than five or so years older than Ari's nineteen. They'd known each other their entire lives.

A large wave rolled beneath the sphere, bobbing it up a good meter. Ari's feet were planted firmly apart, legs stable. Instability couldn't be an issue if you wanted to survive here. "I was ordered to dismantle the UV and bring you with me," Claude said. "None of us want to hurt you. Just cooperate. If you stay here, you'll die."

"I'm well aware of my father's plans," Ari replied crisply. "It's not going to happen, Claude. I'm not leaving, and you're not shutting down this bio. It's our only food supply." It didn't surprise Ari that her father had sent his men after them. Marty Bancroft Jr. had always been a hard, unyielding man, skirting the very edge of sanity. But recently something had caused him to crack, exposing even more madness. In his desperation to get back to the place he referred to as the dark city, he'd become even more of a despot—an overlord hell-bent on achieving his mission at the cost of innocent lives. He had to be stopped. "Put down your weapon and step away from the farmer. If you don't, you're going to pay the consequences, and it's going to hurt."

Claude's hand shook almost imperceptibly. "I can't." His voice held weariness. "I'm not alone. Others arrived with me. If we fail, your father will just send more of us."

"How far did you travel to get here?" Ari had disconnected the farms last week from New Eden, the floating city, thinking they'd finally be free from her father's psychopathic reach. But she'd been wrong. This group of guards was the third to reach them by hydro-skis in the space of six days. "Answer me."

"I'm…I'm not sure," he stammered, his fist quaking now. Feeling bad for him was not an option. "Once you blew up the connections, your father pulled anchor. We're all drifting now."

Ari should've felt surprise that her father had done such an insane thing, but she didn't. Even though he'd grown more erratic recently, he'd always been unstable. By pulling anchor, something that had never been done before, he'd placed everyone in New Eden at risk. And for what? To punish her for disobeying him? They were both beyond that. "Sheer stupidity," she muttered. Claude appeared confused, but Ari didn't take the time to explain. "The guards who accompanied you are gone.

You're the only one left." She wasn't going to inform Claude that three out of the five escaped, likely racing back to tattle to her father that she'd foiled his plans again. "They found their fate beneath the waves." Around here, the sea swallowed everyone eventually. "Drop your weapon and step back. I'm not going to tell you again. You can either join us, or we can toss you over. It's up to you, Claude."

"Please, Ari, don't make me do this—" His hand wobbled, and before he could harm an innocent man, she fired her Blaster. Small pieces of shrapnel exploded outward, spraying into his neck. He tumbled to his knees, his weapon dropping as he gasped.

She holstered her gun, yelling, "Clear!" She hadn't allowed anyone to join her inside. Jake rushed in first, followed by two others. She nodded at the bleeding guard, who used to swap jokes with her during training sessions. "He'll probably survive. See what you can do. Take him to the holding unit on Atlas Three. There's a small medi-unit there."

They'd imprisoned nine guards already. Time would tell if they would join the resistance, but Ari was in no rush to kill anyone. The loss of life that had occurred already made her sick to her stomach. A needless waste.

"Three is almost full," Celia said, her taser aimed at the guard, who was fighting for breath.

"I know," Ari replied. "It's the best we can do until we can figure out another holding place. We can't co-opt another atlas. People need them to live in." When

Ari was a child, the farm chain had been vast, twenty habitats strong, each equipped with a dozen atlases, two hundred and forty in total. People had thrived. Now they were whittled down to four biospheres, only one that was semiworking, and thirty-one atlases. Not nearly enough space for the number of farmers still trying to survive out here.

Celia nodded, yanking Claude up, another resister grabbing his other arm. They hauled him out.

Once they left, the old farmer took a step forward. "Thank you, my dear." William's voice shook with both age and fear. "I couldn't let him get to the lights. They're all we have left. I was prepared to sacrifice myself for the greater good." He clutched a harvesting apron. They were rarely needed these days, as there wasn't much collecting to do.

Ari patted his shoulder. "You did the right thing, William. It was very brave of you to try and protect our last resource. We're the ones who are grateful." The farmers had lived a fairly peaceful existence until the past year. They weren't used to conflict, especially the older folks. "We appreciate your willingness to sacrifice yourself. Without those lights, we'd have no chance of making it through the next few weeks." As it was, the water-cleansing systems were also faulty, the salt water poisoning the crops. Disconnecting from New Eden meant they were nowhere near the engineering ship that could help fix the issues.

It was too much to think about. They'd done what they'd had to do.

William shook his head, his thin white hair brushing his shoulders. "We're thankful for you," he said quietly, grasping her hand. "If you hadn't come to our rescue when you did, all would have been lost. We owe you our livelihood."

"You don't owe me anything," Ari replied, guilt welling in its familiar pocket inside her chest. "I'm just one of many trying to get us to safety." Wherever that was.

"It was you who cut us loose and gave us a chance," he continued, surprising her by touching his forehead to her hand. "Your father was rounding us up, ready to sacrifice us to the sea, commandeering our supplies. We have faith in you. We will live to see another day because of what you've done." He straightened and, much to her relief, released her, giving her a small smile, his eyes misting. "We will not forget it."

The hardest decision of Ari's life thus far had been choosing to sever the farm chain from the floating city. In the end, it'd been the only way to save the hundreds of souls who lived there. William was right. Her father had been willing to end their lives. But by making the choice she had, Ari might've very well killed everyone anyway. They barely had enough to survive as it was, and they were drifting into the unstable sea, away from the protected inlet that had been New Eden's home for the last thirty years.

"Go get some sleep, William," she gently coaxed. "We'll find a way clear of this somehow." He shuffled out, leaving her alone with Jake. As she turned to her partner, she noticed the look he was giving her. "Don't start with me. I'm not in the mood." Jake wrapped his big arms around her, and she reluctantly laid her head against his chest. She'd never been able to resist him and likely never would.

"I'm not starting anything," he murmured in a soothing tone. "You have to get some sleep, too. What's it been? Forty-eight hours?" It'd been longer than that, but there was little time to rest when they were trying to save so many. "Come on. Let's head back to the atlas. Everyone is waiting for a report."

Ari nodded, allowing Jake to lead her out of the sphere. The door she'd kicked in wouldn't close again, but thankfully it hadn't been attached to the airlock. They descended three levels to get to the pressurized exit. Without it, the twenty-centimeter plexi shell couldn't maintain the low-pressure atmosphere needed to keep the heat and water vapor at the perfect temp for growing vegetation.

Outside, the drizzle pattered down on their heads and the cold abraded their cheeks. Ari had lost her helmet sometime during the scuffle, but she would likely find it later, unless it'd floated out to sea. She'd lost more than one that way. Her brown hair, which she kept cut above her shoulders for ease, stuck to the sides of her face. She ignored it. The three pedestrian rings encircling the entire habitat had a bumpy, anti-slide coating, along with handrails, to prevent slipping. It worked most of the time, unless there was a serious downpour. Then you had to be extra careful.

As they walked, they passed bobbing atlases at regular intervals, each secured in its appropriate station. The three remaining farms were linked to this one by long, titanium cables. Keeping adequate space between the habitats was necessary so they couldn't crash into each other, causing irreparable damage. They'd lost more than a few that way over the years. The sea was wildly unpredictable, so the spacing minimum was a standard hundred and eighty meters. Their ancestors had likely had access to watercraft, which would've made all their lives easier, but all they had now was fewer than a dozen hydro-skis, which weren't big enough to transport food or supplies and certainly not big enough to ferry so many people to land—wherever that was.

During the day, when the dim light filtered through the clouds, you could see all the farms lined up, bobbing in the sea. They could be connected by a winching system that used to be automatic, but now took strength and manpower to operate. It was done every five days, so the little food they had could be shared.

Jake led Ari across the short, sturdy platform that anchored their atlas to the walkway. It'd been reinforced over the years. They all had. The constant rocking from the waves had weakened just about every structure.

Once they stepped onto their small deck, they had to steel themselves against the churning movement. These homes were smaller and lighter than the biosphere, thus their movement was more volatile in the tumultuous sea. Ari and Jake had a room here, as did three other couples. The living space was housed above the waterline, the bedrooms and shared waste room situated under.

Four eager expressions greeted them. Brandon, the son of a farmer and a farmer himself until a short time ago, stood. He'd made the transition from tending the gardens and fruit trees to helping with the resistance relatively easily, even without the soldier training Ari and Jake had received at her father's insistence. *The elite must be ready for anything.* That had been a common mantra of her father's throughout her life. Ari was grateful to have the knowledge and skills, though the irony of using them against the man who insisted she be trained was not lost on her.

Brandon was tall, lean, intelligent, and capable. Ari had ordered him to stay behind, and he wasn't happy.

"We heard weapons," he accused. "Was the biosphere damaged?"

"I don't think so," Ari said as she took a seat on one of the integrated chairs situated around a large sleek synthetic-resin table. "There were no telltale hisses or rapid condensation, so we're hopeful it's okay." If cracked, the biosphere's atmosphere would fail immediately. Yet another thing to worry about.

"It was too risky to leave us behind," Brandon continued. "We should've gone with you." Lila, his partner, placed her hand on his arm, urging him to sit back down. Brandon was a few years older than Ari and was generally level-headed. But his mother had disappeared last month, and he was understandably on edge. He had no idea if she'd been lost at sea or taken prisoner by Ari's father. Ari hoped it was the latter, since Marty Bancroft Jr. had been incarcerating people for the slightest reasons.

She met Brandon's gaze, unfazed by his emotion. She was bone-tired. "Listen, I understand it was risky. We had no idea how many were out there this time. But I left you guys back for a good reason. If anything happened to us, you're the next in line to oversee this mission. We can't all be everywhere at once. Somebody who knows what's going on has to stay behind. Survival here is complicated—if not becoming impossible. These people are looking to us for order and leadership. Without that, everything would descend into chaos."

Paris angled her head toward Brandon and in her no-nonsense cadence said, "Sit down and get a hold of yourself. Ari's right. Four groups of six is all we have, spread out over four habitats. We don't risk a whole group at any one time. You know the rules. You were here when we made them." Brandon and Lila had grown up on the farms, while Paris and her partner, Hector, had come from the hulls, the massive underbellies of the ships that had brought them here and the lowest possible regions of New Eden. Their upbringings couldn't have been more dissimilar, and it showed. Paris' grittiness gave her an edge. She'd been fighting for everything she'd ever needed since the day she was born.

Slowly, Brandon took his seat.

"Ari and I go first," Jake said. "That's what we agreed on. Nothing has changed." They always went first. Insisted on it. They had the most experience and training. Tonight's backup had been Celia and Russ.

Paris sat back in her chair. "So, what happened?"

Jake stayed standing, arms crossed, feet splayed. He was so like his father, it made Ari's chest tighten. His tone remained formal, the way he'd been taught to give an intelligence report. "Six militia members arrived on two hydro-skis at four this morning. We commandeered one vehicle immediately. Three guards on the other fled under fire. Two were lost to the sea during the altercation. One is in holding. Ari took that guard down in the UV mechanical room, which was being protected by William Sorenson. The guard is likely to survive his injuries and has been taken to Atlas Three."

As Jake spoke, Ari unholstered her old, battered, barely functioning baby Blaster. She got up to refill it while everyone began questioning Jake about the details of the altercation. Operating without a working weapon these days was inadvisable. As she scooped metal scraps out of a jar, one she had stocked in the last few days, she yearned for her specialized gear. Especially the custom laser she'd gotten at sixteen, presented to her in a silver box.

She didn't have access to it, because she'd been stripped of everything when she'd been captured the last time. The look on her father's face as she'd stood in defiance of him, knowing it would be the last time they'd see each other until this battle was over, was seared into her brain, not unlike a laser brand.

He would never forgive her. Not that she wanted forgiveness.

She only wanted survival.

Chapter 2

"You need to get some sleep," Jake murmured softly, his voice singsonging in Ari's ear as he guided her to their bed. They'd returned to their room below sea level after two hours of discussion on the ever-looming question of what to do next. A question that had no real clear answer. Survival was a day-to-day process. Ari had found that out quickly.

The sooner everyone accepted that, the better it would be all around.

It was dark, save for the green haze penetrating the thick plexi wall of their room and the soft glow of their shoulder lights. The water was too murky to discern the submerged outline of the large biosphere sitting ten meters away, or much else, but the light was ever present as long as the UV was running. The atlases gathered solar through their shells, like the biosphere, but depended on the habitat as a whole for everything to run at capacity. Since this farm was the only one generating any electricity, most of the supplemental batteries had been relocated to other atlases, so they could continue to function.

Ari lay back on the bed. "I'm not tired." She was, of course, lying. She was exhausted. But sleep wouldn't come easily. It never did these days.

Jake began to undress, and Ari turned on her side, fascinated despite the ongoing crisis. Being with Jake like this was still new to her. As he peeled off his syn-leather jacket, his shirt, then his pants, she was struck again by how beautiful he was. She tried, but she couldn't think of a day they'd ever been apart. It was unfathomable to think of a world without him. She was lucky she didn't have to. They'd pledged themselves to each other roughly eight months ago, directly following her nineteenth birthday.

It had been a shock to absolutely no one who knew them, and had always been expected, but it still shocked her that they were together. *Together* together. Not just as best friends and lovers, but as a working unit—a team.

Much to their surprise, they'd been forced to go on the run a short time later. Jake had broken her out of the cell her father had put her in and managed to get her to the medi-ship to mend the injuries she'd sustained, and now they were here, drifting to who knew where, preparing to share the same bed.

Jake draped his pants across a small seating unit built into the atlas' polystructure. Their sleeping room was small and efficient, just like the others. It held one integrated bed, a tiny storage unit, and a short row of seating. The rest of the space consisted of a clear, fifteen-centimeter-thick, microfiber-reinforced plexi wall. It had been the strongest plexi available at the time of its construction and contained an integrated microscopic honeycomb matrix invisible to the naked eye, making it extremely hard to crack.

Ari had learned little about her ancestors on land over the past nineteen years, but there were plenty of resources in the floating city about early hydro-farming. Habitats, biospheres, and atlases had changed throughout history, but whoever had commissioned this particular farm had spared no expense. Everything had been reinforced and constructed with the finest materials, meant to last. But after sixty years at sea, things had eventually begun to degrade.

Jake crawled into bed, immediately gathering Ari into his arms, which had become their new normal. Ari was fully dressed, but Jake wouldn't push her any more tonight. As long as she slept, he would be happy. "If our sensors go off again," she murmured, "you're going to have to fight off the militia in your underclothes."

He chuckled, his chest vibrating against her cheek. "I'll take my chances. Plus, it's almost dawn. I think we're safe from any outside influence for at least tonight."

"I hope so." Ari enjoyed his warmth, exhaling a long, tired breath. "Why can't he just let us go? He should be happy we fled New Eden. We could've stayed and created more chaos. Instead, we left." Her father had begun to target the farms. He'd turned his wrath on the habitats suddenly and without any explanation. If Ari hadn't made the decision to disconnect from New Eden, all the lives floating along with them would've been lost.

"He'll never let you go. Not fully anyway," Jake answered.

"I betrayed him in the worst possible way. He made it clear if I didn't repent this time, it would be the last chance I'd ever get. And I spit in his face. After that, he disavowed me, stripped me of everything but the clothes on my back, beat me, and locked me in a cell to rot." When Jake had found her, she'd needed significant time in a medi-pod to heal. It was pure luck Jake had been able to smuggle her onto the medi-ship. "He's not coming to capture me. He's coming to kill me."

Ari knew Jake was no fan of her father's—he'd endured several of his creative punishments over the years. Not even Jake's father, the second-in-command of New Eden, could save his son from that. As children, she and Jake had had many discussions about it, trying to piece together exactly what was happening on the many levels below them, all the way down to the hulls. They'd realized, almost too late, that they'd been indoctrinated from birth into a strict caste system. People who fell below expectations were never given a chance to redeem themselves. Instead, they and their families were trapped and penalized to live out their lives with less. Much less.

The first time Ari had laid eyes on a bottom

dweller, she'd been shocked. Bottom dwellers—those who were forced to live in the hulls, the foundation the city had been built on—survived on next to nothing, scraping for every last morsel. Each tier higher, a person's status increased. Ari's own home had been high in the sky, at the very pinnacle of the city, nothing else above it but clouds and endless precipitation. Ari had had servants to wait on her, pick up provisions, run the errands, and keep everything pristine and tidy. She'd been eight years old before she'd been allowed to leave her sanctuary to traverse the passageways, gripping tightly to her mother's hand.

What she'd seen then had rocked her to her core.

It'd changed Ari, just not fast enough.

Horrified, she'd asked why children, nothing more than walking spirits, were dressed in rags, their skin pale and scabbed over. Later, she'd learned their unhealthy appearance was caused by a severe lack of UV and vital nutrients and vitamins, but she hadn't known that then. Her mother had chastised her for staring, ordering her to avert her eyes, telling her that she was lucky she lived so high above the waterline and that she shouldn't question what had been given to her as her birthright.

Her mother had never been a strong soul, bound to her father by his quaking will and nothing more. The day she died was memorable, as it had been one without rain. Her mother had simply leaped off their balcony, never to be seen again. Ari had been twelve, and by then she'd been well aware that her mother was sick—not like the children in the hulls, purposely deprived of UV and sustenance—but her mind had never been right, and it had deteriorated over the years, damaged beyond repair.

That very day, Ari had begun to question her own life in earnest, and her role in New Eden. It'd taken her another six years to hone her skills, find her voice, and make the necessary break from her father, which had all led to this—drifting in the sea, tethered to a few hundred other lost souls.

If Jake hadn't been holding on to her tightly right this very minute, she would've let herself sink into hopelessness. But Jake never allowed her to lose herself in helplessness, anger, betrayal, or sadness. Because the two of them shared more than a common goal—they shared a life together. He knew her better than anyone, and she him.

"Your father's not in his right mind," Jake said, pulling her closer. "We both know that. He wants revenge, and he's capable of killing you, but I don't think he will. You're his prized possession, whether he likes it or not. You two are bound together."

Ari arched back, refraining from swatting Jake's bare chest. "We're not *bound* anywhere near each other. What a ridiculous thing to say. If he gets a hold of me, he will kill me…eventually." She rested her head back on his shoulder. "He'll do it, because he can't break me. He's tried over the years with no success. It maddens him more than anything else does." Her father had done his best to groom her in his own image, even though it didn't take. In her late teens, he'd begun to take her along on what he called his "decision-making sessions." They'd been nothing more than opportunities to whip and hurt people who had come to ask—*beg*—for his help.

After that, she'd rebelled. And paid dearly for it.

Her father had often taken his hand to her mother, but he had been careful not to harm Ari. Until she'd blatantly disobeyed him. Following her seventeenth birthday, she'd begun sneaking extra supplies into the hulls, freeing innocent prisoners, and encouraging the people to unite to resist every mandate her father presented to them. When he'd found out what she was doing, he'd punished her brutally, leaving her in pain for days, only to seek her apology and then set her free. It'd become a reliable pattern.

Ari had always managed to convince him that she was repentant, promising to change her ways, agreeing to fall into line. All lies. Her greatest skill, up until the last few weeks, had been her ability to manipulate him. She had known, deep within her soul, that someday she would have one final showdown with her father.

That time was now.

Unfortunately, along the way, she'd gravely miscalculated a few key elements. She'd assumed wrongly that the militia members, who'd been directly involved with her upbringing, and the other elite children who'd been educated and spoiled by their status right alongside Ari, would follow her. After all, she'd been next in line to lead the city, hadn't she? But they'd deserted her, looking out for their own interests, fearful of the retribution her father would mete out.

Everyone except for Jake. She hadn't been wrong about him.

"I don't mean you're bound together, like *physically*." He chuckled. "I mean emotionally. Neither of you will rest until this ends, once and for all. Your goal is to save New Eden and everyone in it. His goal is to destroy it. You'll go back for everyone eventually. He knows it." He planted a kiss on the top of her head. "You know, your stubbornness is one of the things I love most about you. It makes you stronger than gale-force winds."

"What a load of crap." She laughed. "My unwillingness to back down is one of the things you can't stand about me. You've said it for years. Admit it."

"Okay, fine, so it's a love-hate thing. I love that you're selfless and will do whatever it takes to get the job done, but I hate that you get hurt for it. Seeing you injured"—he visibly shivered—"makes me want to retch. I can't wait until this is over."

"*Over* is up for interpretation." Ari turned onto her back, settling one hand behind her head and gazing out into the deep, dark unknown. There was nothing for kilometers and kilometers except empty blackness. "*Over* might mean we all die."

"So we die. It's going to happen eventually." He'd uttered the words confidently, but she knew how he really felt, how he worried, how he ached to have a family and a regular life. "I wouldn't change anything we've done so far. Ever since I was a little kid, my father warned me how this could end. He knew it was coming. Knew your father was unstable. There was nothing my dad could do, even though he tried. He figured the sea would take us all, sooner rather than later, like it always does." Sadness lingered. Jake's father had been the head of the militia and Marty Bancroft's second-in-command until two years ago. The speculation was that there'd been some kind of disagreement. Cormic Dalton had been vocal with his differing opinion, something about optimizing resources on the engineering ship, which floated next to New Eden. He'd disappeared, apparently paying the price for his disobedience.

That had become the norm for the floating city. You disagreed with Marty Bancroft, and you disappeared. The ocean greedily took what it was given, never to return it.

"I wish your dad was with us now," Ari said, trying to reciprocate some of the comfort that Jake was so good at giving. "He had a good heart. Maybe if he was still around, he could've rallied the guards, and all this would've gone differently."

"It's hard to know." Jake turned on his side to face her. "He owed everything we had to your father. Our home, his status, the fact he'd even been allowed to come along in the first place. He would've felt the burden of loyalty. It would've been a hard choice for him."

"I agree that it would've been hard, but I think he would've supported protecting the greater good of all the people, not just the elite. There was no love lost between him and my father in the end. If your dad could see us now, I think he'd be pleased." They'd literally gone from high above the hulls, to existing under the sea itself. "He always loved the farms."

"I like it here," Jake murmured. "It feels safe in a way that our homes never did. Yeah, we had more space, more furniture, and nicer sleeping accommodations. But the wind never quit blowing, the rain never stopped pattering down, and even though the atlases rock, it's nothing like at the top of the city. It's more pleasant down here."

"I agree." Ari smiled. "I like it better below the waves, too." The biosphere and atlases weren't foreign to her. Growing up, both she and Jake had visited the farms as much as they could, partaking in a day of refreshing UV, picking fruit, and enjoying themselves overall. But they'd never lived here. Or even considered it.

Elite members of this community live close to the sky. They do not dwell at the bottom. Words her father lived by, all while swinging his tyrant fist, forcing everyone to abide by his way of thinking.

"Get some sleep, Ari," Jake said on a yawn. "Tomorrow's going to be another long day. Hector said something about the winch being fully down, and we don't have the parts to fix it."

Ari ran a hand over her face. "It's always something. Do you think survival is even possible? Were we foolish to cut ourselves loose? We lost all the resources the city can offer us by blowing the connection." The farm had been tethered to the city by a huge interlocking system made of graphene and steel. In order to free themselves, they'd blown it sky high, so even if they wanted to, there was no hooking back up.

"It was either that, or everyone living here would've died."

"That's true." Ari reassured herself with that daily. "But everyone could still die tomorrow. Without a working winch, we can't feed the other farms. Or the sea could swallow us. There are so many things that could go wrong."

"We did what we did," Jake said, tugging her into his arms again. "No regrets." He kissed the top of her head. "We always make the best decision we can at any given moment. Everyone here knows you're trying to save them. They also know that they could be lost to the sea at any moment. When we blew up the connection, we gave everyone here another day. It matters."

Ari sighed. "Do you think anyone heard us when we radioed the dark city?" She and Jake had broken into the communications room on the medi-ship right before they'd freed the farm. "No one answered."

"It's a tough question. My dad mentioned years ago that your dad had been in contact with people there, so there's a chance."

"If they heard me, do you think they'll help?" Her voice held hope even though her heart didn't feel it. Her father had repeatedly told her that they were on their own. That no aid would ever come from the dark city, even though he was desperate to get back.

"I hope so," Jake replied, trailing the edge of sleep. "Time will tell."

"Our time will be up soon without them."

•HOLLY•

Chapter 3

"We're going," I said, running a hand through my newly washed, not quite dry hair. "I don't care what they say. Since when do we bow down to what the government wants anyway? The fact that we *are* the government is a different kind of crazy." The entire thing was ludicrous, bordering on next-level outrageous. I tried not to pace around my small living space and instead focus on my wall screen, the scene with the building and the wispy clouds, which usually had a calming effect.

It wasn't working. Not even a little bit.

"They didn't say we couldn't go. They just want us to wait a few more days," Case reminded me in his irritatingly reasonable way.

I gave him a look, pondering if he'd lost some brain cells since we'd last discussed this topic, which had been exactly twelve hours ago, before we'd gone to sleep. The night had been fitful at best. "You heard that girl as clearly as I did," I insisted. "You were sitting right next to me. Marty Bancroft Jr. is dangerous. We know that from the history left behind. Ari said he was killing people, that there would be a mass extermination. We've already waited a week. Waiting another one is all kinds of wrong. Who knows what's happened since then? Hundreds—if not thousands of people—could've died while we stayed here and picked protein cakes out of our teeth." Now that we had Maisie, making a long-distance ocean flight wouldn't be nearly as hazardous. Of course, the appropriate amount of worry about traversing a vast space where landing would be next to impossible would happen. But we had high-powered batteries that could keep us airborne for days, if not weeks. And honestly, it couldn't possibly be that far. At least not according to the data we'd already uncovered. "What we need is to get Maisie and head to the barracks as soon as possible." We'd been back only once since Tillman and his crew had tried to blow it up. The entrance had taken a direct hit, but other than that, everything was more or less fine. It'd taken us less than half a day to clean out the rubble. Now we just had to figure out how to resecure it. We'd get to that later. Very few people knew about its existence, so we could afford to wait. "The tech table has excellent mapping capabilities. Coupled with Maisie's access to data, that should allow us to triangulate a location. The floating city has to be within a reasonable distance of the East Coast. It's the only known area to survive the meteor hits."

"We don't have access to Maisie. The government is utilizing her," Case reminded me. "If we commandeer her, Claire is going to know we're up to something."

I shoved off the counter, where I'd situated myself so I wouldn't wander around aimlessly. "They told us to gather intel, so that's what we're doing. We just explain that we need Maisie and don't mention we're leaving. If they bring it up, we deny it. What are they going to do? Throw us in a cell?" The only person who would be beyond hurt if we left without telling him would be Daze. Then, if we didn't return, he'd be devastated. "Maisie technically belongs to Daze anyway. Everybody agrees on that. So we grab the kid and then get the LiveBot, head to the barracks, and do our research. There's nothing suspicious about acting on an order. Then we explain to the kid why we have to go and drop him off with Darby." It was a solid plan.

Case dragged a hand around to the back of his neck, looking doubtful. We were both freshly showered, having just emerged from the cleaning stall. We'd been bunking in my canal residence since we arrived back from the South. Seeing him standing there, relaxed and clean, made me realize how weird it was to have a life partner. If somebody had told me two months ago that this would happen, I would've shoved a jug of aminos down their throat to shut them up. "If we leave without telling the group," Case said, "it's going to create problems."

"I can deal with that," I said. "Isn't the prime objective to save lives? We can't do that if we stay here." I'd been hearing Ari's voice in my dreams, calling for help. Nobody would listen. I'd awakened in a cold sweat each time.

"Yes, it's about saving lives," Case agreed. "But we can't ignore that the city's entering a new era. We're curing seekers, improving our food supply, inoculating people. There are other factors to consider before we leave."

"Bullshit," I argued. "The hard-and-fast rule in this world is still survival. Everything you just listed increases our life-spans. What the people on the Flotilla need right now is a chance at living. Based on the projections Maisie's already made, there could be ten thousand people out there. Ten thousand souls at the mercy of one lunatic. If we wait, the likelihood of their survival diminishes greatly."

"I know." Case took a seat on the bench in front of the screen. He hunched forward, elbows braced on his knees. "But we need more information."

It was hard not to toss my arms up in exasperation. "How many more details do we have to compile? They took thirty ships. Two of those were cruise ships that were built for our vacationing ancestors, who apparently enjoyed life at sea, capable of housing more than five thousand people apiece. They had a plan to construct a floating city, and we know they had the means. We also know they met up with a sustainable aquatic-farming community that housed at least a thousand people, all thanks to your grandfather. The possible locations where they could be are finite—meaning we can find them. At most, it'd take us a couple of days of flying back and forth in a grid pattern." We'd discovered recently that Case's grandfather, the CEO of Bliss Corp, had planned the entire thing, spending upward of one hundred trillion dollars on supplies and vessels. "The records at the Bureau of Truth document what happened, even if we don't have the actual number of people that left. But does it really matter? Even if we were saving ten people, I'd go anyway."

Case stood, clearly as agitated as I was, and made his way to the cooling unit. "I would, too. I don't know why we're arguing, because I agree with everything you're saying. Don't you think I feel responsible? My blood ties me to this lunatic. But if we go rogue on this mission, it's going to place us at odds with everyone."

I leaned up against the wall. "Since when do you care about being at odds with anyone? When all this started between us, you had no commitment to anyone but yourself. What's changed?"

Case seared me with a look. "You."

Chills rushed up my spine. "Are you saying you have an allegiance to me?"

He brought his head down slowly. "Yes. And you have one to your family."

"You're worried I'm going to damage my relationship with them if I leave without saying anything?"

"I am, and they're important to you." He set the water jug down and stalked toward me, grasping me around the waist.

"I appreciate that," I breathed. "But Claire and Lockland don't get to call the shots in our group. It's a democracy. We haven't had a formal vote about this. They just decided. That's unacceptable."

"Then maybe you should call a vote," Case murmured into my neck, his breath warm as it abraded my skin.

A soft moan escaped me. "And risk getting voted down? No way."

Heat radiated deep within as he drew me closer. This was a better distraction than the wall screen any day. "Have it your way." His lips dragged slowly across my throat, up to the corner of my mouth. "In the end, they'll probably forgive you."

His lips were soft, the kiss thorough. I luxuriated in the feel of him. These emotions were brand new to me, but I appreciated every single one. I broke the kiss, panting. "I'm not looking for forgiveness."

"Then we should go." He hovered over my bottom lip.

"Really?" My fingers dug into his shoulders, my tongue stroking his.

"As long as you don't regret it."

I enjoyed his masculinity. "I'm a woman of few regrets."

"That's good to know." His eyes were unfocused, his lips lingering over mine. "I was beginning to get worried."

"Yeah, you look really worried." He looked as relaxed as I'd ever seen him.

His eyes crinkled at the corners. "You've pointed out recently that I'm hogging your towels"—he leaned in—"using your battery power"—his tongue raked against mine—"causing a crick in your neck by sharing your sleeping pod." The last kiss lasted for a good long while, both of us hungry for it. "Those all sound like tiny regrets to me."

"Those aren't regrets," I panted, taking some time to catch my breath. The man could use his mouth in remarkable ways. "Those are cold, hard facts. If we continue to share a sleeping pod, we're going to have to salvage a double. It's getting crowded in there."

His mouth came down hard, and another moan escaped me, more like a groan.

"I disagree," he whispered once we were both out of breath again. "I think it's perfect."

Two loud shrills rent the air. We sprang apart, jolted by the noise, still panting.

Both of our tech phones had gone off simultaneously.

A moment later, Bender's voice rumbled through the speaker from my vest pocket. "It's Johnny. Where the hell are you?"

Chapter 4

"It's Ella," I said, the phone so close to my lips I was in danger of getting the thing wet. It'd taken me more than a few seconds to compose myself. "Where exactly am I supposed to be?" I flicked my thumb off the button, glancing at Case, who had taken a step back. "Did we miss something?"

"Not that I know of," he answered.

It didn't take Bender long to growl his response. "Meeting. Now. Mary's house." Also known as the Pleasure Emporium, the building we'd co-opted from Hutch and the current home to Darby, Walt, and Knox.

My eyebrows rose. There'd been no meeting scheduled.

After we'd disbanded yesterday, the only thing on the agenda had been to gather information. Daze had spent the night with Darby, which he'd been doing more often, claiming that Darby was more fun than we were. Of course he was. The two of them shared a brain, chatting nonstop about things most people would find completely uninteresting. Like the caretaking of ancient farm animals or whether people had been happy driving vehicles with four wheels. Maybe Bender was warning us that something had happened to Daze? I depressed the button again. "Is Rennie feeling okay?"

"Nobody has a temperature," Bender grumbled. "See you in ten."

Ten was doable. I'd taken to parking Tilly out in the open on the roof of my building. Now that we were technically on the same side as the government, I'd decided to relax some of my precautions. That didn't mean traps weren't set up every few meters— stumbling blocks that would render a gutsy intruder half dead or fully dead, depending on what they encountered—but why not take advantage of knowing people in high places? Plus, at the rate we were curing seekers, it wouldn't take long for the canals to become a viable place for folks to live again. Kind of like The Middle—but less uptight. If I had something to say about it. After all, I was here first.

I tucked my phone into my pocket, reluctantly stepping away from Case and his delicious warmth. "Apparently, we're needed at the Emporium." I made my way to the door. "I wonder what's up."

"I guess we're about to find out." Case donned his trench and helmet.

"It's not like Bender to make stuff up," I grumbled as I scooped up my gloves and my Gem, holstering my weapon as I tugged the smooth silia over my hands. Case engaged the heat-sensitive panel, and the door released with a click. We entered the hallway. "He used our regular channel, which means the entire crew heard that missive."

Case was ahead of me, climbing the footholds to pop the roof hatch. "It seems strange," he agreed. "Nobody said anything about getting together. But I think that means we're not the only ones impatient with the way things are going."

Once up top, I automatically walked toward Tilly, Case veering toward Seven. Even though Tillman's craft was far superior to Luce in terms of comfort, speed, and just about everything else, my heart seized each time I saw her. Clearly, I hadn't sufficiently mourned the loss of my beloved craft. Luce had been special. My grandfather had handed her down, through my mother, and she'd fit me like a pair of well-worn pajamas. Articles of clothing my ancestors had loved beyond reason. Case thought pajamas were hilarious, but since I'd salvaged a pair, I understood the affection.

I paused in front of Tilly and crossed my arms. "Are you planning on taking two crafts?"

Case gave me a look, drumming his fingertips on the top of Seven, deliberately not answering.

"You're not automatically winning the craft war every day," I argued. "We took Seven yesterday, and Tilly has a bigger back seat. If we're going to grab

Daze and Maisie and head to the barracks after this meeting, like I think we should, we take Tilly. It only makes sense. Not to mention she's prettier, provides a smoother ride, and my piloting skills are far superior to yours. If we're being technical, the better pilot should always win." It was a true statement. I'd been declared the better pilot. Who cared if it was by a hundredth of a degree? It totally counted.

Case pushed off of Seven, the look on his face settling somewhere between exasperated and resigned. But I knew this particular argument was far from over. We were going to have to find a better way to deal with what were becoming frequent craft wars. My vote was hand-to-hand combat.

My partner made his way to Tilly's passenger side, muttering, "I'm going to kill Maisie for saying that."

I chuckled as I got in, slamming the door. "That's the single best thing I've ever asked her."

"Hundredths of degrees don't count," he replied, a little more hotly than expected. "It's a negligible amount."

"Don't blame me. Winners are winners for a reason." I started Tilly up, her props whirring far more quietly than Luce's ever had. Tillman hadn't installed a failsafe, which had made commandeering this craft much easier. I guess you didn't have to have backup when you thought you were the king of the South. Bender was going to add a false start, and once triggered more than three times, something dastardly would happen to a would-be thief, but he was slated to do it when things calmed down, which was hilarious. So maybe Tilly would never have one. You never knew.

I lofted us into the air. The Emporium was located in the canals, so it literally took less than three minutes of air time before we reached our destination. If we'd used the steel-beam cable swing route, it would've taken us an hour or more.

We parked and entered the building, dodging some of our new traps. Finding no one in the main room, Case and I made our way to the labs. Darby and Walt had side-by-side rooms, which made the world work that much easier. Getting all of Walt's stuff up here had taken a few trips with the mover drone, but we'd managed.

Darby and Daze had their heads together over something on the table, which was no shock to any human left on Earth. I walked in, but before I could say anything, Julian jumped off his nearby chair, smiling so hard the retail bot's straight white polymer teeth clacked not once, but twice. "Welcome! May I get you some refreshments?" Julian had morphed into something beyond jovial, venturing into the realm of manic.

I shot Darby a look. "I thought we talked about this."

Darby shrugged, barely glancing over his shoulder. "His personality is hardwired. Complimentary service is what he was made for. If I try to recircuit his wiring, he could stop working altogether."

I eyed the happy-go-lucky bot, who was still waiting for an answer, an expectant look on his lifelike, unmistakably human face. "Honestly, would that be so bad?"

"He's helpful," Darby said to the project in front of him instead of me, unfazed by his cheerful bot or my disdain. "We've been using him for general tasks around the lab. He makes our lives easier."

Since I was still standing in front of him, Julian tried again. "I can take your jacket, if you'd like."

"No, thank you," I grumbled, turning away from him. "We're fine, Julian. You can go back to sitting." He spun immediately, marching back to his seat. "At least he follows orders," I sniffed.

Daze rushed up to me before I could get to the table. "Look what Darby found," he exclaimed, tugging my arm while gesturing at the pico. The supercomputer on the table wasn't Daze's. It was a new one we'd uncovered in the mag-lev trains. We were suddenly swimming in tech, and the boys couldn't be happier.

I leaned over, squinting at the graphic displayed on the screen. "Is that a biosphere?" It resembled a large globe, half in the water, half out. There were a bunch of smaller globes clustered around it.

"Not only *a* biosphere," Darby clarified, "but likely one of the actual habitats that were under construction right before the meteor hit." He barely glanced away from the graphic. "This pico had a history database installed, and it wasn't by accident. I was able to access all of Bliss Corp's projects. This one was highlighted."

"We have more than a picture of the outside," Daze

announced, excitement front and center. "They included something called blueprints, and they have lots of details." The kid hopped on the balls of his feet. This was great news that meant we could better understand what we would be getting ourselves into.

I was just about to ask where Bender was when he barreled into the room. Even though the world was changing quickly, I could always count on Bender to remain the same. His bald head reflected the illumination in the room, his biceps flexed through his frayed uniform, and he had what looked to be amino stains on the front of his shirt. You could take a guy out of The Middle, but you could never take The Middle out of the guy. "Nice of you to make it," he growled.

"Give me a break," I complained. "There was no meeting scheduled, so don't even go there. What's the deal?" I made a show of glancing past him. "Are Lockland and Claire coming?"

Bender planted his feet a meter apart, crossing his arms. "No. It's just us. You're here because I know you're getting ready to take off, and I don't like it. We need a plan first."

I inclined my head. "Judging by your tone, I'm assuming you approve rather than disapprove? You don't think I should wait for the government to give us *permission* first?" The word *permission* came out with a teensy sneer. Okay, maybe more than teensy. A moderate sneer.

"Hell yeah, I approve," he answered. "But I'm not

letting you out of my sight until we come up with something solid. Going in unprepared, you'll get yourself killed. That would be a fucking waste of everybody's time."

"Um, I agree," I replied. "Getting killed is not the front-runner for hopeful outcomes. But calling over the open airwaves for us to meet wasn't the smartest way to go about this. Lockland and Claire have to have heard that. They're not stupid."

Daze bounced around. "They don't know he called you on the phone! Because Walt fixed it."

I angled my head to the side. "What you mean he *fixed* it?"

Case had taken a seat on a stool within Julian's compulsive to-be-of-service range. It was his funeral. "Did he confiscate their tech phones?" Case asked. It was a logical conclusion.

Walt helpfully entered the room then, clearly having overheard our discussion. "No, I didn't take their phones. I simply made some improvements to your bandwidth. Some *selective* improvements." He winked. The old man had some serious spunk. Leave it to Walt to be the oldest, most conniving guy among us. That man could look you straight in the eyes and tell a lie, all while manipulating you with his old, withered, feel-sorry-for-me wrinkled face and rheumy eyes. Add a halo of white hair sticking up all over and a slight hunch from a bump over his shoulder, and you were lulled into complacency faster than you could take your next breath.

"I'm not going to ask how that's even possible, because I won't understand the answer," I said. "But Lockland is going to be pissed when he finds out." Not that I really cared. But still.

Walt clucked. "It needed to be done. If we are to save those people, you must leave sooner rather than later." Walt's priority in the last sixty years had been trying to save people, so he understood how I felt even better than I did. His saving came in the form of bioengineering new inoculations and pain medication and administering healing boosts. Not to mention perfecting slurry production and updating and rebuilding necessary tech. Once upon a time, he'd been an astrophysicist. Now he insisted he was a simple scientist. We all knew he was much more than that.

"I agree with you," I said. "I'm happy you guys are affected by the urgency of this mission. Honestly, I was beginning to think everyone had lost their damn minds."

Knox came in, his face drawn. This kid wore his emotions on his sleeve and was as easy to interpret as a flashing digital readout. He'd tragically lost his first love, Gia, at nineteen and had been instrumental in the reorganization of the former militia base down South. He had proven his loyalty and had become an important part of our crew in a very short amount of time. "I know that face," I told him. "What's wrong?"

He halted, seemingly surprised we were all gathered here, and cleared his throat, hedging for a second. "Um, I just came from Government Square.

AMANDA CARLSON

I was there to give an update to Lockland and Claire on the last of the goods we've inventoried from the South. We're on track to get them up here within a week."

"*And?*" Bender's tone encouraged Knox to get to the point quicker.

"A message may have come from the floating city in the last day or two."

I gave Bender a look. "I hope that's not true," I said to Knox. "Claire and Lockland wouldn't keep something like that from us." They knew we'd been waiting for further communication before we launched our rescue mission.

"I can't be sure." Knox appeared uncomfortable. "But I heard a couple of people talking. They said someone named Marty had been trying to communicate, but they weren't supposed to reply."

This was big.

As far as we knew, Martin Bancroft Jr. was in charge of the floating city. He was also Case's estranged father.

Instead of extending my leg and sending a chair flying, which was my first inclination, I sat, trying to maintain my composure, which was hanging by the barest polymer fiber. If Lockland and Claire had kept this vital information from us, it was a deep betrayal. "Okay," I said after a moment. "What exactly did you overhear?"

"I didn't catch it all. But it seemed like something was going on. Something about the farms being cut

48

loose. I'm not sure. I don't think the people I overheard really understood what they were talking about either. Then Claire came back, and I moved away from the door."

I muttered under my breath as Bender swore. Darby brushed imaginary lint from his pants. Case wore an unreadable expression. The only one who looked thoughtful was Walt.

I didn't trust myself to speak, so I was glad the old man decided to jump in first. "We can't interpret this as a betrayal," Walt started in a knowing tone. I was about to pontificate my exact thoughts on that, when he held up a single finger and shushed me. He had the ability to do such things, because he was an old man with a hump on his shoulder. "From what I understand about the inner dynamics of your group, your relationships have been built on a foundation of trust and respect. Am I correct?"

Bender and I both spoke at the same time.

"They were—"

"Damn straight—"

Walt didn't let us finish. "Then it's safe to say that integrity is still intact." He shuffled his way to a stool and sat. "It's my feeling that they're trying to protect you from something, rather than deliberately withholding information. It's a possibility that Claire has uncovered some facts through her workings in the government and has deemed this mission too perilous. She would be extremely concerned about your well-being and safety, would she not?"

Bender jumped in with, "She might. But there's no excuse for Lockland. He knows we can take it. Withholding a communication from the floating city is unacceptable."

A heavy pit wallowed in my stomach.

I stood, heading toward Daze, who was tinkering with something on the counter, even though he was taking in every single second of this conversation as much as I was. Even this kid realized all we had in this world was trust. Once that was dumped out a scraper window, you were on your own. "Maybe whatever Knox overheard was brand-new information." I sighed. "Maybe Lockland's on his way over right now to share it with us." Playing the devil's advocate wasn't my forte, but there wasn't much else I could say without becoming red-hot. Receiving this information was a blow, but even though it stung, it was important to remember that nothing was definitive until we knew what had happened.

"Tell us what else you overheard," Bender ordered Knox. "The aquatic farms are loose? What the hell does that mean?"

Before Knox could comply, Darby nearly leaped out of his seat. "I can help with that!" He was more than his usual overeager, proving that we were all on edge. A fracture in the group, especially now that we were linked to the government, would be bad all around. Darby took in a breath. "Sorry. What I mean is that not only do I have the blueprints of the farms they were building, but also some detailed graphics about the floating city they planned to build. Bliss Corp purchased a number of cruise ships, and four were parked in the harbor here when disaster struck. Two of those had special anchors and flotation apparatus installed, as if they'd been retrofitted for an epic disaster." Darby tapped on some keys, and we all gathered around. I was thankful to have something to do. Even though the pico screen was small, renderings of a floating city stuck out in stark contrast, a white background with precise, black lines delineating the schematic.

It was incredible, and surprisingly elaborate, at least thirty stories high.

"Did they use these drawings as a guide to manufacture the city?" Case asked.

"I have no idea," Darby said. "But we now know for a fact that Martin Bancroft Sr., your grandfather, made sure his warehouses were stocked with the materials that could build this." Darby tapped the screen directly over the graphic. "We found one of his stashes in the mag-lev trains thanks to Tillman. But we think he had two more on the East Coast. There's no way to know if they survived the meteor or the aftermath, but my feeling is if we found them now, they'd be empty." That meant that whoever had been organizing the Flotilla had known where to get the necessary supplies. It all made sense. Wrapped up in a fiber carbon bow.

"Remember, I was alive back then," Walt wheezed, his voice containing wistful knowledge.

We all turned. *"And?"* I asked in a tone similar to Bender's.

"A number of ships, including military vessels, showed up in the harbor one night out of the blue. The next day, they were gone."

·ARI·

Chapter 5

"It's broken," Hector told his assembled audience. "The wormgear has been completely destroyed. No amount of manpower is going to make this winch functional again. We need the right tools and a replacement part in the form of a chunk of steel." Hector had grown up in the hulls and had spent years working on the engineering ship in exchange for tiny rations a day. He was in charge of all things mechanical at the moment.

"Are you sure?" Ari asked, her eyes flicking into the distance where the rest of the farms rocked in the waves. It was time to reconnect. Those people needed sustenance. She had farmers inside picking crates for them this morning.

"As sure as fruit on the vine," Hector replied as he stood, wiping his greasy hands on a rag that was black from use.

"How in the hell did it break in the first place?" Paris stomped in a circle, gripping a rail as a wave swept beneath them.

"It's old and caked with salt. It was only a matter of time. We're going to figure this out," Jake concluded. He was forever the voice of reason. Except, Ari didn't think it was going to work out this time. The winch wasn't the only issue they had at the moment. Food and clean water were scarce, and the sea was getting increasingly wilder as they drifted into parts unknown. That was a lot to contend with.

"There might be a way..." Lila started, surprising them. She had a tendency to say little when it came to strategizing.

"A way to what?" Paris said, her voice edgy enough to intimidate.

Lila looked uneasy, beginning to fidget. Ari stepped in. "It's okay to speak your mind, Lila. Paris does it all the time, and we all suffer through." Paris shot her a look, but smartly kept her mouth shut. "If you have any ideas that could help, we want to hear them."

Brandon set a hand on Lila's arm, giving her his support this time. "Last night, you told us that you commandeered another hydro-ski," she started. "That means we have two. You also said that your father pulled anchor and is drifting along with us."

"That's correct," Ari said.

"Well, then New Eden is probably not too far away, since the guards arrived here in one piece. That means you could—"

"Are you suggesting we go back to New Eden?" Paris gaped. "If we get caught, they'll kill us on sight. No waiting around. No opportunity to defend ourselves. Just plain death."

"Let her finish," Jake said, arms crossed. He was clearly interested in the direction Lila was headed.

"Not New Eden, exactly," Lila continued. "The engineering ship has always been attached on the west side of the city. It's quieter there. My dad used to deliver goods and supplies to that ship when our farm was docked. As a young girl, I accompanied him. One time, I climbed up on a box of crates and peeked over the edge of that big ship. It was the highest I'd ever been above the sea in my life." She blushed, darting a glance between Jake and Ari, knowing that they'd spent most of their lives well above that height. Ari nodded to encourage her to continue. "I noticed that the ship had handholds set into both sides, ladders leading from the water to the rail. I imagined horrid sea creatures, from the tall tales we'd tell each other growing up, coming from the depths to devour us whole." She chuckled softly. "The fantasies of a little girl. But if we could get the skis—"

Hector picked up her thread, clearly excited. "Then we could get up and over, get the supplies we need to fix the winch, and disappear out of sight before they even notice we were there. She's right." He turned to the group. "There are ladders on both sides of the ship. They came standard on military vessels, so they could rendezvous with the ultrasubs. It could work."

"It might, but it's risky," Jake said. "For one, we have no idea how far away the city is, and we'd have to navigate at night. The waves are choppier now than they've ever been. Not like when we were kids, playing in a buoy-protected area."

Brandon took a step forward. "Those skis were ours. They were stripped from the farms when your father first arrived. But knowing how to operate them gives you a chance."

Lila added hastily, "We realize and accept that none of us can change what's happened in the past. But if we truly want to help those poor people get food"—she gestured toward the habitats floating in the distance— "skiing to the engineering ship is our only hope."

"Hell, I'm up for taking a trip on a ski," Hector hooted enthusiastically.

"Me, too," Paris said. "You're not leaving me behind. We've got two drivers and two passengers. Four should be more than enough to get the job done."

Ari glanced down at the broken winch.

She now found herself in the position to make yet another life-altering decision. But what choice did they really have? There were too many crates of food to transfer between all the farms by skis alone. She and Jake definitely had enough skill to pilot them to the engineering ship. Her father wouldn't be expecting them anywhere close to New Eden, so they held an advantage. She glanced up at the sky like it might possibly rain down some better answers. All it gave her was precip.

"Okay," she sighed. "Taking the skis might work. But we're going to have to do a lot of planning to execute this without placing ourselves in jeopardy. Our weapons are pathetic, we barely have any flotation devices, and none of us can see in the dark. Those are all obstacles we have to contend with, as well as how to get everything back here safely."

"I agree, planning is a must," Jake said. "If we start now, we can formulate something by twilight. Hector's familiar with the engineering ship, so that'll give us another edge. I've been on it a few times, though not enough to know its inner workings. But as far as I know, no one patrols the decks. There's never been any outside interference, so no need to be paranoid. If we're stealthy, we'd be able to get in and out without notice."

"While we're there," Ari added, "we pick up as much as we can strap on our backs or fronts. We're not going to get more than one chance at this. When they discover we've been there, they'll add security." She glanced around. "Does anyone know if they have extra UV stored there? I know the big bulbs that were custom-made for the farms have all been used up, but small UV might be helpful to some of the plants. Or are those only available in the merchant area?"

"The merchant area is not that far away," Hector said. "We could just cross over—"

Ari lofted her arm. "No way. Please tell me you didn't just suggest that." Hector gave her a lopsided grin. "We're not risking our lives any more than necessary. This is a crazy plan as it is. Jake and I haven't piloted skis in years. The engineering ship is as far as we go. Under no circumstances are we entering New Eden. Paris is right. Not only the militia, but any loyal citizens would kill us on sight. We've been declared outliers, an imminent threat to the city."

Paris shook her head. "I can't imagine how New Eden is faring knowing that they're drifting. There must be widespread panic. I'm certain that bastard locked the main doors, too, securing the hulls. They're probably dying down there trying to get out." Her voice held sadness and disgust.

Deciding to save the remaining farms, and not staying with the people in New Eden, had been a tough choice for Ari—the toughest of her life. But the number of guards and elite on her father's side had made it impossible to stay. They would've been caught and killed. But her heart ached for the people suffering in her city. She wanted nothing more than to help them. She knew they had enough food for the time being, but it wouldn't last. Unless help arrived, they would all perish.

Paris' eyes gleamed with mischief. "We don't have to *actually* enter New Eden to do some damage. I mean, why not shake things up while we still can, right?"

"What kind of damage do you have mind?" Jake asked, his eyes narrowing.

"The engineering ship is tethered on the west side, just like Lila said," Paris replied. "The hulls on that side contain the isolation chambers. You know the people locked in there are suffering. Most—*if not all*—of them are innocent of any wrongdoing. We could sear a few holes in the side and give them a fighting chance. It would create just enough chaos."

"If we interfere with the city, we're going to bring down the wrath of its leader," Brandon stated flatly.

Paris shrugged. "He's already sending militia after us, and if you hadn't noticed, we're free-floating. As far as I see it, based on how rough the sea is getting, the longer we drift, the sooner we encounter destruction on a large scale. We have no idea how big the waves will swell. Why not go out with a bang? At least we can give those folks a fighting chance. New Eden is more capable of surviving the larger hits from the ocean than we are—that is, before it cracks apart once and for all. He can't kill us if we're already dead."

Ari wasn't ready to weigh the pros and cons of damaging the hulls just yet. "Brandon's right. My father sending a few guards after us is not the same as sending an army. If we retaliate, he would deem us a direct threat, which we would be. But if we can do something under the radar, I'll consider it."

"Let's brainstorm inside," Jake said. "We're going to have to send a message to the other farms and tell them it will be another day or two before we can deliver the food. Let's get Celia on that." Celia and Russ were in charge of communications, as well as watching over the prisoners on Atlas Three.

"It'll take her time to get the message across," Ari said, falling into place next to him. "The radio connection between biospheres has been intermittent. The sea is making everything much harder." Thirty years ago, her father had chosen the location for New Eden based on nearby land masses, which had provided protection from the rougher seas. As they'd been drifting, that protection had dwindled.

"The ocean also brings advantages," Jake said. "They won't expect us to come by ski."

"Do you think we can actually do it?" Ari asked. "It's been a long time since we've taken a ride out there." It seemed like a lifetime ago. In their early teens, they'd been allowed to play on the waves on calmer days, always with supervision and adequate personal inflatables. Her father had thought it supremely important for members of the elite to know how to use these devices in case of emergency. Ari was certain he'd never thought skimming the waves would help prepare his daughter for a fight against him.

"If I remember correctly, you could out-ski us all." Jake chuckled. "I'm sure it'll come back to us as soon as we hit the waves."

"I hope so," Ari said. "If not, this won't be a recovery mission. It'll be our final mission."

Chapter 6

Ari adjusted her headgear. She wore an aqua helmet made of thick neoprene, complete with a crystalline face shield and a built-in oxygen valve. Normally, the personal inflatable she wore came standard with chem-generated oxy cells, feeding directly into a tube that could be inserted into her mouth, but those cells had long since dried up. Instead, she was using a diox-rebreather, which had limited capacity when fully submerged.

So she'd have to make sure she stayed mostly above the waves.

"Be careful," Lila said. Brandon stood next to his partner, wearing his usual stoic expression.

Ari nodded from her place in the pilot's seat. "You guys as well. We have no idea if my father will be sending more men tonight. If we see them, we'll try to get you word, but communication once we're more than a kilometer out will be sporadic at best."

Each farm had a single weak radio antenna.

"Our plan is to travel ten kilometers," Jake said. "No farther. If there's zero sign of New Eden and the engineering ship, we return. No diversion from that."

Hector pounded his chest, which was covered in a comically patched inflatable, the best they could do on such short notice. In the last month, Ari's father had ordered the farms to be looted of their supplies. Almost all of the inflatables had been taken. On the hunt, the group managed to find two intact inflatables. The other two had to be constructed from other vests that were no longer deemed usable. Jake insisted that he and Hector take those, as they were the strongest swimmers.

Paris grumbled, "Why did I get the tiny one?"

Ari grinned. "Because you're the only one who comes close to the size of a child. Be thankful you have one at all." Ari grabbed the safety belt that would connect her to the ski. "Are you ready?" Paris was riding with her. Ari knew how to ride the waves, but the extra weight would make it challenging. They'd decided as a group that Hector and Paris would wear backpacks, and Ari and Jake would take smaller bags clipped to their waists. "Remember what we told you," Ari cautioned Paris, who stood beside her. "Your body motion has to mimic mine exactly. We work as a team." When these skis had been manufactured sixty years ago, they'd come with a sealed dome that provided an airtight space. The pilot could either coast across the waves or dive beneath them, an option that had been essential to maintaining the farms when they'd been in the business of harvesting seaweed. But the domes' seals had long ago broken or cracked, so they'd been removed. Riding on the surface was the only option now.

"I get it," Paris said, her bravado front and center. Ari knew that once they were actually in the sea, there was a good chance Paris would panic. Coming from the hulls, Paris had never even visited the farms before last week. Ari had spotted her gripping the rails on more than one occasion, walking with her hand splayed against the shell of the biosphere for stability. The hulls, deep beneath the sea, rocked the least in the city. This was all new to Paris. The ocean was terrifying for anyone, the strength of the waves fierce, but it was especially terrifying for a bottom dweller.

Ari wasn't willing to take any unnecessary chances. The safety belt locked the driver in, keeping them stable side to side, but she'd had Hector quickly fashion another belt that would keep Paris anchored the same way. "We won't be able to communicate verbally over the whine of the motor and the noise of the ocean," Ari told her. Ari and Jake were communicating by amplifier, as were Hector and Paris, so they would be connected that way. "I can't have you losing your mind, so you have to promise to keep it together." Watching Paris' face, Ari began to second-guess her decision to bring her friend along. They needed at least four to get the job done, and the pool of able-bodied people to bring was extremely small, but Paris might be the least prepared for this.

"I'm not gonna lose my mind," Paris insisted. "I promise. I'm up for this. Like I told you earlier, we're going to die anyway. This is as good a way to go as any."

Ari gave her a hard look. "We're not dying. At least, we won't as long as you follow the plan. Picture yourself aerogelled to me. When I lift up, you lift up. When I sway, you sway. Your body needs to act like it's made of elastomer. I've only ever taken two people on the back of a ski, and they were both seasoned riders." Mara and Sabine. A lifetime ago. Ari handed Paris the extra belt. "Wrap this around your waist. It will stretch as far as mine and will keep you stable on the craft. It's strong, so it won't break."

Paris took it, threading the banded material around her back. If she'd been wearing a specialized hydro-ski inflatable, there would've been additional hoops to lock onto. But she was wearing a child's emergency vest. "I'm not gonna let you down." Paris' voice dropped a few octaves, causing Ari to glance her way. "I owe you my life, Alaria. If you hadn't found me and let me out of that cell, I'd already be dead. I'm in this till the end."

Satisfied, Ari gave a single nod.

She wasn't about to make this emotional. Paris had helped Ari when she'd been in bad shape. When Jake had broken Ari out the last time, Ari had insisted he unlock the cell next to hers. Paris had been imprisoned for theft and still wouldn't tell Ari how long she'd been there, or what had happened while imprisoned. Judging by the clothing she'd been wearing and her gaunt appearance, she'd been down there a long time.

Paris hadn't left Ari's side since.

Ari had never had a friend like her, loyal and giving, and she wasn't about to lose her tonight.

Hector adjusted Ari's safety precautions. In addition to the belts, they would be using leg harnesses. They *should* be wearing polythermal suits, but since they were unavailable, they had to settle for their standard syn-leather. They'd be cold and soaked when they returned, but the end would be worth the means. At least, that's what Ari kept telling herself.

Hector announced, "All set. We're going to get you two on first, then we'll follow." Hector was fearful of exactly nothing. In fact, he was the most keyed up Ari had seen him. But she'd known him only a little longer than she'd known Paris. Jake had come across Hector by chance on his way to break the law by setting Ari free. Hector had agreed to help Jake, no questions asked. Their friendship had been duly born. In a mild coincidence, Hector and Paris had known each other as children, and their affection for each other had grown quickly. With no bashfulness whatsoever, Hector leaned over and planted a kiss on Paris' lips. She swatted at him, but was clearly pleased.

"I'm fine with going first," Ari said. "But once we're out, we ride side by side. We use the running lights, along with the shoulder lights, until we get close." New Eden would provide enough ambient light for them to see once they arrived. Ari adjusted her position on the ski. They were parked next to a docking station. Normally, the platform underneath the station could be lowered into the waves with the flick of a switch. But the farms hadn't used these stations for skis in years. Ari's father had commandeered the skis early on for use in the construction of the city. The platforms had long since rusted out, caked with salt, so they had to enter the water from above, which meant Ari had to launch them off the side, timing it perfectly so they landed in a swift-moving crest.

Ari double-checked her belt. The vehicle felt good and sturdy underneath her, familiar and comfortable. Thank goodness for that. Predisaster, operating the skis would've been manageable without any safety features, but that had never been the case for them.

Jake bent over and rechecked everything. For the first time, Ari read the worry on his face. She knew the threat of losing her overwhelmed him, and she shared that same chest-tightening when she imagined losing him. Doubt swirled in his eyes once again. "Hey," she said, touching his arm. "You can't flake out on me. We're in it too far now to go back."

"I'm not changing my mind." Emotion tumbled out. "But I'd be okay if you did."

She grinned. "There's no chance I'd let you do this alone." She was saved from having to reassure him that they would be all right by the arrival of Celia and Russ.

"It took us all day, but we finally got through," Celia announced as she grabbed the rail behind them as the water shifted below. "The other habitats are hanging on. They understand the supplies have to wait. They're grateful you guys are willing to do this."

"How long do you think it's going to take?" Russ asked. Russ grew up on the East Commoner side of the city. Commoners were the people who lived in the ready-made cruise ships, which were the anchors of New Eden to the east and west. Over the course of Ari's life, she'd visited the ships sparingly and had never entered a personal dwelling. She was aware of the horror stories about their upkeep—that they were nothing more than broken-down hovels. Russ hadn't elaborated on his upbringing, but everyone agreed that the cruise ships were better than the hulls. But, by her guess, not by much.

"Depending on the distance, we're hoping the entire round trip takes us no more than an hour or two," Jake answered. "That's if we're lucky and nothing goes wrong."

"If we're unlucky, give us six," Hector said, holding up all five fingers on one hand and the thumb of the other. "After that, we ain't coming back."

Paris grumbled, "Don't say that." She nodded toward Celia. "Give us eight. Once we get the goods, there might be time left over to help the people locked up in New Eden." The group had decided to sacrifice a few of their magnetic hot-laser keys. Their plan was to lob them against the ship wall, which would activate the hot laser inside, designed to melt a crescent-shaped hole in the steel. With any luck, after about five seconds, the prisoners would spot the newly formed spots and find the laser keys. After twelve hours, each key's chemi-capacitor would recharge, and they could be used to cut through the steel bars of the cells.

It was a long shot, but it might work.

Paris had attached personal messages to a few of the laser keys. She and Hector carried them in their pockets. This was a better plan than blowing things up and making noise. After all, they had to do something. But that plan would work only if they got onto the engineering ship undetected. If they were spotted, they'd be lucky to escape with their lives.

Ari patted the small space behind her. "Get on."

Paris obliged, her small body fitting into the space behind Ari with plenty of room to spare. The seat was actually made to hold three adults. Ari grabbed one side of her safety belt, Hector grabbed the other, and they secured it into the same slot Ari had used for hers.

"It's a little tight," Jake said. "But you should be able to unclip no problem once we arrive."

Once they got there, securing the skis to the side of the engineering ship would be tricky. Each hydro-ski was equipped with a magnetic cable that was stored in a special housing. They just weren't sure how loud the sound would echo on impact, so they had to toss them from close range. How much the ocean was rolling at the time would affect that endeavor.

Jake still looked unsure. Ari reached out and grabbed his hand. "It's going to be okay," she assured him. "It's this, or we all starve." They'd already said their goodbyes in private. Public displays of affection didn't happen often in their world.

"I know it's going to work, because you're a better pilot than me." Jake grinned. "You've always been the fearless one."

Once upon a time, Ari had indeed felt fearless. She wasn't going to share with her partner that everything had changed once the resistance began. It'd been easy to live free from fear when she hadn't cared about herself. It was another thing to carry the weight of the welfare of others heavily on her shoulders. Fear was her motivation now.

Ari switched on the ski. The motor was powered by electricity, but the boosts were triggered by fuel cells. It was lucky these hadn't been drained, because they had no replacements. Ari and Paris were on the ski they'd confiscated from the guards. It was clear that whoever had been piloting it before hadn't known how to use the equipment efficiently, or the cells would've been burned. Instead, they were almost full. "And don't forget. I wasn't the only fearless one when we were kids," Ari told Jake. "If I remember correctly, your prowess on the skis was unparalleled."

Jake chuckled. "I'll show you prowess." She thought for a moment he would kiss her after all, but he stepped back, giving her a salute as he mounted his ski. Hector practically danced around it, waiting for his turn.

Ari turned to Celia. "If we don't return, you're in charge, along with Brandon and Lila. Your last resort is to turn on the biosphere and atlas propellers and hope the sea doesn't break them apart too quickly." It was a long shot, as the strength of the propellers was greatly weakened by the lack of power to any of the farms, and the sea was rough. If they found land, there might be hope for survival. But they had no idea in what direction it lay.

Celia nodded. "It will be done. Ride safely. We'll eagerly await your return."

Ari was surprised to see a small crowd had gathered behind them. William, the old farmer, lifted his hand. His face was solemn, as were the others'.

They couldn't fail. Ari couldn't disappoint these people.

She faced forward. "Get ready," she told Paris. A wave swelled beneath them from behind. Even though she couldn't see it, she could feel it. It was as if she was a child again. "One, two—"

On three, they plunged two meters into the angry sea.

·HOLLY·

Chapter 7

"Two more hours." I held up two fingers, then swung my hand around so everyone had a clear view. "That's it. Two. Then we're grabbing Maisie and heading to the barracks." After Darby had shared the plans for the floating city, along with an itemized list of every supply the Flotilla had had access to—an amazing amount of materials—there was no question in my mind that the city had been built. And it had to be massive. A city like that was meant to thrive.

Now all those people were in trouble, and I was beyond sick of waiting.

We'd voted to give Lockland the benefit of the doubt. Whether or not that was the right thing to do remained to be seen. But I wasn't waiting any longer than the time I'd just specified for Lockland to show. With the new information Knox had overheard about the communication from the floating city, it was

Lockland's responsibility to let us know what was up. As Claire's second-in-command, he was privy to all the inner workings of the government, which in and of itself was completely bizarre, but that meant it wasn't our job to ask him what was going on. It was his job to *tell* us what we needed to know.

I comprehended, on some level, that Claire might be worried about us surviving the mission. After all, it was full of uncertainty. But Lockland owed us the truth. There would be no excusing any lies or manipulation.

Bender had parked himself on a chair in the main room of the Emporium and hadn't moved for the last forty-five minutes. He was likely going over the same scenarios I was. In all of our years together, a crisis like the one with Ari and her people had never reared its helmeted head. We'd never been at odds as a group before. All we had in this world was each other. Messing that up was unthinkable.

"Maybe the taste of power got to him," Darby said from his position on the couch next to me. We all had sort of miserably congregated in the main room, while we waited for our partner to make the right choice. "Not everyone is immune to the headiness of ascending the ladder of command."

My hands were steepled. "It's not about the power. If anything, he's doing what he thinks is right. He's just choosing wrong."

"Yeah," Bender said, finally breaking his silence. "I never saw this coming. And that pisses me off even more than him not showing up."

"We voted to give him the benefit of the doubt," I argued, surprising myself. "You know, like Walt said."

Bender arched an eyebrow at me that stood out because it was the only hair on his head, and it was kind of bushy. "Since when are you the voice of fucking reason?"

"I'm not," I answered defensively. "At least, I don't want to be." I stood, shaking out my arms. "What do you want me to say? We all know this sucks. But like Walt said back there"—I jerked my thumb toward the labs—"our relationships were built on trust, and trust doesn't evaporate overnight. What's his motivation? Why is he keeping things from us? He must have a good reason, right?" The last part came out a little weaker than the rest. Was it right? Hell if I knew.

"If we knew his motivations, we wouldn't be sitting around here waiting like a bunch of assholes," Bender fumed. The fact that Bender had stayed seated was the scariest part of all. Bender, being Bender, would normally be tearing the place apart. His anger came out physically. He liked punching stuff. Plus, he was closest to Lockland. He'd brought him into the group. They were friends on a different level. Yet, Bender stayed seated. I didn't know what to make of that.

"He could've been ordered to keep quiet," Case offered. My partner with the incredible lips sat across from us, Daze on the floor next to him. Case was frustrated, like we all were, but it wasn't the same for him. We'd been his crew for only a short time, and working as a team was not his happy place.

"What do you mean?" I asked. "The only person above him is Claire. Plus, the last time I checked, Lockland didn't take orders from anyone."

"The government has different departments," Case offered. "In order to get access across all places, he might've had to make a promise he doesn't feel he can break."

"He wouldn't make an agreement like that," Bender argued. "He wouldn't choose them over us."

"Well, he chose something—" I started.

All of our tech phones went off at once.

As I grabbed for mine, relief flooded through me.

We were hardly ever in the same area together, so it was almost comical. Lockland's voice cracked through next. "You're needed at the bureau. Enter through the basement." Then the phone went dark, meaning he'd shut off any further communication.

"The basement?" I sputtered, trying to analyze the message. "Entering that way means we use the tunnels we lasered through to get there undetected last time. Tell me that doesn't mean he wants us to *sneak* in."

"That's exactly what he means." Bender scowled, already heading toward the door. "Something's up if he wants us to come in under the radar."

"We may have underestimated him too quickly," Darby said sheepishly, scrambling after us. "I'll be the first one to admit it."

"I wouldn't go that far," I shot back. Case and Daze were already up the stairs. "To ensure nothing goes wrong, we're going in armed. I can't believe I'm saying this, but there's a chance he could try to detain us. The best way to do that would be to gather us all in an indefensible location."

Case tossed me a glance as we exited to the roof. "The chance of that is fairly slim."

"A chance is still a fucking chance," I muttered.

My Gem and HydroSol were positioned out in front of me. We'd just made our way through the last challenge in the underground maze, a tough spot where we'd haphazardly supported a crumbling wall with sheared-off beams we'd constructed on the spot. Getting to this point had been slow going. I hoped Lockland hadn't sent for us because he had an emergency, because if he'd needed us fast, we were arriving late.

"What now?" I asked. We'd left Daze at the surface with orders to pick up Maisie if we didn't communicate within two hours. The status reader-turned-LiveBot had loyalty to Daze first and foremost, and if she found out something had happened to him, she would come to his aid, then he would direct her our way. That was the theory anyway.

I guess we'd see. Having a LiveBot was new to all of us.

"This is strange as hell," Bender said, dusting off his shoulders after getting through the last bit of tunnel. "I understand about meeting in a stealthy location, but we have quite a few of those that don't require crawling around in the fucking rubble."

"Well, this is what he picked," I said. Our shoulder lights were the only illumination in the dark space. "Now that we're here, how do we let him know? He turned off his phone."

"I suppose we can knock," Darby suggested.

We all peered at him like his intelligence had finally failed. "I'm not sure that's the best idea," Knox replied generously.

Case chuckled. "No, it's not. I'll take the lead. If I don't come back, you'll know something's up."

Before we were able to hash out the matter, solving it by me going instead, a voice popped out of the darkness. "Hey, guys, over here."

"Mary?" My visor was down. I searched for a heat signature, but found none.

She stepped from behind a large partition to our left. It must be some kind of insulation-coated concrete. No heat came through. "Yes, it's me. I'm supposed to take you to Lockland."

This was getting stranger by the moment.

We all lowered our weapons, so they weren't pointing at the poor woman. We followed her, picking our way through the debris farther into the tunnel, because what else were we going to do?

"What the fuck is going on?" Bender grumbled. That about summed it up for all of us. "Somebody better tell me soon, or there's going to be trouble."

We crunched along a broken trail of stones in silence for a full thirty seconds before Mary came to a halt. "I don't really know what's going on," she whispered, "other than he told me there are too many eyes and ears upstairs and to bring you here. He doesn't want to arouse suspicion."

"The government won't let him leave?" I asked.

"Like they could keep him," Bender sneered.

"I'm sorry, Mary," I told the nice lady trying to help us. "We're just having a tough time figuring out what's going on. It doesn't make sense."

"I understand, and I'm sorry," she said. "I don't have any answers for you. I wish I did. But I want you to know I'm thankful to all of you. I wouldn't be here if it wasn't for you." She made a turn, surprising us by heading through a small opening. Once inside, she gave a door on the left a tentative tap.

It swung open. Lockland stood there, looking relieved. He took a step back, ushering us inside. My inclination was to start the conversation by yelling my grievances at him, but instead I took my place and waited for him to speak.

He bowed his head. His way of showing regret. "I want to start by apologizing. I've been caught up in some business here, and it got the best of me. I rationalized it by saying that what I was doing was for the good of the entire city and all its inhabitants, but I can see that my priorities are not in the right order." A freely given acknowledgment of an error in judgment from Lockland sounded like it'd been uttered in a foreign language. My ears were confused, but luckily my brain had tracked the conversation like a pro.

"Cut to the protein. You're irritating me," Bender said, his arms crossed. "What business are you talking about? And you damn well know whatever this is, you should've told us from the start. We don't keep shit from each other. Not now, not ever."

"I realize that," he began. "It was a gross lapse of judgment on my part, and it won't happen again. I give you my word. I fell in line with everyone else on this. Understandably, the government has to keep certain information under wraps," he continued. "They can't afford widespread panic."

"What panic? What sensitive information?" I asked. "You're not talking fast enough."

"Messages have come in from the floating city," he said.

I crossed my arms, matching Bender's stance, a weapon still gripped in each hand. "We know." I let that sink in, and judging by the look on his face, Lockland wasn't extremely surprised we already had that particular information. "You kept that from us. On purpose."

"I did." Lockland ran a hand over his face. He looked extremely tired, like he hadn't slept in days. That was no excuse. "The radio missives from Marty started five days ago."

I balked. Five days? I'd assumed they'd come in more recently. "So, you're telling us," I started, my voice ringing with anger, "that at the time of our *last* meeting, you *knew* this and didn't share it? Please explain. I'm assuming someone had a laser to your temple? Or there was a threat to wrap you in a burial shroud and set you on fire? Or possibly they threatened to cut the sensitive parts from your body with a rusty blade? Because anything short of that, then you're fucked."

He shook his head, his eyes pinned to the ground. "I made a bad choice. The first call came in when I wasn't around. The people manning the communications board were supposed to alert me first, but instead they called a meeting. Word got out about Marty's rantings to a large government faction before I could vet it. Then the panic set in. I was trying to quell it before I told you."

"What did the damn messages say already?" Bender said through an almost fused jaw. I'd honestly never seen the man so angry.

"Marty Jr. declared war on this city, our city," Lockland said. "He threatened to blow the entire place up from the comfort of his ship."

"Why would he do that?" Bender fumed. "Doesn't he want to come back? Didn't they have some pact or something? That he'd bring improved resources to a city of willing followers? Or whatever the hell they decided."

"What were his terms?" Case interjected.

"What do you mean terms?" I said. "I don't think he's looking for terms."

"No one threatens to blow up a city without a

reason," Case said. "Bender's right. He wants to come home. But there's no home if he blows the place up." Case's voice was filled with disgust. If he and his father ever met up, it wouldn't be a loving reunion.

"He gave no reason. That's the problem," Lockland said, running a gloved hand over his hair, which was in need of a trim. "But we suspect he knows his allies are gone. Someone must've tipped him off before we could shut the communication down. Without his group, he realizes he won't be welcome here. I swear to you all, nothing has come over the line in the last few days. During Marty's last rant, we heard another voice, a younger male. He said something about the farms being disconnected from New Eden. That must be what they call the floating city. No one in the government here is sure what cutting loose the farms means. Then the mystery man mentioned something about an internal war. Then Bancroft got back on and shouted more threats. He listed off a huge arsenal of weapons at his disposal. It's clear he could raze this city if he wanted to." It wouldn't take too much firepower, since our fair city was already pretty much in shambles.

"We already know they're at war with each other," I pointed out. "The girl, Alaria, was crystal clear about that when she called for help. She said there was going to be mass extermination. I wouldn't be surprised if she is the one behind setting the farms loose. She's obviously trying to save her people. I bet everyone's terrified." I shifted my shoulders, dropping my arms.

"Honestly, to hell with the government workers and their panic. Why isn't anybody thinking about the people losing their lives at sea?" I locked eyes with our head of security. "Telling us this now doesn't explain why you kept it from us initially. I don't care if all the people in this city are up in arms, this is something we needed to be in on. So why did you keep silent?"

Lockland looked miserable. "Because Claire asked me to."

Chapter 8

Everyone started talking at once. Bender was furious, Darby was concerned, Case was practical, verging on irritated, and Knox was trying to ask informative questions. The only one who wasn't adding any bits to the chaos was me. I glanced around, noting that Mary had left, shutting the door behind her.

I gave a sharp whistle as I lifted my hand. "We're wasting time arguing about this." Everyone quieted down somewhat. I inclined my head at Lockland, my eyes conveying my intent. "You made the wrong choice, and it can't happen again. We all understand Claire is a member of this group and is now the president of our city. But we either choose to keep the team together, or we don't. But we decide now. What's it going to be?" My hand remained aloft. "Raise your fist if you're committed to remaining a part of this group, and we continue to run like we always have.

Every vote counts." Voting was an ode to our ancient ancestors. It'd been well documented in the history left behind that during the time of democracy, the world had thrived. After that, pure oligarchies, hand in hand with big businesses like Bliss Corp, had taken control. The world, and the people in it, had been worse off.

Every hand rose in the air. Knox looked unsure if he was supposed to participate or not, and I nodded with a smile.

"That settles it," Bender announced. "It doesn't matter what the government does in the future, this group shares every piece of sensitive material we encounter. And we make decisions accordingly." His tone broached zero discussion.

Darby addressed Lockland. "Why do you think Claire wanted you to keep quiet? Surely she knows we're just trying to help."

"She's got a lot on her mind," Lockland said, trailing a hand behind his neck. "Her first priority is to keep panic to a minimum. But ultimately, I think she's scared Holly is going to barrel into this situation and get herself killed."

"Why single me out?" I asked gruffly, totally offended. "I'm not the only one who wants to help those people. Not to mention, it's the right thing to do." The last part came out in a semiwhine. All eyes were on me. "What? It is. And I'm not planning to head out to sea unprepared. That would be stupid. Maisie will be heavily involved. She can guarantee a strategic plan that gives us a positive rate of success.

That status reader was made to crunch the odds of complex missions. If you hadn't been withholding information," I accused Lockland, "a fucking plan would be in motion already."

"Promising Claire you wouldn't give us the information doesn't explain why we're sneaking around in this basement," Case continued on my behalf. That was a very valid point. "Why couldn't you leave this area and come to us? There's more you're not sharing." An even more valid point. Case was flush with them.

Lockland appeared increasingly uncomfortable. "Well," he stalled, "Claire didn't just ask me to keep this confidential, she ordered me." We were all stunned. He continued, "She also secured Maisie. She knows you're ultimately going after the threat, whether she wants you to or not, but she knows you can't do it without the LiveBot." His shoulders drooped. He looked beyond tired—he looked fatigued to the bone. It seemed Lockland had been trying to placate two factions, and it had worn him thin. About time he came to his senses.

"It doesn't matter if she locked up Maisie," I countered. "The kid can contact her, no problem. Daze is in possession of her receiver button, from when the LiveBot was Priscilla. There's not a lot of places in this world that could keep Maisie for long." Maisie wasn't just a LiveBot, she was a military-grade status reader programmed for combat. It was a wonder we'd survived so long without her. She was that good.

"Once we order Daze to tell her to break out of wherever she is, we rendezvous at a secure location, and we go about the business of saving the people of New Eden before that madman floats into our harbor and blows everything up."

Lockland glanced at me, a skeptical look on his face. "That sounds easy, but Claire is prepared to put us all under what she's calling quarantine to prevent us from going, if it comes to that."

Bender swore. "What the absolute *hell*? She's one of us. She can't lock us up!"

"She's well aware we don't take orders from the government," I groused. "Something's going on here we still don't understand." I turned, trying to get some much-needed room to move around in this pitifully small space. "Maybe if she and I sat down, I could talk some sense into her. It might be worth a try."

"We can't risk it," Bender said. "If what Lockland said is true, we don't want a war with the government. If they lock us up, we retaliate. That's how this will play out. Claire or not, we can't trust them if they *quarantine* us against our will." He ended on a snort, like going up against Claire was even an option. It wasn't going to happen, but I wasn't willing to argue that point at this very moment. It was hard for me to believe Claire had even suggested confining us to Lockland. Things must be completely messed up.

Lockland's pissy expression conveyed his thoughts on the topic that Bender thought he might not be telling the truth, but he refrained from commenting. Smart man.

"I've tried talking to her, but Claire won't be dissuaded. She doesn't think there's a way to save both New Eden and our city. She's choosing to save her people."

"It's noble that she wants to protect us, and that *is* her job now, we can't forget that," I said. "But how is she effectively going to defend against Bancroft blowing up the entire city once he sails into the harbor? She can't. We don't have enough compressed fuel or long-range launchers. The only real option is to find and eliminate the threat before it arrives on our doorstep. It's the *only* option." I holstered my weapons, squeezing my hands open and shut. "We're the closest thing to a war council she has. Why would she trust panicked government workers over us?"

"I don't think it's about trust, exactly," Lockland said. "She already knows what we want to do. She's not stupid. She just doesn't agree that the best course of action is engaging Marty directly."

"She's willing to go to great lengths to keep us here, which is telling," Case said. "Locking Maisie up is also an issue. She knows we'll come after her sooner or later. She has to be readying for a fight. She realizes if she tries to contain us, there will be retaliation."

I drew out my tech phone. "Maisie won't be restrained for long." I depressed the button. "Rennie, I need a favor." I waited for the kid to fish his communicator out of his pocket.

A dash of static crossed the line first. "Can I bring you a gift?" His voice sounded sweet and small coming out of the speaker. I wasn't used to it.

I smiled. The kid was using our code. Bringing us a gift meant we needed help, and we did. "Yes, I'd love a gift." For the next part, I had to make sure that if Claire was listening, she wouldn't readily understand my meaning. But I had to choose something the kid could decipher. "I need you to fetch the negative resource with the bell. Order it done quietly. Meet me at the station."

It took the kid all of two seconds to catch my meaning. "I'll be there." His excitement was palpable. He would complete his first order with glee.

I stuck the phone back in my pocket, surprised to see all the inquiring faces. "Maisie is the negative resource," I explained. "Daze and I had a big discussion recently about her not eating or drinking or needing much of anything from us. Thusly, according to Daze, she increases our net positive, rendering her somehow negative. Don't ask. I didn't even understand. As for the bell, Daze read something on the pico about our ancestors summoning servants hundreds of years ago with a bell, a cone of metal with a movable weight inside. He thought it was hilarious they had no access to any tech and likened Maisie's summoning button to a bell."

"Where's the station?" Bender asked. "You can't mean the old main mag-lev hub at Government Square."

I chuckled. "No, I don't. It's where I've been parking Tilly. Daze gave it the nickname of the station. I think because it has pillars around it or some such thing. Daze's brain defies explanation. It's a vast, complicated web of synapses, which I don't pretend to understand." I shrugged. "But it worked. The kid understood. If you guys didn't understand, Claire shouldn't either. Though, she's probably too busy locking people up to listen in on our conversations."

"She's not too busy. The only reason she's not listening," Lockland replied, "is that I took this." He reached into his trench and pulled out a tech phone. "Otherwise, she would be. When she realizes it's missing, she's going to be pissed."

I gave him a look. "I'm thinking it might be time for you to quit the government. Doesn't seem like a good fit to me. You and Claire being at odds is only going to worsen everything."

Darby shook his head before Lockland could answer. "Oh, no. He should stay. How else are we going to know what's going on? If Claire is in control of everything, and making these kinds of decisions, Lockland has to be there. We love Claire. She'll get through this, but we need answers."

"Darby's right," Bender growled. "Lockland stays." Bender pierced Lockland with a withering look. "But if you ever keep a single thing from us again, we're going to have issues." The way Bender said *issues* was more like *irreparable damage.*

Lockland got the point.

"All information will be shared," Lockland answered. "By abiding by Claire's wishes, I convinced myself that I was working for the good of everyone. I wasn't."

My head rocked back and forth as I tried to figure

out why this was happening and what I was missing. "Maybe Claire feels backed into a corner. Moms protect their children, right? The stress of trying to pull this city off of its road to implosion must feel like an enormous task." It was hard to find fault with Claire. I knew that, in her mind, whatever was really going on, she was doing the right thing for all inhabitants here, not just us. "Then couple that with the threat of Marty and his firepower, and she feels like she has no other choice. The people of the city are her children."

Bender grunted. "She's not *my* mother."

"Stress could be a factor," Lockland said, easing back into his role as head of security. "At any rate, we're going to need to keep moving. Once you get Maisie, head to the barracks. You're going to have to go without me. Claire knows that location. I'm going to stay behind and make sure no one follows you before you get a chance to depart for New Eden. Knox will stay with me. He'll rendezvous with you at the barracks later tonight and give you an update on what's going on here."

"Is that okay with you?" I asked Knox. He nodded. He was young and innocent. No one would suspect him of anything. "The intel we gather at the barracks with Maisie will determine how quickly we move. I wish we could hear those radio messages from Bancroft. That would help."

Lockland grinned. "Maisie has copies of the recordings. I made sure she was in the room when I had them played back. Keep me apprised. I'll do my best to maintain stability here. Once the threat to the city is dealt with, I'm certain things will even out."

"Let's hope so," I said. "And when they do, I'm going to have a long discussion with Claire. We can't find our way back to this place again. If she chooses not to have us involved in the governing moving forward, I'm fine with that. We go back to the way it was before. It's worked all these years. It will certainly work again."

"Agreed," Bender said.

Case inclined his head toward the door. I caught his meaning. "We need to go meet Maisie and the kid," I said. "If for some reason the LiveBot can't break out on her own, we're going in to get her. We'll keep the damage to a minimum. Bender, you and Darby go pick up Walt. We're going to need all available brainpower on this to figure out a viable plan. Knox, we'll see you a few hours after blackout. Everybody stays overnight at the barracks. If the odds are in our favor, Case, Maisie, and I leave first thing in the morning."

"Don't cut us out of the journey just yet," Bender said. "If Maisie can pinpoint exact locations, we all go. That madman doesn't get a chance at *my* city on my watch."

I nodded. "We'll discuss it if the odds are in favor of a group mission."

Case pulled the door open, ducking his head out to take a look, his Pulse drawn. "Let's go," he said. "I hear movement."

Something clattered from above.

A large weight sounded like it'd been dropped on the floor. Everything rattled, and dust filtered down around us. "Where are we anyway?" I asked.

"We're below the new housing unit Claire opened up," Lockland replied, following us out. "In the building next to the bureau."

"Is that where Maisie is being held?" Darby asked.

Another couple of clunks echoed above, and more debris sprinkled down.

Lockland eyed the ceiling. "Yes."

I smiled. "It sounds like she's already sprung."

"Let's go find out," Bender said.

We hurried toward the tunnel. Before we'd gotten more than ten meters, Mary's voice called out in alarm. I drew my Gem, running her way.

"You will not be punished for letting me pass." Maisie's distinctively modulated humanlike voice flowed out of her borrowed silicone vocal cords at a fairly loud level. "I'm free to go."

I ducked around the corner and into the hallway in front of the medi-pod room where the Seeker Rehabilitation Program was administered. The wall that used to be there had been blown out by a bomb that Bender had set. I spotted Mary. She was doing a valiant job of trying to keep the LiveBot where she thought she should be, standing her ground, arms splayed. Claire must've informed the staff that Maisie wasn't allowed to leave.

"It's okay, Mary," I murmured from behind. "She's with us."

Startled, Mary immediately stood down and turned around. "I'm sorry," she said, a hand on her heaving chest. "I was told she had to stay." Then she recovered, chuckling under her breath. "It's not like I can do anything to keep her here anyway." As Maisie walked past her in her brisk, no-nonsense way, Mary called, "Good luck, you guys! I'll keep you in my thoughts as you travel."

"How do you know we're traveling?" I asked over my shoulder.

"Oh, everyone does," she replied. "The rumors are that you guys are going to save our backsides, yet again, from that crazy guy on the boat. I think when you come home, we should give you a trophy or something."

"A trophy?" I said. I had no idea what that was.

Darby cleared his throat. "A long time ago, when people won competitive games, they received things called trophies. They were meant as recognition for something well done."

"Huh, well, my trophy will be living, breathing human beings and a city still standing. Well, half standing, you know, like it is now." Maisie stopped in front of us. I gave her a once-over. She looked pretty badass. We'd outfitted her in synthetic leather. Her streaked red hair was pulled back at the nape of her neck, her green eyes calculating and otherworldly.

"Are you ready to go?" Maisie gave me the same once-over, complete with a small cock of her head. I knew it well, because it was one of my own. She'd nailed my key facial expressions, which was as cool as it was spooky. This look clearly said, *Took you long enough.*

"Of course," she replied. "I was created ready."

·ARI·

Chapter 9

The impact of hitting the water had tossed Ari and Paris around on their seats. Ari vaguely heard Paris' cry of distress. Jake's voice landed in her ear a moment later, but she couldn't make out what he was saying and couldn't take the time to focus on it just yet.

The swells were enormous, the biggest she'd ever ridden.

Ari realized her speed was too slow. The only way to avoid sinking was to fly across the surface of the water. Ari forced the propulsion to its max. The waves were high, but the troughs were wide, giving her ample time to ramp up for the next trip up and over.

"Paris!" Ari shouted above the din. "Hold on tighter!" Paris got the message, clasping Ari's waist. Ari took the next ascent even faster, racing up the side of the swell, cresting the top, launching them through the air and back down, expertly angling the nose of the ski to match the steep downslope of the backside of the wave. As her body flung forward and backward, Ari remembered how much she had loved the exhilaration of the ride growing up.

Ari felt her friend's face buried in her back as Paris' moans became louder. That was fine, as long as her friend kept her body flexible. After the next peak, Ari spotted a dot of light to her left. Jake and Hector sped into view. Jake was focused. Hector's head was thrown back, and she was pretty sure he was yelling with glee.

They were really doing this, and they were going to succeed. There was no room for failure.

After a few more waves, Ari found her rhythm. She was able to stay in her seat more, using her upper body and shoulders to do the work for her.

"Just like when we were kids," Jake said, his voice humming through her earpiece, crackling with static and echoing slightly.

"Yeah," Ari agreed. "I can't believe this is happening. We're not as wet as I thought we'd be. That's a bonus."

"If we skim the tops, we should be okay," Jake said. His voice sounded close, which was comforting as they zoomed through the vast, churning sea. "My gauges are working. We've gone half a kilometer. At this rate, we should get a visual on the city in a few minutes." They were following the currents, assuming New Eden was trailing along after them.

"Let's give it fifteen," Ari said. "You scan left, I'll scan right."

AMANDA CARLSON

They rode for a few more minutes in silence before Jake intoned, "I think I see something."

Ari glanced in the direction of his outstretched arm. She squinted into the darkness. "I think you're right," she said. "There's definitely a glow, but it's faint. Let's head that way." They both veered northwest. Ari's ski didn't track kilometers anymore, but her directional indicators were alive and well.

Shifting their direction meant changing the angle they rode the waves. It was a little trickier coming in at forty-five degrees, but not impossible. As they raced closer, the city began to solidify—a hazy, jagged outline bobbing along the horizon.

They'd found it.

"We keep the running lights on until we get a kilometer away," Jake said. "There's a chance they'll see us, but we can't ride blind. The swells are too big."

"I have an idea," Ari said, something she should've thought of sooner. "When we get a little closer, let's switch on the underwater sub lights. They're blue and muted. But I think they'll allow us to see far enough ahead."

"Good idea," he answered, his breath coming in spurts from the effort it took to navigate the churning ocean.

"Do you think we'll be able to board the ship? The waves are pretty big." Ari was having doubts. If the waves were this massive next to the ship, they could smash them and their skis into the hull.

"If they have the buoy wall out, we'll be fine," Jake

said. "If it's gone, we'll have to make a decision when we get there."

For their entire lives, partitions made of a heavy-duty foam had protected most of the city. The buoy walls had been installed years ago to keep the sea from battering the sides of the ships all day long.

"Their anchors are up," Ari said, amping her voice as the wind whipped around her face. "Now that New Eden and everything along with it is drifting, the buoy wall could hinder them. My guess is they took it out. Without that protection and calmer surf, we're going to have a hard time getting close enough without these skis smashing to pieces."

"The guards have to have a place to depart and return," Jake said. "They wouldn't be foolish enough to make it impossible to get back."

Ari had agreed on that during the planning session, but she couldn't help worrying they were wrong. "If there's no floating wall, we abort."

"Agreed," Jake replied.

As they continued, Ari and Jake avoided the swirling white foam as much as possible. At this speed, the skis were skimming the surface, which was ideal.

Ari spotted something in the distance. "What's that? To the right of the city."

After a brief pause, Jake answered, "I think it might be the medi-ship. That's the only ship that has a tower on the top."

"Why would they disconnect the medi-ship from the city?" For her entire life, the medi-ship had been accessible by a steel bridge connected to New Eden. Behind Ari, Paris relaxed her death grip around her abdomen. Ari wouldn't go so far as to say Paris was enjoying herself, but her fear had subsided, making the job of guiding the ski easier.

"It's hard to know," Jake said. "Maybe it broke apart on its own?"

"I don't think so," she replied. "If it was adrift, it would have floated farther away. It looks like it's keeping a close proximity to the city. You don't think my father has taken command of it, do you?" When the original group of ships had first rendezvoused with the farms thirty years ago, several of them had been set up to be separate from the construction of New Eden. The engineering ship was one of them. It'd been custom fitted with state-of-the-art technology and tools. The medi-ship was another. It had saved myriad lives over the years and was stocked with inoculations, surgery pods, 3-D organ printers, medi-pods, and much more. Ari wasn't sure what, if any, of that was still functioning, but she'd used the medi-pods many times in her life and had been thankful for them. "He wouldn't be that heartless to take away medical services, would he?" But she already knew the answer. Of course he would. She had no earthly idea why her father wanted to destroy all those innocent souls. If his goal was to get back to the dark city, fine. He could take one of their ships easily enough. But why take down an entire city full of innocent people? It baffled all logic. "Don't answer that," she muttered, taking a long jump off a particularly big swell, tilting the ski back down into a dive. Paris squealed in renewed terror.

"If the medi-ship is on its own," Jake said, his voice breaking apart and sounding fuzzy, "that means we might have a chance to do something more while we're here."

Ari had been thinking the same thing. "Do you think it's still on board?"

"Of course. Why wouldn't it be?" he answered.

The thought made Ari's heart skip a beat. Communication with the dark city might be within their grasp, floating on the medi-ship and apart from New Eden. "We go to the engineering ship first," Ari decided. "We'll decide after that."

"Sounds good," Jake said. "We douse headlights in less than one kilometer." They were approaching the city rapidly.

As they sped closer, Ari could see the buoy wall in place. A huge relief. "I see the wall, but it looks like it only extends around the back side of the city," Ari relayed.

"I see that, too," Jake answered. "But it should provide enough protection to dock the skis." After a brief pause, Jake ordered, "Switch your lights off."

Ari punched a button, and her headlight went out. Then she flicked the knob next to it, and small bulbs dotted around the rim of the skis blinked on. With less light, Ari was forced to concentrate harder to keep the ski stable as they continued to traverse wave after wave.

As they skirted New Eden, they entered the hazy glow cast on the sea by portholes and light pouring out of residences high in the sky. The floating city had never been short on battery power. The farms' continuous photovoltaic output had made certain of that. But eventually, without the farms, the city would suffer as the batteries weakened.

"How close do you want to get?" Ari asked.

"Just outside the illumination. Let's head left," Jake said. "The East Commoner side doesn't have much access to views. We should be able to slip in under the radar."

"If someone spots us, they might think we're militia coming back from a raid on the farms," Ari said as they circled around the city. Once they passed the East Commoner ship, they should be in sight of the engineering ship.

The waves were choppier here. It took more effort to keep their balance. At least Paris was doing well, all things considered.

They took their time along the curve, then once they cleared the corner, they found what they were looking for. The buoy wall was wrapped almost entirely around the engineering ship, with a gap between partitions large enough to ride the skis through. They'd made it.

Seeing the city this close made Ari's heart ache. She'd never known anything different. It was her home. She knew that if her father would've let her, she could've made this a better place—a thriving city where all the people had a chance to prosper and grow. Instead, it was nothing more than a shell, polluted by greed and condemned by neglect.

Jake continued in the lead. "Turn off all lights," he instructed. "I see the way in."

Ari flicked the knob, and her ski went dark. Luckily, there was enough ambient glow reflected on the continually breaking surface of the sea to guide them straight to their destination. Ari followed Jake closely through the small separation in the wall, the water extremely choppy at the intersection as the rougher water slapped into the buoys.

Inside the enclosure, the waves immediately became muted. The buoys were weighted at the bottom, so they dropped well below the waterline, providing a more stable environment within.

Jake slowed, and Ari did, too. "Get ready to launch your anchor cable and enact the air cushion," Jake instructed.

Each ski had a cable that, when released, secured the vehicle to a metal object, usually a rod positioned around a farm. But in this case, the magnet would anchor them to the side of the engineering ship. The skis also came standard with protective cushions made of an inflatable chemi-foam, so if they bounced against whatever they were moored to, they wouldn't get damaged.

Ari scanned the ship, but didn't detect movement, nor any lookouts. New Eden had never needed to guard against intrusion, because there'd never been a threat. The very few humans left in the world hadn't been searching the seas, as far as she knew. So there was no guard watch, and it was unlikely that her father, or any of his men, would assume Ari would venture back, especially since they were the ones being pursued.

It all made for a perfect opportunity.

Jake maneuvered in and out of the well-lit areas, weaving his way toward the ship instead of taking a straight line. Once he was within three meters, he lofted his hand. "Launch your cable," he announced in her ear. In the next instant, a hollow *thunk* rang out as both their anchors landed against the ship. The impact hadn't been overly loud, but they'd have to wait to see.

Jake cut his motor, allowing the cable to automatically drag the ski closer to the ship. Ari followed close behind. They'd managed to land within a meter of the ladder. Hopefully, no one had heard them.

"Holy hell," Paris moaned, her head sagging against Ari's shoulder. "Are we finally here?"

"Yes," Ari answered. "You did well. You should be proud of yourself."

Paris replied by leaning over and vomiting into the sea.

Chapter 10

They sat on their skis for a good five minutes, bobbing in the swells, thankful the water wasn't any wilder, waiting to see if there would be any call to alarm. Paris had been sick twice, but had rallied. Ari let her do her business, refraining from consoling her. Her friend would hate that.

Earlier, Hector had mapped out the interior of the ship in detail for them, and they each had a job to do. Ari was going to collect some needed tubes of PlexiFill, which the farms had run out of, and whatever else she could grab. Paris was going to gather some hand tools to fix the winch. Hector and Jake were going to retrieve the steel part they needed and anything else they could stuff into their sacks. The entire undertaking wasn't meant to exceed fifteen minutes, if all went well.

Jake's voice sounded in Ari's ear. "Hector and I go first. Once we're up, you guys follow. We will sound the alarm if anything goes wrong." Ari watched him flip up his mask, reach into his pocket, and don his chromoscope glasses. All four of them had a pair, but unfortunately, they didn't fit when the crystalline face shield was lowered.

"Will do," Ari replied. "Be careful. Remember, only fire if absolutely necessary." They each carried inferior weapons, but they worked. They'd agreed to keep the noise to an absolute minimum. The odds of escaping before any violence erupted were in their favor, as the engineers were not armed. But if they were detected, her father would bring his militia down hard in retaliation. They wanted to avoid that at all costs. As far as the engineering ship went, things had a tendency to go missing all the time. They wouldn't automatically assume they'd been looted by the resistance.

Jake used a retractable pole that came integrated under the ski seat. It was fashioned with a hook on the end for harvesting seaweed and facilitating maintenance work. In this case, Jake used it as a guide, hooking onto the bottom rung of the ladder. Once he was close enough, he hit the bottom of the pole against his leg, which made it contract immediately. Instead of sticking it back under his seat, he tucked it in his pocket. He'd need it to snag the ski once they were finished.

Ari and Paris watched the boys climb. They took their time, stopping to listen at regular intervals. Ari held her breath as Jake crossed over the top, disappearing from sight. A few seconds later, he said, "All clear. Nobody around. Do you want us to wait?"

"No," Ari replied, donning her own chromes, nudging Paris to do the same. "You have the toughest job. We'll follow. I'll alert you if anything happens." Ari already had her pole extended. She unhooked their safety belts and repeated Jake's movements, careful to guide them in a wide berth around Jake's ski. Even though the air foam was employed, she didn't want to take a chance on a collision. They couldn't get back to the farms without them.

Ari had to stretch a little higher, standing on her tiptoes and angling her body, to grab the bottom rung of the ladder. The swells bounced her around, making it hard to keep a firm grasp. "You go first," she whispered to Paris. "You're shorter than me. I'll give you a boost."

"Fine," Paris said, her voice resigned. "Anything to get off this damn ski. But I'm warning you, my legs are shaky."

"You'll be fine," Ari coaxed. "Once we start up the ladder, adrenaline will take over, I promise. When I get a grip, you climb on my back and use my shoulder as a step. Go quickly. I'm not sure how long I can keep hold."

Paris stood on the seat behind her, clutching Ari's back to keep her balance as the water rocked them. Ari had to use her entire body to get a firm clasp, finally grabbing the bottom rung with two hands, trying her best to stabilize them. She gritted her teeth. "Go."

Paris didn't waste any time. She scampered up, stepping lightly on Ari's shoulder as she deftly grasped the handhold above Ari. Paris was extremely agile. Daily scavenging in the hulls as a child had prepared her for stunts like this. Paris had confided to Ari, briefly, that because of territory disputes over the years, the once mainly open hulls had been transformed into a clutter of mazes and tunnels, hidey-holes, ladders, and makeshift hard-to-reach openings, constructed from remnants of steel and other metal scraps. To traverse to the top, which was the only way to exit the hulls, one had to bypass the many living quarters. You had to step lightly if you didn't want any conflict. Paris had spent her life deftly traversing these places.

Once Paris climbed higher, Ari hoisted herself, using her upper-arm strength. It was harder than she'd expected. Thank goodness she wasn't sopping wet. Ari's conditioning wasn't what it was when she'd trained every day. Fitness, defense, along with good health and nutrition, kept the status tiers in place. More of her father's words. Those who occupied space below her didn't have access to the same resources, therefore were weaker. That was the theory anyway. But Paris and Hector had proved otherwise. Their survival had been based on fierce determination coupled with ingenuity and intelligence. What they needed, they took. Ari was in awe of their strength and abilities.

Ari bent her body, hooking her legs through the rung. From there, she was able to start climbing, even though she was huffing with the effort. Paris had paused halfway, waiting for her to catch up. Ari nodded as she neared. Paris reached the top, poking her head over to scan for heat signatures. Then her friend disappeared over the side.

Once on the deck, they both crouched low, settling their backs against the solid steel barrier to get their bearings. Ari flipped the dials on her chromes, checking for any potential pitfalls, then left it on infrared. She hoped she'd spot someone before they detected her.

Ari pulled Paris in close, whispering, "I'm heading to the supply room. We meet back here in ten." Ari felt better knowing that Paris was communicating with Hector and would get the same warnings she would from Jake if there was any danger.

Ari and Paris moved together, splitting at the first stairway. Ari entered the small space. Heading down three levels, she would reach the supply closet. Paris needed to move past this area, toward the middle of the ship, to get to her destination.

Giving Paris a small salute, Ari descended the stairs, treading slowly and cautiously. Once she reached the right floor, the room was four doors down on the left. That was, if they hadn't moved the supplies since Hector had been on board, which was a possibility. She'd have to wait to see.

Ari gripped the railing as she crept down, her shoulder pressing against the cool metal of the ship. As she rounded the second landing, she heard voices. Jake had been extremely quiet in her ear, doing his best to keep this a stealth operation. The amplifier automatically tuned out ambient noise, picking up only human speech.

The voices echoed upward, making their way toward her from a few levels below. Dim bulbs located at the base of each stair tread were the only lights illuminating the area. She slid off her chromes, glancing around. There was nowhere to go. She was stuck. With only one option, and the voices getting nearer, she backtracked to the small landing she'd just traversed. A shallow indent beside a large column of metal was her only hiding option. Light was muted on the landing, full of shadows. If whoever approached wore chromes or a visor, they would spot her body temp immediately. But if they didn't, she might remain safe.

She held her breath as she squeezed into the tiny space, making herself as compact as possible. She wore head-to-toe black and still had her neoprene head covering on. She hoped it would be enough to keep her camouflaged.

The voices continued. A man and a woman. They were arguing.

"I don't trust him," the female said as they came up the last few steps to the landing.

"I don't either, but what choice do we have?" the male answered.

"We have to look out for ourselves. Nobody's going to do it for us," the woman said. "Things are changing so fast. It's hard to keep up."

"The newest rumor is that Bancroft is taking the medi-ship to the farms, then back to New Eden. He's going to leave us here to rot with no food."

"Well, that's better than killing us outright, isn't it?" The couple stopped less than a meter away from where Ari had stuffed herself into the small space. The man grabbed the woman's arm, efficiently turning her toward him. Luckily, they were facing away from Ari, too caught up in their discussion to notice anything amiss.

"Leaving us here *is* a death sentence," the man insisted, his voice stressed. "There'll be an uprising in the hulls, and the commoners will follow. Even though we don't trust Ernie, staying here is our only option. If things go to hell, he's prepared to captain this ship away."

"And go where?" the woman huffed. "We can't follow Bancroft. He'll probably blow us out of the water if we tried."

"Well, we can't cross over into the city either. This is our safest option."

The woman wrapped her arms around the man's shoulders. He pulled her near as her head settled into the crook of his neck. "We can only hope that the resistance network will stop him. I hear it's growing by the day."

That was news to Ari. Most of the people on Ari's side had left with the farms. Knowing that a resistance was growing in the city would make a difference.

"Those kids are going to have a hard time

defending against that medi-ship once it reaches the farms. Bancroft had all the laser cannons and the frequency-seeking missiles installed in the last few days. There won't be much left when he's done."

"It's such a shame," the woman murmured, her voice muffled against the man's neck. "I had high hopes for Alaria. She's the only one who has ever stood up for the people. She could've brought a lot of good into this world. Now the madman's going to win, and we're all going to die."

"We're not going to die," the man said firmly, kissing the top of the woman's head. "Not if I can help it. But for right now, we need to get back to our cabin before anyone finds us. If we get caught out this late without permission, we'll be cleaning the waste rooms for a month."

"It was worth it," the woman replied, drawing away from him, linking her arm through his. "The little one needed a snack." Ari watched her hand settle protectively over her abdomen. From her angle, Ari could see a tiny swell.

The couple turned, continuing up the stairs to the main deck. According to Hector, the residence quarters were accessed by the middle stairway. Once they were out of earshot, Ari spoke into the mic to Jake. "Did you catch that?"

"Affirmative," he responded. "I passed the info on to Hector, so he can alert Paris." Paris was in the quadrant that housed the quarters, and she needed to know that someone was approaching. "We're inside the main warehouse," Jake went on. "We found what we're looking for. Meet at the rendezvous point in six."

"Got it," Ari replied, sliding out of her spot to hurry down the stairs. "I'll be at my destination in less than one minute. I'll see you in six."

Ari reached the level she needed and glanced through the small round window, her chromes back on. No light signatures. She cracked the door, cringing as it squeaked, then angled her head into the hallway. All clear.

Like a ghost, she eased inside. At the fourth door, she paused, listening again. According to Hector, this was a supply closet designated to keep all sorts of fillers. It was extremely lucky their ancestors had perfected liquefied composites. A squirt from a nozzle could fix literally anything, from plastics to metal. Ari tried the door handle. Locked. No surprise there. She tugged a hot-laser key out of her pocket and aimed it inside the mechanism, depressing the button. In less than five seconds, a click sounded as the melting internal components malfunctioned.

She slipped into the room, shutting the door and using her foot to keep it closed. She found a switch, and a pale yellow light blinked on from above. "Goods located," she murmured. They'd gotten lucky. The entire room was stacked with shelving, and on each platform, tubes were organized in neat rows. Ari unzipped the pouch around her waist with one hand, grabbing a fistful of PlexiFill with the other. Then she continued down the line, plucking up tubes of liquid metal, EpoxyAll, PlasterIt, and the old standby, hydro-gel. The farms were short on all these supplies, but particularly the PlexiFill. A little went a long way. Each tube was six centimeters in diameter. When her pouch was crammed full, she forced it shut, working the nylon glider back in place with effort. A larger sack would've been better, but with Paris behind her on the ski, balancing would be tricky.

She was just about to leave the room when Jake's voice settled softly in her ear. "We found something," he whispered. "I think you should come and take a look." Her eyebrows rose at the request. It must be important if he wanted her to risk detection. She didn't question it, as Jake wouldn't put them in jeopardy if it wasn't worth it. "Make your way to the last stairway. I'll be waiting for you outside the door on the bottom."

"Have Hector tell Paris there will be a delay," Ari said. "I'm on my way." She exited the storage room, reaching into her pocket and bringing out a steel pin. She jammed it into the lock, securing the door in place. The break-in wouldn't be discovered until somebody needed a tube of filler, which she hoped wouldn't be for a day or two. Luckily, this area wasn't residential, and no one was about.

Ari hurried back up to the main platform, ducking around the side as she raced down the deck to the last set of stairs. The engineering ship stored supplies out in the open, strapped down on large pallets with waterproof coverings. The only way someone would spot her was if they were charging directly toward her. She made it in less than a minute. "All clear down there?" she asked as she tugged open the passageway door.

"Clear," Jake answered.

Ari was relieved when she found Jake safe and sound at the bottom right where he said he'd be. She noticed his front pouch was as full as hers. Hector exited through the door behind Jake, his backpack sitting low on his shoulders. Ari reached up and clipped her mic off so they wouldn't get feedback this close. "What do I need to see?" she whispered.

Hector nodded to the right. "Once I got down here, it triggered my memory. There was a top-secret room when I worked here. Off-limits to workers, official personnel only. I asked about it a few times, but didn't get much of an answer. I forgot all about it until I saw this place again. While Jake was gathering some tools, I decided to check it out." He began to walk. Ari followed, Jake coming behind. Hector paused before a plain steel door and cracked it open, having already unlocked it with his laser key.

The scent was distinctly musty. Nobody had been here for a while.

Ari's eyes widened as she hurried inside and tugged out the desk chair. "I didn't think he had more than one of these units," she exclaimed, flicking on the power. The circuit board jumped to life. The microphone was large, shaped like a cylinder nestled on a small tripod. "Do you think it still works?" The communications system was just like the one she'd used to hail the dark city on the medi-ship.

There was movement outside the door, and Jake pulled his weapon. A moment later, Paris' voice echoed, "Where are you guys?"

A squeal of feedback followed immediately, and Hector ripped his amplifier out, rubbing his ear. "*Ow,*" he moaned.

Jake opened the door, gesturing her inside. "Turn off your mic," he told Paris. "We found something."

Paris came in, adjusting the tiny bud on her inflatable, her pack making a jangling noise. They'd all achieved their goals. "Holy mother of sunshine, is that a *communicator?*"

Ari nodded. "This one looks like it hasn't been used in a while, not sure it will work. The channel is set to a different one than the medi-ship. I'm going to try it first." Ari brought the microphone close, engaging the button on its neck, leaning over so her lips were mere centimeters from the dark steel mesh. "This is Alaria Bancroft. Can anyone hear me? We're in danger of extermination. Without any help, our city will be wiped out. Is anyone out there?"

·HOLLY·

Chapter 11

"How'd you break out?" Darby asked the LiveBot as we walked. After bidding Mary a farewell, we were navigating our way through the tunnel to reach street level.

Maisie shrugged in yet another humanlike gesture. "Daze summoned me, and I obeyed. I detected your signatures below and concluded this route would be the quickest exit for a rendezvous point with him."

"You chose right," I agreed. "But what Darby is asking is: How did you escape, *technically*? Were you trapped behind steel bars? Or did they just lock you in a room?"

Maisie paused a good five seconds before answering.

I was learning her tells, and this was one. When she didn't want to divulge would-be military-grade classified information, the kind she was programmed to protect had the world survived and she'd been utilized on a military base, she stalled.

But a LiveBot stall lasted far shorter than any human's. At the six-second mark, she answered, "I was detained in a holding cell. The titanium barriers were twelve centimeters in diameter. There was one way to exit, through a lock requiring a physical key made of steel." She'd given us a technical answer, but still not the one we were looking for.

"Enough delay. Spit it out," I ordered, mildly irritated. "We already talked about this. We need all the information you have, one hundred percent of the time. What are you keeping from us?"

Two seconds later, she said, "I melted the lock with my eyes." She'd relayed the news calmly, as though all LiveBots had the capacity to melt metal with their orbs alone, and we should've known better.

I stumbled, catching myself at the last minute before falling flat on my face. But I wasn't the only one. Everyone came to an abrupt standstill, too stunned to speak.

Maisie continued moving like nothing was amiss. "Stop right there," I called. She halted, turning, managing to form a convincing look of surprise that we weren't following. Her mannerisms were becoming so familiar that it was only a matter of time before we forgot she was a robot. She knew it, too. Of course she did. She was programmed for that. Easing soldiers into relating to her as a peer was probably hardwired as a military safeguard. My voice came out pained—pained that I had to even say this. "Can you please explain, in great detail, how your eyes have suddenly become hot lasers? And is this capacity shared by all LiveBots?" The thought of Julian having the wherewithal to sear tiny holes into my body at any given moment gave me the shivers. I ran a hand over my arm in an effort to calm down.

"No," she answered immediately. "Other LiveBots do not share my internal programming. I am hardwired to remediate all available resources when necessary. I determined that lasers were the only course of action to free myself from captivity, so I used my optics."

"But *how* did you manage that?" I complained. "I know the retail bot you're occupying didn't have laser eyes to begin with." My frustration was at the bubbling point. "You're not telling us what we need to know."

Darby took a step forward, nudging me gently out of the way, coughing into his fist. "Maisie, give us detailed parameters involving tactical military assets, integrated and otherwise." He was *so* much better at this than the rest of us were. It wasn't fair.

She answered quickly, firming up her shoulders like she'd been given an order by a high-ranking officer. Double unfair. "Integrated assets come in the form of weapons-creation data for assembly with known parts. Physical assets are acquired and assimilated upon discovery, for future use to facilitate missions, provide protection, and minimize bodily harm for the entire squadron."

"What the hell does she mean by *acquired and assimilated?*" Bender charged. "Does that mean she's going around swiping stuff, then cramming it inside her head?" Bender was the least excited about having a LiveBot milling around. He understood their value, as we all did, but was the most leery of them. For good reason, it seemed. This one had turned her eyes into custom lasers.

There was so much we didn't know about Maisie. Every status reader should come with a detailed manual, but the military ones should come with an entire digital databank outlining the pros and cons before even turning them on. Her handler would've known everything about her, but we were at a considerable disadvantage. It didn't help that she'd been silent about what she was truly capable of.

Maisie addressed Bender directly. "I've processed the use of the word *swipe* in reference to *steal.* That could be considered a truthful definition, although it's not considered a crime when the item is without an owner. I did not cram physical objects directly inside me. Instead, I broke down the components and adapted what I needed to construct an upgrade."

My brain was aching. I rubbed my forehead, glancing at Case to get his take. He was appraising Maisie in his own way, taking it all in, waiting to make an assessment. "So," I said, "you're *technically* not stealing, but when you suddenly find yourself in a place where a useful item is unclaimed—for instance, a hot-laser key—you then bust it apart and do what?

How in the world did you know how to construct a new eyeball in the first place?"

Darby made a jubilant sound in the back of his throat before loudly exclaiming, "That's exactly what she's saying, and it's completely brilliant!" His face became animated. "All LiveBots are constructed with extremely durable materials, including state-of-the-art plastic and complex circuitry made from bendable, pliable metals. With that type of construction, every part of her could be transformed into a potential weapon." That didn't help any part of this situation. "Eyeballs are particularly good conduits, constructed with diamond crystalline tubes, complete with input and output chambers. All she would need to do would be to set the plasma generator of a hot-laser key behind her eye sockets and align the light refraction with the output path. With her power source, the eyeball laser would be immediately operational. Complete genius!"

"Well, I'm glad somebody is excited about it," I muttered as I walked up to Maisie, knowing that this stunning information Darby had just laid out would complicate everything between us and the robot. "Even though other LiveBots don't share your internal hardwiring, are they capable of doing what you did? Could they break things apart and integrate them into their systems, essentially performing a self-upgrade?"

She didn't stall this time. She was adept at understanding and evaluating human emotion, and she could tell by my voice, heart rate, expression, and rapid intakes of breath that I meant business. "No," she said. "Although Julian is made up of similar materials as the LiveBot I inhabit, he does not have the technical database, nor are his intention parameters set to initiate this kind of specific integration. In essence, he does not have the instinct or the means to perform such tasks."

"Is it something you can teach him to do?" I asked. "Feeding him your diagrams and explaining how to build an eyeball laser? Or some other crazy thing that could harm us?" We had to get this straight. Maisie had been in charge of Julian in the past, giving him orders through her airwave communication, something, again, that we didn't completely understand.

"No," she answered. "He would resist. He is hardwired only for exemplary service and nonviolence."

"But you're not," I said. "Clearly." I braced my hands on my hips, turning in a small circle, trying to read everyone's take. I faced the bot again. "I'm sure you're aware, but this complicates things. You're arming yourself in secret." Picturing Maisie in some back room, removing her eyeballs and packing things inside her skull, gave me a gruesome mental image. It also exemplified her careful calculation. "Your integrated weapons could be used against us. Keeping this kind of information from us erodes our trust in you, and we're going to have to do some serious debating about what to do about it. You might not like the outcome." Shutting her down would be the only reasonable option, even though it would be a sad day. It seemed this status reader turned LiveBot had gotten under my skin. I liked her.

She bowed her head in a show of human remorse. "I detect your disappointment. Whether to reveal my capabilities or keep them from you has been based on a ratio of carefully calculated odds. The outcome ratio weighs a full detailing of my technological advances against the likelihood of you ending my life." She met my gaze, her green eyes sparking with her lidar, which was constantly scanning. "The ratio is, of course, in favor of me keeping certain key aspects of my nature a secret and detailing them as needed, instead of all at once. If I told you of the full extent of my abilities, the odds would be less advantageous to me."

I glanced at Darby. He shrugged. "She has a point," he said. "If she breaks down all viable scenarios—and in my opinion, those options might be limitless depending on the material and tech she has access to— our fear could very well overpower the logical parts of our brain. Meaning we could lose an extremely valuable asset because we're scared shitless of what she can do."

"Damn right we're scared," Bender snarled, lifting his beefy arm and jabbing a finger at the LiveBot. "She just confessed that she can weaponize any part of her body, and she kept that information from us on purpose. What's not to say she wouldn't use her power and smarts to take full control of the city and everyone in it? We all see it—she's becoming more human every day. Not only that, she lives forever. She can afford to bide her time and wait for all of us to be set on fire in our burial shrouds before she makes her move. She's too fucking dangerous."

Case chose this time to take a step forward, right in between Bender's finger and the LiveBot. "I agree with you," he said, partially placating Bender. "But determining how dangerous she is to us is the key here. I think it's something we can solve right now."

My eyebrows rose. That was a lofty statement, and my skepticism was front and center. But Case had an excellent tactical brain. He deserved to be heard.

"How do we do that?" Darby asked. If Darby didn't know, solving this right now was going to be a large task.

"We know because she used the words *ending my life*." Case directed his next comment at Maisie. "Why did you choose that particular phrasing? Instead of something like *shut me down*? Or *turn me off*? That would've been the logical response. If we took away your power supply, you would cease to function for a time, but as soon as you were rebooted, you'd still be you. Your life would be intact. But you're fearful of your life being destroyed. Why?"

We all glanced at Maisie, waiting for her response. I had to hand it to him, Case was good.

Maisie hedged a teensy bit, so we knew sharing this with us put her at a disadvantage. "Before I explain my word choice, I will note that my allegiance to this group cannot change," she started. "I am programmed as an intelligence officer and a combat soldier. I am designed to take orders from humans, not give them. Even though my software contains detailed schematics to equip myself with the necessary means—not only to protect myself, but my team—I am no threat to you. My database is aware of how civilians view robots." Her eyes landed on the ground, her hands clasped in front of her, her voice noticeably softer. "I chose to say *ending my life* because shutting me down, if you desire it, would not satisfy you, for all the reasons you've already stated. If you deem me too dangerous, you will destroy me. If that is your wish, I will do nothing to prevent it from happening. Not now and not ever. It's your right as my superiors to decide when that time comes, unless I'm destroyed in combat." She glanced up, her expression imploring. "But as I'm adapting into a human counterpart and team member, I find I am…enjoying it." That was a surprising admission coming from a robot. "As you continue to view me as more human, my program has unexpectedly adapted, inserting human emotions into my thought processes. I had not anticipated that and cannot find a record of it in my database. It has been…a surprise."

Darby made another noise, this one close to a baby gurgle, before clapping his hands excitedly and shouting, "Symbiosis! They were experimenting with that right before the dark days. The program was called SymBot and was designed by a geneticist, as well as a brilliant software engineer. The program can only be activated once a relationship has formed and can't be manipulated by the droid itself. They were trying to make all robots not only more humanlike, but more loyal. The original research was sparked by the real fear that robots were gaining superior intelligence and power." Bender wasn't the only one afraid of that, it seemed. "Their theory was, if LiveBots experienced quantifiable human emotion, they were more likely to be sympathetic and empathetic. Creating bonds with humans, hypothetically, would prevent them from being cold and calculating. I'm happy to say I think it's working." Darby turned to Maisie. "As a military-grade status reader, you were clearly meant to be inserted into various bots, as needed. You would've formed a human bond with your handler, as well as your team. It would've made you an incredible asset. If my theory is correct, you might be the only activated SymBot on Earth and certainly one of the early trials. It's simply amazing." Darby was all but gushing.

Maisie smiled at our resident scientist. "My database shows detailed information about the SymBot program, but I'll have to take your word that it is integrated into my system. I have no detection of it. The engineer must've been very clever, but it would explain many otherwise unexplainable things."

"With this information," Case concluded with a hint of satisfaction, "I'd say she is not an immediate danger to us. But we should continue doing due diligence to make sure it stays that way."

"My brain honestly hurts," I said. "Processing all this information is making it ache right here." I pointed to my forehead. "Darby, if we choose to believe that Maisie is a SymBot and an invested team member who's now bonded to us, it's going to be based on your information alone. None of us have any knowledge when it comes to this. We have to put all of our faith in you. Can you handle that responsibility? It's your word we're going on, whether to keep her alive or not."

I expected Darby to crumple under the pressure of taking our lives into his hands. If Maisie went haywire and turned on us, we would blame Darby. Instead, he looked gleeful, which was not an expression he wore naturally. Darby was contemplative, leaning toward dour, most of the time. He certainly didn't present himself as an overly energetic, happy man. "Yes, I take full responsibility!" he all but yelled. "I will continue to work with Maisie, through Daze, updating her program, making sure plenty of safeguards are installed. In turn," he said to Maisie, "you must reveal all of your capabilities to us, without fear of loss of life. That's an order."

A squeaking sound, like a beep interrupted by static, came out of nowhere.

Then a voice echoed into the tunnel.

It seemed like it was coming from Maisie's torso.

"Hello. This is Alaria. Is anybody out there?"

Chapter 12

Hearing the girl's voice erupt out of Maisie's chest was nothing short of astonishing. We were riveted. Ari continued speaking, her voice imploring. "This is the last channel I'm trying. We need help. People are dying. Their plan is to use the medi-ship to attack the farms." Static buzzed out of Maisie's body. "Give me two more minutes," she pleaded with someone in the background. "Someone has to be out there!"

Then the mic picked up another female voice. "We don't have three minutes. We have to get out of here!"

We couldn't miss our chance to make contact with her, not now.

I rushed toward Maisie, my hands splayed in front of me, sweeping in circles around her midsection. "How are you doing that? What's happening?"

Maisie replied matter-of-factly, "I breached the communications channels, rerouting their correspondence to divert through me." She'd done something similar on our trip down South, connecting with the radio towers so I could communicate with Darby. She had also intercepted the South's radar system, causing a blip so that I could fly through undetected.

Case asked urgently, "Can anyone in the bureau hear this?"

Maisie shook her head. "As long as I'm within range, the radio signals will feed directly here. Once I'm out of range, they will revert back to the main communications center."

I was frantic. Ari had gone silent. "Can you send her a message? Quickly, before she leaves!"

"Of course," Maisie said. "Speak directly into my receptor, and I will relay the recording."

Darby stepped forward. "Her ability to reroute the communications system is attributed to the status reader, so this is coming from that source. It has nothing to do with Maisie's LiveBot capabilities. Just so you know."

"I got that," I said impatiently, trying to think up the best words to efficiently communicate with Ari. "Maisie, start relaying: Hello. My name is Holly. My friends and I have received your message. Help is on the way. Where are you located?"

I held my breath and waited.

No response.

"Dammit, they already left—" I started as static erupted in a harsh blast of white noise.

Then the girl's voice came back, sounding farther

away this time. "I can't make out what you're saying…it's not coming through clearly. Please repeat."

"What's wrong?" I asked Maisie. "Why won't it go through?"

"The outgoing signal could be impeded by the fact that we are underground," Maisie replied.

I grabbed her arm and began to run. "Then we need to get the hell above ground. Maisie, relay what I'm saying: Ari, my name is Holly. We are on our way. What are your coordinates?" We all raced through the tunnel like lives depended on it, which they did.

After we'd crawled through the first barrier, Ari's voice sputtered out, "Are you still there? Everything is…jumbled." Panic and fear were forefront in her reply. "No, we can't leave now," she yelled to someone in the background. "We won't get another chance. People can hear us!"

"Please, let this girl be smart and give us information without being asked," I muttered, pumping my arms harder to help propel me along. "Maisie, keep relaying the last message I gave you until we reach street level." When we arrived at the next obstacle, we were forced to make our way through the rubble on our hands and knees, which slowed us down considerably.

"Send Maisie up without us," Case ordered once we emerged in the vicinity of the train. This journey ended in one of our safe places, an old mag-lev that had survived the initial destruction of the city.

"Maisie, go ahead of us," I told her. "If Ari responds, ask her for any detailed information you think is pertinent. The mission is to reach the floating city and try to save the inhabitants."

Maisie pulled ahead easily, her body made for speed and long distances, with no living parts needing such menial things as regeneration and oxygen. She disappeared into the train, which would lead to a hatch. From there, she would climb up an old maintenance shaft to reach the surface.

We caught up to the train several minutes later, most of us huffing and puffing from the exertion. Darby bent over, clutching his thighs, wheezing like someone had punched him in the gut.

"Take it easy, Darby," I cautioned, placing my hand on his back. "We don't want your heart to stop beating. We need your big, beautiful brain to remain fully functioning."

He sputtered, "I'm fine. I just…need a minute."

Bender and Case entered the train ahead of us. I lagged behind, waiting with Darby even though I was impatient to keep moving. "Come on, Darb," I coaxed. "If Ari is still there, we have to communicate with her if we can."

"You go," he said, gasping like I would imagine a sea creature would if it was deprived of oxygenated water. "I'll be right behind you."

"No way," I told him. "We go together or not at all. Your shoulder lights barely work. Plus, you're going to need a boost up to get out of the train. Like I said, without your brain we'd never be able to figure anything out. I'm not leaving you alone."

"Okay, okay," he panted. "I'm coming." He straightened, only to hunch back over, this time coughing. "It's nice to know you only care about my brain."

"That's not true at all," I feigned sweetness. "I also adore your ability to extrapolate facts, as well as your uncanny ability to engage Maisie."

"Ha-ha," he said. "Still my brain."

"Come on." I studied him, placing my arm around his shoulders, propelling him forward. "I like each and every part of you. Though we need to get you on a training regimen. Sitting in the lab all day has done you no favors. You've gotten mushy."

"I'm not *mushy*," he sniped. "I prefer the term physically challenged. Exercise makes me uncomfortable."

I chuckled. "It won't once you do it regularly." We entered the train, making our way to the middle, where the roof was hacked out. I was relieved to spot Case waiting above the opening, obviously anticipating that Darby was going to need a hand. "I'll hoist him up," I told Case. "You drag him through. There's not much left in his fuel tank."

The outskirt had the nerve to grin, popping a dimple. "It'll cost you."

"I always pay my debts," I snarked as I turned to Darby. Being a couple wasn't so bad after all. A flash of his smile was a welcome distraction as I laced my fingers together and dropped to one knee. "Come on, let's do this." Darby obeyed, springing up on rubbery legs, barely managing to ascend less than a meter. Luckily, it was enough to get into range of Case's waiting arm. The outskirt pulled up our mushy computer scientist like he was a child rather than a full-fledged adult of seventy-five kilos. I followed, jumping up on the nearest seat and easing through the hatch on my own.

We hurried up the maintenance shaft as fast as Darby's legs would take him. That led us into the basement of a building. Bender was nowhere in sight. We hustled to the main level and found Maisie and Bender huddled next to a blown-out doorway leading to the street.

I raced up to them. "Any luck? Did you get through?"

Instead of answering, Maisie aimed her chest at me, playing back Ari's voice: "I know you're out there. The message is scrambled, but I can hear your voice. We're in danger. Our last known location, told to me many years ago, was in between what our ancestors considered the state of Cuba and the Caribbean Colonies. The land around us was mostly submerged, but New Eden was located in a protected area up until a week ago. We cut the farms loose from the city in an effort to save human lives, and the city pulled up anchor and followed. We're adrift, and once we float into the sea, I'm not sure what's going to happen." There was some shuffling in the background and a shout. Ari's voice became hurried. "It might be too late to save us. My father is pursuing us in a medi-ship equipped with missiles and cannon lasers. He intends to wipe out the habitats. New Eden will be left with no food or clean water. Help them if you can!"

Sounds of a scuffle followed, and a male voice shouted, "Ari, we have to go. Now!" Then static, followed by one final message from Ari at the end of a single breath.

"He's armed and dangerous! Please don't let my father win."

The recording cut off.

A clear picture of Ari formed immediately in my mind. Fierce, battle-weary, intelligent, and capable. This girl had guts, which wasn't a surprise. We were quiet as we thought about what we'd just heard.

In the meantime, small footsteps shuffled up to us. "There you are!" Daze exclaimed. "I was waiting and waiting, then I decided to just come to where you guys were, instead of staying by myself. If you weren't here, I was going to use my phone, but talk in code so no one would know what I was saying." He grinned at Maisie. "You broke out. I knew you could! Nothing can hold you for long." The kid had no idea laser eyeballs had been involved. In the next instant, Daze took in all of our stoic expressions. "What's going on?"

"We just heard from Ari." I peered at Case, trying to gauge his reaction.

"What did she say?" Daze asked excitedly. "Are they gonna be okay?"

"They're still in trouble," I replied, placing a hand

on the top of his head. "But we're going to help them as soon as we determine where they are." Since she'd given us a general area, we had a solid place to start.

"That's good, right?" Daze fastened his attention on Case, sensing his discomfort. Deciding to fix it in his Daze-like way, the kid walked up to the outskirt, reaching out to grab hold of his arm. "You look sad. What's wrong?"

With Daze's approach, Case shook himself out of his reverie, his expression softening. One of the few times it ever did. Since the two of them shared blood, their bond had grown into something thick and cohesive, like hydro-gel on growth stimuli. "It seems you might have an aunt out there, and I might have a sister." It was huge news, but Case was right. We'd all heard it. Ari had indicated that her father was the madman bent on destroying the city.

That could be only one person: Martin Bancroft Jr.

I decided to diffuse the moment to let Case have more time to sort through everything. "Let's get out of here. We shouldn't linger. We can discuss this back at the barracks. Bender, you take Maisie and Darby," I instructed. "Daze, Case, and I will meet you there. We're going to have to leave Walt back for now. There's no time. Park in the trees. The back entrance will be open."

We started out, but Daze didn't make a move to follow, his eyes wide and unblinking. "We...have family? Like, by blood? The girl in trouble is your *sister*?"

Case placed both hands on Daze's shoulders to steady the kid, who looked woozy from the impact of it all. "We don't know for sure," Case relayed calmly. The man hardly ever got flustered. You had to admire his titanium backbone. News like that would've taken me off-balance. I'd be rocking on my feet like Daze. "We won't know until we get there. But from what she said, yes. It seems my father had another child once he built…New Eden and got it up and running. They left thirty years ago, but she sounds younger than that. It's not unusual for men to have children later in life."

"We have to help her." Daze's voice was elevated. "She has to be okay! We have to save her! She *can't* die." Daze's heart was as big as his head. It was amazing it stayed stuffed in his chest. Having blood relatives in this cruel world was highly unusual. Life-spans around here weren't overly long, and couples having more than one child was rare.

I wanted to step in and comfort him, but decided to let Case handle it.

"We're not going to let her die." Case's tone was firm. "Do you trust me?"

The kid nodded vigorously. "Yes!"

"Then you have to believe me when I tell you Holly and I will find them. Alive."

"And bring them back?" Daze's voice held a plea.

"Yes," Case affirmed as he stood. "Now we have to head to the barracks, so we can figure out the best plan. Then we leave as soon as possible."

The kid went from excited to crestfallen in a single beat. "Can I go? I really want to."

Case shook his head. "No, kid. We need you to stay here."

"But...but what if you don't come back?" Watching Daze's face crumple was hard. Bender grunted, agreeing with my assessment and choosing to step outside. Maisie remained impassive, though I knew she was extrapolating data from this interaction to use later.

I knew exactly what was whirring around in Daze's mind. Why choose to keep breathing when your family was gone?

Before Daze could plead anymore, I hurriedly said, "There's a chance you can come. Let's see where Maisie places our odds." Case met my gaze over the urchin's head, his expression resigned.

Daze sprang onto the balls of his feet. "I know they'll be high! That means I can go!"

"Don't get ahead of yourself, kid. Come on, let's go." The first time I'd met Daze, he'd been ready to terminate himself off a cliff. He might've been acting for some of that scene, but in those few moments, I'd caught a glimpse into his soul. He believed there was nothing to live for without family.

And we were his.

"I had no idea you were such a softy," Darby muttered as he limped after me.

I took umbrage. "I'm not soft," I replied. "I'm *practical*. Having Daze along might work to our benefit. Everyone underestimates that kid. He could be an asset."

Darby snorted. "Yeah, keep telling yourself that. It'll make you feel better."

"Oh, don't worry. I will."

·ARI·

Chapter 13

"Ari, *now*," Jake urged. Paris and Hector were already outside. They'd been discovered by a maintenance worker. Jake had brought him down, stunning him into unconsciousness, tying him up, and stuffing him into a closet.

Ari nodded, reluctantly letting go of the microphone, her fingers stiff from gripping it so hard. She'd done all she could and hoped it would be enough. If the dark city had heard the details of her plea, hopefully they'd arrive. If not, no help would be coming.

She exited the room after Jake. Paris and Hector were already starting up the stairs. They made it to the top deck quickly. Hector placed a finger over his lips as he eased the door open, surveying the outside with his chromes. He made a beckoning gesture, and the four of them began to race between the storage crates and supplies tethered to the sides of the ship by long ropes, their packs jangling. The noise couldn't be helped.

When they were just about to the ladder they'd used to climb up the side of the ship, two people stepped in front of them.

Both parties gasped, shocked by the encounter.

Jake was in the lead, his weapon out.

Ari recognized them immediately. The couple from the stairwell. "Don't harm them," she said, easing forward, placing her hand on Jake's arm. He obliged, lowering his weapon a few centimeters. Ari tugged down her neoprene covering. "I'm Alaria. I overheard you in the stairwell. We're here getting supplies. We mean you no harm."

It took a moment for the couple to grasp the situation, the woman coming around first. She nodded rapidly, her eyes darting toward her partner. "Yes, yes. You need supplies. How can we help?"

The man pulled the woman protectively into his grasp, his eyes flashing with fear. Before he could respond, Ari said, "If you tell anyone we were here, there will be repercussions. The farms are in jeopardy. Only one working habitat remains. Now that we know my father's plans to come after us in the medi-ship, we'll do our best to retaliate. If we succeed, our first priority will be to reunite the farms with New Eden." She glanced between them. "That means survival, at least for now, for everyone." Ari's eyes deliberately landed on the woman's abdomen, her meaning clear.

The man's expression changed. After a few seconds, his head bowed in resignation. "We will do anything we can to help you."

"Good," Jake said. "Now we need to get to our skis before anybody else discovers us."

Hector and Paris had slipped by, making their way toward the ladder. Jake glanced at Ari. She nodded for him to follow.

Ari moved toward the couple, grasping the woman's hands, surprising her. "We will defeat my father and do our best to make everyone safe. Or die trying. I hope you believe that."

"Praise you, Alaria Bancroft," she said. "We will help you to the best of our abilities."

Ari appraised the couple. They were no more than thirty years old each. The man had a weathered look about him. He was used to hard work and likely did it with little complaint. The woman was strong, confident, and ready to protect her child at all costs. "You said something in the stairwell about not trusting Ernie," Ari said. "Were you speaking of Ernie Adelson?" He was a staunch supporter of Ari's father.

"Yes," the man answered. "He's been in charge of this vessel for the better part of a year."

"He is not your ally," Ari cautioned. "My father would never leave this ship behind. It's far too valuable. If he succeeds in finishing off the farms, he will probably come back to retrieve it. I'm not sure what exactly he will do, or how many souls it takes to power this ship, but you are in grave danger. You must install someone you trust to take over, someone who is not under the thumb of my father. Is there anyone here who fits that description?"

Paris and Hector disappeared over the railing. Jake was waiting for Ari to finish. She had to make this fast.

The man hesitated. "I...I am the ship's steward, the second-in-command. I've never captained a ship on the open sea, but my father brought this one here thirty years ago. I'd like to think he taught me well enough."

Ari nodded. "How do tempers fare here?" The two of them would not succeed in this mission unless the majority of the ship had resistance in mind.

The woman answered, "There are a fair amount against your father. But rumors are controlled tightly. If there is even a whiff of radicalization, there will be severe punishment. Ernie has implemented stricter rules recently, even though he says the welfare of all is his priority." She glanced at her partner while cupping her swollen stomach. "We have never trusted him."

These two were smart. "If you want to survive," Ari instructed, "you have to get rid of Ernie and his comrades. It will take some time. Gather those closest to you and build a network. You must arm yourselves. Do it as soon as possible."

"Once it's done, how do we get a hold of you?" the man asked.

"If we managed to defeat my father, we will drop anchor and wait for New Eden to drift closer. I've just signaled the dark city for help, and I'm fairly certain it was received." She wasn't certain how much got through, but she needed to do her best to bolster this couple. "Once you're within range, our radio signal will work."

Jake made a motion for her to join him. They were running out of time.

The woman pulled Ari into a quick embrace. "We are Janel and Justin. We will do our best."

"I hope to hear from you soon," Ari said. "I have to go."

Before she could step clear, the man said, "Your father has taken the majority of the militia on board the medi-ship. The city is spiraling into panic and chaos. I fear for the lives that will be lost there."

"I fear for them, too," Ari said. "We will do the best we can to get to them." She began to walk away. "There's a maintenance worker locked by the main workroom downstairs. Go find him and try to sway him to your side." If the man refused, the couple would have to make a decision about what to do with him. Ari wouldn't tell them what that decision should be.

By the time Ari and Jake arrived at the bottom of the ladder, Hector had already gathered the skis. Ari and Jake each climbed on. Ari adjusted her head covering and clicked on her mic.

"Let's get the hell out of here," Paris urged, gripping Ari's midsection like a vise.

Ari chuckled. "I thought anywhere was better than on this ski."

"I was mistaken," Paris said. "Being alive is better, and vomiting up my guts aside, you're not such a bad pilot."

"Thanks," Ari said as she jammed the throttle and punched the propulsion. They took off, soaring over the tips of waves, following Jake and Hector as they veered toward New Eden before making their exit through the buoy wall into the unprotected ocean.

Ari felt Paris release her grip, reaching for the little aid they had to give to the inhabitants of the isolation chambers. Hector and Paris each had five magnetic laser keys in their pockets. Ari watched as Hector hurled his, the magnets finding their marks against the steel of the old ship that had become the base of the city she'd known her entire life. Red lights issued out, but there was no way to tell if the lasers actually penetrated the steel.

Paris did the same as Ari steered them closer. If the hot lasers cut through the metal, the prisoners should be able to utilize them once they recharged. No guarantees, but they'd had to do something to try to help them.

Jake led them out of the enclosure and back into the sea. "We'll reach the farm in thirty minutes," Jake stated in her ear. "It's a little rougher, but we can do it."

"We need to increase our speed," Ari said. Jake obliged, and as they rounded the outside of the city, Ari eyed the floating medi-ship in the distance, thankful they wouldn't have to board it. Yet. "The ship hasn't moved," she commented. "Hopefully, it will stay put for a little longer. That will give us time to mount a defense against what's coming."

Paris was lifted off the ski by Brandon and Russ, faring better than she had initially, but still not great. She held up a hand to Lila, who came toward her with a look of concern on her face. "Don't touch me," she warned. "I need a minute. Maybe a few more."

Celia looked pleased they had returned so quickly. "Back in record time."

Ari connected her anchor cable to the old bracket with a loud *thunk*, so they'd be able to pull the ski up and over the side after she was on deck.

Brandon gave her a hand. She took it gratefully, steadying herself on the rocking causeway once on board, her body still swaying from being so close to the ocean. She unzipped her inflatable and pulled off her head covering, wresting the amplifier out of her ear. She was wetter this time and ached to get into some dry clothes.

Hector bounded by with his full pack, looking no worse from their arduous journey. "I'm going to get started on the winch immediately," he announced. "Russ, you're with me, and find some lights while you're at it."

Jake climbed on deck, with a hand up from Brandon, looking worn out, but content. Ari unbuckled her front pack and handed it to Celia. "I managed to get a bunch. It should last us awhile."

Celia nodded. "How did it go? Did you encounter any trouble?"

Paris was doubled over the railing, her head bowed. She lifted it, her skin pale in the low light. "Let's head back to the atlas. We'll debrief you guys there. I'm freezing and sick to my stomach. I need food."

The group began to move. Ari fell into step with her friend. "Usually, food and upset stomachs don't go together."

"Yeah, well," Paris muttered, "when you spend your whole life scrounging for the smallest morsel, sustenance pretty much cures all my ails. I'm sure everything will settle down once my legs stop shaking."

Brandon gently hooked his hands beneath Paris' shoulder straps, easing the pack off her back as they went. He glanced inside. "This is just what we need," he said, sounding impressed.

Lila patted Paris' shoulders. "Did everything look the same?" she asked. "Is New Eden still intact?"

They arrived at the atlas, heading inside. "We need to change into dry clothes first," Ari said. "Then we'll fill you in."

Paris, Jake, and Ari headed down the central staircase, a tight spiral made of white compressed polymer to conserve interior space. Once at the bottom, Paris went to her quadrant, while Ari and Jake went into theirs.

Before Ari could even close the door, Jake had her in his arms. He buried his face in her hair, taking several deep breaths. She could feel his heart racing through his clothes. Adrenaline had pretty much taken control, and now that they were back, Ari's body vibrated with the aftereffects just as Jake's did.

"That was crazy," he murmured. After a moment, he arched back. "I could've easily lost you." His face was stark.

"Yes, but you didn't," Ari said. "The same goes here. But by going, we accomplished our mission and people won't starve." At least for another few days. She pulled away, needing some breathing room. She didn't want to hurt Jake's feelings, so she leaned up and placed a small kiss on his lips.

He moved, granting her the space she needed, and immediately started disrobing. When he was finished, he headed into their small waste room.

Once Ari had changed, into an identical but dry outfit, she followed.

Jake stood with his head bowed over the sink. The mirror covering the wall reflected his broad shoulders, the tight muscles of his arms, and the arch of his neck, his hair beginning to dry in half-curled tufts around his head. He didn't straighten.

She came in close, molding her body against his, resting her head on his back, her arms encircling his waist. She knew what he was thinking. "They're going to come."

Jake was quiet for a long moment. "If they don't, this is the end. We can't fight off the medi-ship, and we'll never make it to land."

"I know."

Chapter 14

Everyone at the table was silent. Jake had just finished detailing what had transpired on their journey. Ari had added some of her own details, including her conversation with the couple on the ship.

Celia spoke first. "If the man and woman can gather enough resistance, we might have a fighting chance."

Ari ran a hand through her still-damp hair. "Maybe, but that ship's not equipped with much artillery. So, even if Justin is able to commandeer it and break away from the city to rush to our aid, it would be no match for the medi-ship. Which my father knows perfectly well."

"You said your message to the dark city went through," Brandon said, his tone hopeful. "You heard a voice."

"Yes," Ari replied. "But there's no way to know if whoever was receiving it heard what I actually said.

My plea could've been scrambled on their end. We have no idea how sophisticated their tech is. We won't know unless they show up. But I did give them our coordinates, as best I could." Her father had always kept certain things secret. Their exact location in the world had been one of them.

"Unfortunately, we have to prepare for the worst." Jake rose from the table. "We don't know when the medi-ship is coming. It could be a few hours, or it could be a few days. The only thing left to do is gather up any items we can for defense. Celia, you radio the other farms. I want each biosphere and atlas turned inside out. Once the winch is working again, and we connect with the others, we amass the supplies here."

Celia nodded. "Will do. Bancroft confiscated almost everything, but these farmers are wily. They likely have hidey-holes we know nothing about."

"Once the farms are reunited," Ari said, "we'll call a meeting to address everyone at the same time, let them know what our plans are." Ari took in the concerned faces, knowing her expression mirrored theirs. "I will be voting for disengaging from the other habitats and standing our ground alone. There's no reason why everybody should stay in harm's way." The table erupted with chatter, everyone speaking at the same time.

It wasn't a surprise that Brandon's voice came through the loudest. "If you do that, you're effectively sending them to their deaths!"

Ari steeled herself, readying for a fight. She and Jake had gone around about it before they met with the group. This was their best option—their only option. "If my father reaches us, he'll wipe us out, and we all die. Letting the other farms go gives them a chance, however small, to get out of his line of fire. If we somehow survive the attack, we find a way to reunite with them. If we lose, and my father knows he's won his personal battle against me, he may decide to leave them alone. The way I see it, there's no other reasonable choice. This way, we are at least giving people a way to stay alive for another day. It's possible, if my message was received by the dark city, help could arrive. We can't count on it, but it's a possibility."

Before Brandon could refute Ari, Jake said, "She's right. But I suggest we swap biospheres. We leave this one to the people, to keep them safe, and we take Habitat Four."

Paris shook her head. "That biosphere is taking on water. It's slowly going under. The walkways aren't even exposed anymore. People don't leave their atlases. We can't fight from there."

Ari had an idea. "What if we cut Habitat Four loose for good, since it's beyond repair? Then we have Hector connect this habitat to Habitat Two. We make our stand on Three."

Lila made a noise, and Ari turned. "I think that would work. Habitat Four could be a decoy. The propellers don't have much power, but if we turned Four in one direction, and we went in the other, it would be the first thing your father sees from that direction. He is likely to go after it, not knowing who's on it. It could give us a little bit more time."

Ari was impressed. "Lila, it seems we've underestimated your tactical abilities. I like the way you think. That's exactly what we'll do. We cut Four loose, turn on its props, and see what happens. We can refine the plan in the morning." Ari rose from the table. "Now I think it's time for everybody to get some sleep. It's been a very long night. We take three hours and meet back here. We'll hope Hector has good news about the winch by then." She turned to Celia. "Let the other farms know we need firepower, anything they have, and that we'll be pulling them in soon."

Celia nodded. "I'll do that now."

"Let me introduce you to our new and improved winch," Hector announced, brandishing his arm in front of the machinery. It'd taken him all night, and he had large black circles under his eyes to prove it, but he'd achieved his goal.

"Is it ready to go immediately?" Ari asked hopefully.

"Yep," Hector answered. "Just a few minor things to shore up, but the men have instructions on how to work it." He gestured to a trio of farmers standing behind him.

Ari turned to Celia and Russ, thankful they were in charge of delivering information to the others. "Let everyone know. When the other farms arrive, call a meeting inside the sphere." She addressed Jake. "Now let's go meet William. Then we can go over what we're going to say to the people once they get here."

Jake nodded, and they began to walk. "William was pretty insistent we come alone." Jake had assigned some farmers to watch the sea as soon as it was light enough to catch a glimpse of the horizon. They had to know the moment the medi-ship came into view. William had been one of those, but the old man had something else he wanted to tell them in private.

"I think we're the only outsiders he trusts," Ari said. "There's been such upheaval here, so many new faces. What happened the other day with Claude, and my intervening, solidified his view of us, hopefully for the better." When the resistance had boarded the farms, not all the farmers had embraced them equally.

They entered the airlock. Once it pressurized, the inside door popped, and they went in. Immediately, the warmer air brushed against Ari's skin like a kiss from a sun they would never see. The inside of the dome was ringed with a freestanding circular platform, leaving the interior for the tallest of the plants and trees to grow. The middle started out level, then flowed upward, forming a large, terraced hill, each level growing a different kind of tree, vegetable, or fruit. It was very organized, but sadly in a state of rapid decline. The stench of rotting vegetation and stagnant compost rushed up Ari's nose, and she couldn't stop it from twitching, barely refraining from sneezing.

She unzipped the top of her jacket as the mugginess seeped in.

Maintenance rooms had been incorporated into the steel platform that encircled the perimeter. Most were for storage, but some contained smaller UV lights, along with tables filled with pots used to coax seedlings into early growth. They headed toward one of those rooms. William was the head farmer on Habitat One and had overseen the entire farm before Ari's father had even arrived.

When they reached the appropriate location, Jake rapped on the door.

"Come in," the familiar voice beckoned.

Jake stepped through first. Ari had been inside this room before. It was full of old containers made of what she'd been told was poly-infused clay, from an era she knew very little about. UV bulbs were strung across an unadorned steel table roughly two meters in length and scuffed from years of use. Tools and dirt were heaped in the corners of the room, the dirt spreading like a blanket along the floor. Crates were haphazardly stacked along one wall, almost to the ceiling. It was a well-used workplace.

William wore a one-piece outfit, the common garb of hydro-farmers, in a drab green and affixed with an abundance of utility pockets, most of them full, small trowels and seed injectors sticking out. He smiled as he rose from his seat, holding out a hand in greeting. Jake and Ari both shook it. "Glad you could make time for me," he huffed in a voice worn by hard work and age. "I've got something important to say. Why don't you two have a seat?" He gestured to the chair he'd just vacated and the one next to it.

They obliged, sensing his seriousness.

"We're happy to hear whatever you have to say," Ari said, trying to put the old man at ease as William took out a three-pronged rake the size of a fist and began to twirl it.

"I'm not so sure you'll be happy when I'm finished with my tale, but it needs to be said all the same." William leaned back against a large crate, still spinning his tool. "The buzz on this farm, starting with your request for everyone to pool their resources, is that maybe after you gather our firepower, you plan to leave us behind so you can take on your father alone."

Jakes said, "It's the best chance you have for your survival—"

"I'm gonna stop you right there," William intoned, cutting Jake off with an easy wave of his wrinkled hand. "This has been my home for the last sixty-three years. I came here as a boy, not even ten years of age, along with my parents, who had a notion to build a better, brighter future for our family. I'm not leaving my farm, nor is any other farmer worth the oxygen he or she breathes. We're going to stay right here and fight alongside you, defending what's ours until the sea takes us under."

This didn't come as a complete surprise. The farmers were fearsome in their love for their homes. "I would expect nothing less," Ari said, clearly surprising him. She guessed he'd been expecting a fight. "It's my wish that you will stay here and continue to defend Habitat One, with its working biosphere, and Habitat Two with everything you have." She paused, trying to will the old man to understand what she was about to say next. "That's why we will be heading to Habitat Three, with the firepower, and cutting everyone else loose. We're choosing to do this, because after my father is finished with me, he might decide to ignore the rest of you, choosing not to waste his precious artillery. If that happens, we hope you continue to live. And if he decides to come after you, we hope you fight."

William's eyes drooped for a moment as he processed what Ari had just said. He stuffed the small rake into a pocket almost as an afterthought. "Wait...wait a second here," he stammered, fixing Ari with a brooding look. "You plan to abandon this habitat and go to Habitat Three? Alone?" Ari was unprepared for William's rush of anger. "Didn't I just tell you that we are willing to fight for what we believe in?" He patted his chest. "In no good conscience can we allow you to be a sacrificial branch for that man!"

Ari was immediately overwhelmed by the caring and loyalty that had been bestowed upon her in such a short amount of time. She didn't deserve it. She had lived her entire life as an elite citizen of New Eden, benefiting from every advantage throughout her childhood. She owed them, not the other way around. "We appreciate that," she replied carefully. "Me, especially. But I'm imploring you to look at this objectively, William. The survival of *all* people is more important than my life or the lives of a scant few. We have a plan. We're sending Habitat Four out empty, hoping my father will destroy it first. It's beyond repair, so we risk nothing. My father will figure out eventually that we're not on board, but during that time, Habitats One and Two will have a chance to use their props to get out of range. You won't get far in this rough sea, but hopefully far enough out of reach of a laser cannon. We will stand our ground on Habitat Three, with only enough people to ignite whatever firepower we can amass. William, you *must* stay here. We need you to oversee the retooling and any fixes we can make so that this farm has a chance to thrive. If you don't, the people—*your people*—have no chance of surviving. Without your knowledge and experience, it's a death sentence for everyone."

William was quiet, studying her with so much intent Ari began to perspire, though that could also be because of the warmth. Sweat was pooling in certain places under her syn-leather.

Being in charge and calling the shots felt right. Easy for Ari in the way breathing was automatic, but it was still new. The man she was addressing was fifty years her senior, and she was basically ordering him to do something he didn't want to do.

After a good, long minute, William finally tossed up his hands with a loud snort. "To the blessed giver of all sustenance, this is a conundrum! I can't in good conscience let you face that evil without—" Jake tried to interrupt, but William waved him off impatiently. "I know what you're going to say, boy, and I'll go along with your plan." Ari's eyebrows rose. "But only because I have this." With a flourish, he tore off the side of a crate behind him. Inside were large metal boxes stacked three high. Ari knew what those shiny containers had inside.

Explosives.

Ari grinned, jumping out of her seat, moving forward quickly. "Are they all full? How did you manage to keep these hidden during the raid?"

William chuckled. "If you spread a bunch of spoiled refuse all over the place, people don't go looking too hard. When they marched on board, this room was in shambles, and the stench was overpowering. Even if they'd taken off the sides of the crate, they wouldn't have seen this. They would've seen what I wanted them to see, which was a bunch of old junk not worth anyone's time. It took me a while to clean it all up afterward, but it was worth it."

"Is this the only stash?" Jake asked, standing next to Ari.

A gleam hit William's eye. "There are a few more here and there. Once the others arrive, I'll have a chat with them. By full dark, we'll have an accounting of everything we can use against that madman and his ship."

Ari held her breath as she asked, "Are there launchers in there?" Hydro-bombs were an excellent asset, but only if they could fire them at the ship. They wouldn't make much difference otherwise.

"Oh, yes," William said. "Top-grade military." He caressed the outside of a box like he would the bark on a tree.

"How did you get your hands on those?" Jake asked. "My father had access to only a handful of launchers in the city."

"Your father was a good man," William replied, reaching out to give Jake a pat on the shoulder. "I had the chance to spend time with him on a number of occasions. He was conflicted, but his heart seemed to be in the right place. In his chest, where it should be. A lot of good that did him." William shook his head sadly. "What Bancroft and his lot have never understood, was that these farms were designed by the same man, for the same purpose—survival. Martin Bancroft Sr., your grandfather"—William nodded toward Ari—"made sure we had a way to arm ourselves, if needed, after the meteor hit. Of course, this kind of arsenal was never needed before now. No one else in the whole world is out here except for us, bobbing along in the feral sea. Marty Jr. never bothered to take inventory of the farms once he arrived. He was too focused on constructing his city, his brand-new Eden. By then, it was too late. We got a clear picture of what was coming, damn near from the very first day, and kept what was rightfully ours."

William was right. Upon his rendezvous with the farms, her father would've been laser-focused on commanding people to achieve his goals. Building a city he deemed worthy, nothing less. It had been an oversight not to check the biospheres and atlases. One that would cost him. Ari smiled at William. "Thank you for trusting us with this information. Compile an inventory and choose a handful of farmers you trust who want to join us. We all meet tonight to devise a plan."

·HOLLY·

Chapter 15

"How are we supposed to figure out where they are?" Bender asked, as frustrated as the rest of us. He stood behind Darby, legs splayed, arms crossed. Everyone was gathered around the tech table at the barracks, which had generated a nice 4-D hologram half a meter above its surface, utilizing its tiny cameras seamlessly incorporated into the four corners. It was incredible to see our ancestors' technology in action. It didn't happen nearly enough. The table was considered 4-D because it provided audio, and you could manipulate it with your hands.

We all focused on the graphic, a 3-D display of the tiny islands that made up the Caribbean Colonies.

"The terrain won't look like this anymore," Darby asserted. "Ari said that their inlet was protected, but those islands are underwater now. She also said their location was between the Colonies and the state of

Cuba. That would put them somewhere over here." He inserted his hand into the hologram, red points dotting where his body temperature connected with the picture. "Computer, adjust water levels to increase by thirty meters."

"Can it do that?" I asked.

Darby shrugged. "I have no idea, but it's worth a shot. It's military grade, after all."

Nothing happened.

"Apparently, that's too tough an order," Case said. "But that's okay. We can assume a likely location based on—"

A map about a meter square lit up in front of Maisie, similar to the one hovering over the table, but with more detail. I shook my head. "Is there anything you can't do?"

"My capacity is vast," she agreed. "I could not pinpoint the radio coordinates from Alaria, because of the great distance separating us, but the general directional data has allowed me to extrapolate within a finite radius, give or take two hundred kilometers. That would place the location inside this region." The diagram began to spin, detailing some outcroppings of land still visible after taking into account the rising sea. The imagery wasn't as clear as the 4-D hologram, but it worked.

"Darby, manipulate the holo map until the features look similar to what's in front of Maisie," I said. "That way, we can compare the two. Maisie's is showing increased water levels, but the land is hard to see.

Between the two images, we should be able to get a better idea."

Darby did what I asked, and we all leaned forward.

Bender gestured toward the image hovering above the table. "That doesn't look near the Colonies to me. The land still showing looks like it's right off the coast of Cuba." Cuba had become the fifty-fourth state of the United States in the year 2108, not very long before the meteor strikes, but long enough for Martin Bancroft Sr. to get the farms installed there relatively easily, since it was part of the United States.

I moved toward Maisie, eyeing the smaller, but more accurate diagram in front of her. "Here would make sense." I indicated the spot, circling it with my finger. "It looks like it was a protected inlet once upon a time, and there's still some land poking out around it. Not enough for anyone to live on, but enough to keep the ocean a little quieter. When they cut the farms loose, they could possibly be drifting this way." I swished my hand downward. "And once they pass this place at the end, it would lead to rougher seas. Maisie, can you display wind and water currents? Then we might be able to figure out which direction they're actually going."

"The flows of the wind and water were greatly disrupted after the cataclysmic event," she said. "It is not something I can determine until I am within range to take data samples."

"Even if she's right, and this is the location," Bender stated in a gruff tone, "where do you land? From the blueprints Darby has of those biosphere things, there isn't any room to park a craft."

I'd been thinking the same thing. "Maisie," I instructed, "pull up anything you have on medi-ships constructed right before the disaster. The ship would've been state of the art and likely commissioned under the name Bancroft or Bliss Corp. Maybe it was mentioned in the news. I would think every ship from that era would have a landing site on deck. Everyone traveled by craft back then. In order to get goods delivered while at sea, they would need a place big enough to land a supply drone."

"Your plan is to set down where Marty has an arsenal waiting?" Bender grunted. "Smart."

"Do you have a better idea?" I asked, irritated. "We can use the element of surprise. No one on that ship is going to assume *any* craft will suddenly drop out of the sky. If we arrive under the cloak of darkness, it could work."

The imagery in front of Maisie blinked, and a large ship solidified. It was enormous. At least twenty stories high, with not one, but two landing pads, one on each end. They were marked with large white X's.

"Okay, so they have them," Bender said. "But that doesn't mean they're available. They probably have stuff crammed all over those decks. After all, they don't need that space for aircraft."

Before we could debate the landing issue any further, the graphic in front of Maisie morphed again, blinking into an aquatic farm. "According to my data, a habitat is equipped with a drone pad, which can be extended from underneath the walkway." A little stunned, we watched what was clearly a stock video from a manufacturer as something unfolded next to the farm. It looked adequate enough for landing, even though the structure was made of panels instead of one solid piece.

"That…seems like it's constructed on a flotation device," Darby said, his voice cracking. "I can't imagine it's very safe. Remember, these biospheres were built over sixty years ago. As far as we know, they didn't come equipped with any kind of craft, and if they did, they probably don't work anymore. The last time they had to utilize that landing pad would've been years ago, making it highly unsafe today."

"This entire mission is risky," I said. "There are things we can't plan for until we get there. Knowing they have the capacity for landing is enough for now." I made my way toward the kitchen, which consisted of a large cooling unit, a utilitarian shelving unit, and a long steel countertop. "Ari indicated her father was coming after them, but he hadn't engaged yet. Once we arrive, and see what's happening, we will decide what to do. If they're engaged in a full-blown battle, we focus on taking out the ship. If there's yet to be a battle, we rendezvous with Ari and come up with a plan to save the people on the farms." I grabbed a jug of water out of the cooling unit and slammed the door. "Anyone else want water?"

Case said, "I'll take some."

"Me, too," Darby said.

Bender grunted, and Daze shook his head no.

Case took out three cups, setting them on the counter. I filled them. After, we headed back to the table. "Listen," I said. "I'm not trying to make this trip sound easy. It's not. In fact, it's far from it. Not only are there people trapped on those farms, but she said New Eden is in jeopardy. We have no idea how many people in total are in trouble, and the logistics of getting them back here makes my brain hurt all over again. But the first thing we have to do is eliminate the threat. That's what we're good at. We do that, we can figure out the rest."

"Do you think there's a chance Bancroft will surrender?" Darby asked, taking a sip of his water.

I shrugged. "I have no idea. Is he rational? Is he crazy? Everything points to him being unstable, but we won't know until we arrive." My gaze landed on Case. "What do you think?"

Case took a seat on one of the couches. He shook his head. "I don't know. I really don't. I remember only bits and pieces of my mother. The man she was with, who I knew to be my father, was not Marty. He was a kind man, but even so, I don't really remember him. If Marty is responsible for the deaths and suffering of these people, I don't care what happens to him. I don't care if we ever speak. I harbor no illusions that he's a good man. If he goes down with the ship, so be it. He's nothing to me."

We all appraised Case. What he'd said was the truth, but it didn't make it any easier.

"We need to discuss how to take out that ship," Bender said. "Our crafts don't have tactical equipment to fire from the sky." It was illegal for personal dronecrafts to have artillery integrated. "So, let's say you get there and a battle is happening, how are you going to take them out? You would have no choice but to land. And once you do, you'd have to employ the biggest hydro-bombs we have as soon as possible, which would take too much time. The militia would be on you before you could set the timers."

"Not exactly," I said. "We have launchers. I could get within striking distance, and Maisie and Case could shoot from an open door." As a safety precaution, the integrated locking systems on most crafts wouldn't allow the doors of the craft to be lofted unless the drone had significant pressure on its landing gear. "We've never had a need to bypass the locking system before, but I'm sure you can do it." Bender could do just about anything when it came to altering machinery.

"I could. I could even mount launchers to the outside, but it would take more time than we have if you want to leave in the next few hours," Bender answered. "And don't even suggest breaking a window. You'd freeze to death on the way back." He walked over to the cooling unit and grabbed a jug of aminos. I tried not to cringe as he took a long swig. Instead, my tongue lightly spasmed in my mouth. If the smell of garbage had a flavor, it was aminos. Walt had said he had a way to improve the experience. I was looking forward to that, because aminos were actually very good for you, as they were a fortified drink that provided vitamins and minerals in one swallow.

I took a seat next to Case. Maisie still had the projection of a farm in front of her. "Can you switch back to the medi-ship?" I asked. Without hesitation, the ship took its place. "Did you find any news articles about a ship commissioned by Bancroft? It would be nice if we know what we're dealing with and if it has any weaknesses."

"My data scan provided more than one hundred articles matching your request," she said. "Here is a screencast recording."

A polished female voice flowed out of Maisie's torso: "The Bliss Corp foundation is funding a radical new medical ship intended to help those with complicated illnesses all over the world. It's expected to be christened next winter. No expense has been spared on this lavish vessel. It contains three state-of-the-art organ-regeneration pods, a dozen brain-to-bodylink scanners, and even has an intrabody gene splicer, which is illegal in over seventy-three countries. Bliss Corp has issued a statement that the ship will comply with each country's laws before requesting entry into any port. It is said this endeavor will cost in the ballpark of forty trillion standard world currency. But some critics are asking whether such an endeavor is really necessary. This has been a once-hourly screen update brought to you by SensiTouch. Have you had your dose of pleasure lately? I'm Melinda Socorro. Up next hour: Is it finally the end for public animal sanctuaries?"

The audio cut off. It was hard to know what to say.

"Holy crap," Darby whispered. "If the medi-ship we're talking about really has that much tech on board, it would be devastating to lose it. That kind of medical equipment would save so many lives. Even if some of it isn't working, I bet Walt and the other scientists could fix it."

Darby was right.

Technology like that would be a once-in-a-lifetime score. There was no way to manufacture anything like it in the entire world. It was the ultimate scavenge. "Damn," I swore, running my hands over my face. "This creates a whole new set of problems. Defeat Marty, but keep everything on the ship intact, all while trying to save the people. I doubt all three things are achievable."

Daze interrupted, "What's a ballpark? The lady said ballpark. What did she mean?"

"I think she was talking about games people used to play," I said, distracted, my mind trying to figure out too many things. "But I don't know why she used it when she was talking about the cost of the ship."

"The term ballpark," Maisie replied smoothly, "refers to a place where people played games and spectators watched. Ballparks were also referred to as stadiums and arenas. A ballpark estimate, the manner in which the announcer used the phrase, comes from terminology coined over two hundred and twenty years ago, relating to the proximity of landing a US spacecraft within a designated area after a research mission. If it landed within an area the size of a ballpark, it was on target."

"Great," I said. "Now that we've got that ancient lesson out of the way, how do we save the ship *and* take out the bad guy? Any ideas?"

"You could use a jet pack," Darby said. "The ship would have to be close, but it would get you there. I've been working on some prototypes."

Trying not to look completely appalled, I gaped at Darby. "You're kidding, right? You want us to jetty over the ocean? Your mind must finally be cracking under all the pressure."

Darby grinned. "It's only a suggestion. I didn't think there was anything you were scared of. Too bad you can't just cable-swing over from the farms." He chuckled loudly, proud of his snark.

"Funny," I said. Darby hated cable swings more than just about anything else. "Jet packs are highly unreliable. They use both battery power and liquid fuel to operate. Plus, they're clumsy and loud." I shuddered while thinking of doing such a thing, my stomach roiling at the suggestion.

"I told you," Darby said. "I've been working on a prototype. It's much quieter and more stable. It could be a viable option, if the ship was in close proximity. Don't rule it out."

"It's totally out," I said. "Next."

Chapter 16

"Darby and his damn jet packs," I grumbled. "We aren't using these." I shoved the cumbersome harnesses Case had just handed me—that Darby insisted we take as a precaution—into the back of Tilly. It was daybreak, and we were parked on top of the Emporium, gathering supplies. After a night of zero sleep, we'd come up with a plan of attack. It consisted of packing as much artillery as we could in the craft and figuring out what to do with it once we arrived. It was the only way, since we were at a loss until Maisie analyzed everything with her lidar and NeuDAR, which thankfully had a much longer reach than regular eyeballs.

Daze hurried out onto the roof, carrying a slim titanium container I'd never seen before. "What's that?" The kid had dark bags under his eyes. Even though he should've rested, he'd been too amped to take a break. Just like the rest of us.

"It's from Walt," Daze answered. "It's full of darts." The kid shifted the thing in his arms, unclipped the sides, and tilted the lid open so I could see the contents.

There were at least fifty injectable darts in a bright array of colors. Some I knew well, like the potent pain blockers in nuclear orange, yellow, and blue. I'd used those on our last trip down South when I'd totaled Luce, and the medi-pod in Walt's dome hadn't been enough to heal me completely. Those darts had taken the pain away nicely. I recognized the blue Quell, a serum that made someone extremely easy to deal with. Others I hadn't seen before, like a sickly yellow and a color so dark it seemed to absorb any and all light.

"How are we supposed to know—"

Daze flipped a panel to expose a color-coded chart. I chuckled. Tranqs, Babble, nerve agents, inoculations, antinausea, and soothers. Leave it to Walt to think of everything. "Excellent. These will come in handy." Daze shuttered the lid and handed the container to Case, who stuffed it in the back of Tilly with everything else. We were getting short on room. "Head back in and see what else he's got for us."

The kid hesitated, shuffling his feet.

I knew that look, but I was going to make him work for it. After another thirty seconds, he finally spread his arms, his face crumpling. "You never said if I could come or not!"

"That's because I haven't made up my mind," I replied honestly. Half of my brain was arguing with the other half. Should I take this innocent child into the unknown or not? "I told you when I figured it out, you'd be the first to know."

"But you're leaving in a few hours," he complained.

"We all agreed we need to get sleep first," I said. "When we wake up, I'll let you know."

"I can't wait that long." His voice held a long, worrying plea. "Holly, *pleeeease.*"

Case was next to me. The outskirt and I hadn't had a chance to talk about it privately. Case crossed his arms. "Do you think you're ready for a mission like this?" he asked the kid.

Daze pretty much shot off the ground. "Yes, *yes!* I can help you. I know I can. Please, don't leave me behind." The starkness of his request surprised me. It was filled with emotion, but something else stood out. Desperation.

"There's a chance we won't come back," Case said. "Are you prepared for that?"

The kid's eyes drifted downward. "I don't want to come back if you don't."

"Are you sure?" I asked. "That's a pretty big decision to make. At twelve years old, all I wanted to do was survive. Bender, Lockland, Darby, Walt, Knox, and all those guys are staying here for now. They're your family, too."

He shook his head. "It's not the same." Then he surprised both of us by rushing forward, tossing one skinny arm around each of our waists. "I don't want to lose you." His voice was muffled between our bodies, his warm breath tingling into my side.

I gave Case a look before gently untangling Daze. The kid stumbled backward a couple of steps, his eyes red. I settled my hands on his shoulders, leaning down. "The first time I met you, you were ready to launch yourself off a cliff because you wanted to find the Flotilla. I know you're dedicated. Against my better judgment, I've made my decision. You can come with us." I held up a single finger. "Under one condition. You do everything we say without argument as fast as you possibly can." He nodded vigorously. "The only reason I'm willing to allow you to be in this kind of danger, is that Maisie will be with us. If something happens to us, she can get you home." He opened his mouth to protest, but I waggled the finger, cutting him off. "Before you complain about not getting the chance to die in spectacular fashion alongside us, I have news for you: You still might. As much as I want to, I can't guarantee your safety. The craft could be hit by a rogue wave, we could run out of battery power, the medi-ship could blow us up. But if I have any say, you *will* survive. I understand that losing us would be very hard. I'm not denying that. But you'd get over it." He opened his mouth, and I shook my head. "*Eventually.* I'm sure it would take you a while. But if you died, what would Maisie do without her handler? And who else can we depend on to get word back here about what happened to us? Don't you think Bender, Darby, Lockland, and Claire would deserve to know how everything went down?" Very slowly, he nodded. "We'll count on you to make us sound like heroes. I'm

giving you freedom to embellish as much as you want."
He didn't look convinced. "You know, your dad would
be extremely proud of you if he could see you now."
The kid's surprise mirrored my own. Bringing up his
father, Case's brother, hadn't been planned. "He would
be happy to know you inherited his large brain. And
I'd like to think your dad would want you to continue
living, so you could use that brain to help lots of other
people. I'm certain he'd be upset if I didn't do my
best to protect his greatest gift." I stood, hoping he
absorbed what I'd just said. "Now, head inside and bug
Walt for more fun stuff that will help keep us all alive."
For a moment, Daze looked like he would dive back
into my arms, but then he stiffened, his chin resolutely
rising.

"I'm on it," he said as he zipped back toward the
building, stopping right before he went through the
door. "Thank you, Holly. I won't let you down. I
promise." Then he was gone.

I turned to see Case giving me a strange look.
"What?" I felt defensive. "You know we have to bring
him. I'm sorry we didn't get a chance to talk about it
first, but I made the only decision I could. But that
doesn't mean I'll willingly let him die. I'll do anything
I can to make sure he keeps breathing."

Surprising me, Case slid his arms around my waist,
drawing me close. He brought his lips to my neck, a
deep throaty sound growling into my ear. "Seeing you
handle that kid is nothing short of extraordinary."

Flustered, I pushed him away. "No, it's not. You would do the same. He has a big heart. Daze would be devastated if something happened to us."

The outskirt wasn't ready to let go. He held me firmly, his lips meeting mine in a soft caress. "Not even close to how big yours is."

A sound much like a cough erupted behind us as Bender came through the door. I sprang away from Case like I'd been jolted by a sensory node. "This is the last of it," Bender said. He carried a huge box that jangled with tools and other supplies. Walt trailed, holding something that smelled delicious. Every one of Walt's special concoctions had a different scent. I was enjoying discovering each one. Thankfully, the smell of cupcakes was first and foremost. Bender handed Case the goods.

Walt gave me the food. "This should last for a while," the old man said. "But it will spoil much sooner than any protein flakes. So consume it readily."

"Not hard to do," I confirmed.

"The boy brought out the darts," he said. "Familiarize yourself with each color. Carry them with you. The black one is courtesy of Nareen. It's her own formula, one that efficiently brings an adult male down in seconds, followed by death within three minutes. After a dose of that, they don't get back up. Only use that if there's no other option available." Walt valued life, but he wasn't above causing pain to gain compliance if need be. He understood that our world was rough, and what we were going up against was going to be a challenge. "There's also something in there for seasickness. I wish I had access to the wristbands we used to use. They were very effective. But the darts will do if you need them."

"Thank you. I appreciate it," I said. "We'll be sure to keep them close. Thanks for putting the pain blockers in as well. Our goal is to commandeer the medi-ship, if at all possible. I know you'd love to see that technology."

"It would be an incredible discovery, indeed," Walt agreed. "Before the dark days, I witnessed organ printing firsthand. Since the process uses a patient's own cells, it's always an exact genetic match. Having that now would save many lives. Not to mention that gene splicer. Highly controversial back in the day. Now, we could use it to eradicate illnesses once again. The scope is unlimited."

I nodded. "I hope, for all our benefits, those machines are still in working condition. I'm certain that's why Marty took that ship now, instead of another. He knows the value of the medical equipment as well as we do."

Walt settled his hand on my forearm. "I believe you will complete this mission. I've seen you in action. There's little you can't overcome. For you, it's only a matter of logistics. We will be awaiting your quick return."

"Luck is going to play a big part this time," I said. "We won't know what we're getting into until Maisie tells us. There might be too much to overcome. We don't even know if the craft will have an adequate place to land. We might have to abort the mission and fly back here to figure out another strategy."

"I don't think so," he said with a shake of his head. "You'll figure out something. I've never met another individual more stubborn than you." He chuckled. "I almost pity this man." He flicked his eyes toward Case, grinning. "Almost." His expression shifted. "What Marty Bancroft Jr. is doing is wrong. No human should be allowed such power. Handing out pain and punishment as they deem fit is unnatural. It's our job to be compassionate, to help others, to make this world a better place. Bring back the survivors. Once they arrive, we will have much work to do." He dropped his hand, drawing me into a quick embrace. "May the sun shine on your endeavors, Holly. Even though we can't see the orb, it grants us life all the same." He turned to Case, reaching out to shake his hand. "Take care of yourselves." Then he shuffled back inside. I watched him, amused. Finding Walt had been a blessing. The old man was teaching us so much.

Bender took a step forward. "I was overruled last night," he said, "but that doesn't mean I like it. I still think two crafts is better than one. If you can't find a way to help them without sacrificing yourselves, come back. That's a fucking order."

I snickered. "Since when do I take orders from you? That hasn't worked since I was nine. By then, I figured out that you're actually a giant softy. Heavy on the giant." I widened my stance, settling my hands on my hips, matching his take-no-prisoners pose. I was well-versed in this game. "And two crafts *isn't* better than one. Not this time. The only advantage we have against Marty and his arsenal is surprise. We can barely accomplish that with one craft. But even if more crafts were better, there's no way for us to communicate out there. Tilly's at capacity with Daze and Maisie in the back, but you'll get your chance soon enough. Getting those people to safety is going to be a huge endeavor. It's going to work out. I promise."

Bender snorted, hardly convinced. "By Maisie's estimate, it'll take you ten hours of flying at max speed to get there. I'm giving you twenty-four hours. If we don't hear from you, expect company."

I couldn't argue with that. The plan was to engage with Marty almost immediately.

Darby, Maisie, and Daze came out onto the roof. I gave Bender a quick nod. "Make sure Lockland comes with you." Knox had shown up at the barracks to give us a report. Nothing had changed. Not knowing what was going on with Lockland before we were to take off made me uneasy.

Darby handed me Daze's pico. "Here, take this. All the diagrams and maps of the ships and structures are in marked folders. You can access any of it at the click of a button. If you can't figure it out"—he smirked—"let Daze handle it."

"My brain functions pretty good," I said. "I think I can click a button." I tucked the extremely thin, lightweight piece of machinery into the front of my vest. It was hardly noticeable. "I'm assuming you gave a copy of everything to Maisie as well."

"Yes, she plugged in herself and downloaded the info directly onto her hard drive." Darby hesitated a moment. "Holly, are you sure about this? Isn't there another way? Maybe we can send a bunch of the LiveBots down there first, so we don't risk anyone."

"You want a bunch of Julians handling the job?" I asked, trying not to laugh, since his expression was so sincere. "All they'd do is offer everybody refreshments and try to sell them baubles and fancy clothing. Now, if they were military grade, I'd consider it. But we can't let these people down, Darb. You heard Ari. With that many lives at stake, not to mention all the technology we could gain, we have no choice but to go."

"I know," he said. "It just makes me nervous. I mean, you're going to spend hours over the ocean with no place to land." He visibly shuddered. "What if you run into a problem?"

"Maisie will be on high alert," I assured him. "If anything goes wrong with the craft, we'll know about it ahead of time. It's going to be fine. I'll be back here to make your life miserable in no time at all."

"You better be," he said. "I don't know what I'd do without your constant nagging."

"I don't nag," I said. "I encourage with finesse."

Darby gave me a quick hug. "Your finesse needs work. Travel safe, Hol. Come back in one piece."

"That's the plan," I told him.

Case closed Tilly's back compartment. "Time to go," he announced. "After we get a few hours of sleep at Holly's residence, we leave. If we're in the air by noon, ten hours will get us there at dark."

"We'll contact you as soon as we can," I said. "If Maisie can hack into any radio towers, we'll do that. If not, hopefully we'll be hailing you from the medi-ship shortly."

Daze wrapped his arms around Darby's waist. "See you soon, brainiac," the kid said. Daze had taken to calling Darby that after he'd found out Cozzi had given Darby that moniker a while ago.

Darby mussed the kid's hair. "Not before I see you, wiz kid."

Daze giggled. "Maisie told us that word when Darby asked her for another word like brainiac. It's short for wizard. It means you're really smart."

"That's an appropriate nickname," I said. "Why don't you and Maisie hop in Tilly? We'll be taking off in a second." I faced Bender. There'd never been a time or place where we'd needed a goodbye longer than a salute. I wasn't about to let this be one of them. I held three fingers up to my forehead, giving him our traditional sendoff. "I'm coming back, you know."

"You'd better."

I walked to the passenger side, Case already at the helm. I shut the door as Case lofted us upward.

Bender held three fingers in the air.

·ARI·

Chapter 17

The biosphere was full. People were crowded on the platforms. Children had gathered at the edges, feet dangling over. Some had found spots in the branches of trees, while others had taken refuge on the roofs of various structures.

It'd taken nearly six hours, but the farms had finally been linked. People were hungry. After everyone had taken their small share, they'd settled in to hear what Ari had to say.

Ari stood near the tallest railing, the door behind her leading to the UV mechanical room. The same place she and Claude had had their encounter only a few days ago. Jake and Brandon stood on either side of her, William next to Jake, Paris and Hector next to Brandon. Lila, Celia, and Russ were behind them. The other resisters, the ones who helped maintain the other habitats, fanned out along the edges.

"I appreciate you coming here," Ari announced to the crowd in a strong voice. She wanted to get people organized as soon as possible. "As most of you know by now, we are under attack." Low murmurs filled the air. She scanned the crowd, spotting fear clearly etched on most of their gaunt faces. "We've put a plan together to save as many lives as we can, but to do so will take work from all of you. After I'm finished speaking, if you have any questions, we'll get them answered as quickly as possible. After that, it's important we act immediately." She took a deep breath and plowed on. "Habitat Four is beyond repair and is slowly sinking. It's currently home to six atlases. Our first task will be to disperse those six homes across Habitats One and Two." There were a few shouts of alarm. "Hector, our head of maintenance, has assured me we can accomplish this safely." Hector nodded his agreement, lofting his thumb in the air in the universal sign of agreement. "We don't have enough docking stations, but we will make sure they are safely connected using steel cables, as well as anchor lines." Murmurs increased. Surprise crossed some faces. "Once this is completed, we will disengage Habitat Four from the group permanently and turn on its propellers. It is our hope that my father will encounter this sphere first and will take the time to destroy it, before continuing on."

"You're sacrificing our home!" one woman shouted.

"How are we supposed to survive all crammed together like that?" a man yelled.

Ari had known this wasn't going to be easy, because none of the solutions were perfect and each one required sacrifice. She had no choice but to continue with her message and deal with the fallout after. "Once my father finishes destroying Habitat Four," she continued, "and turns his attention toward us, we will have already isolated Habitat Three away from the remaining farms. We will make our stand there and do our best to defeat him. It is our hope that he will leave the two remaining habitats alone once he accomplishes his task of getting rid of us—particularly me. In the end, we hope that all of you survive, untouched. That is the conclusion of our plan."

The room erupted, voices jumbled together, some people beginning to openly weep. This was not the reaction she'd been hoping for.

Before Ari could formulate a response to reassure them, William stepped forward. He leaned over and said into her ear, "Let me have at 'em. They'll respond better to one of their own."

Ari nodded and stepped back.

The old farmer raised his hand, fist clenched, above his head. Very slowly, the rest of the inhabitants did the same, quiet descending over the entire biosphere like noise-canceling headgear. Once every last murmur had evaporated, William lowered his fist and intoned, "I think it's safe to say that none of us wants to die if we can help it." He paused, letting his words penetrate. People nodded, but they refrained from responding. "In the face of this unprecedented adversity, I'll be damned if we're quitters. We've worked too hard all these years to give up without a fight, and this here girl"—he motioned to Ari—"is doing her best to save us. If you don't believe that, there's the door." He made a sweeping gesture toward the airlock. "Nobody's stopping you from getting into your atlas and floating away. Nobody's holding a laser to your temple to force you to remain in the fight. And in my estimation, anyone willing to sacrifice themselves for the good of others, especially women and children, is to be commended." He made a show of peering into the crowd, focusing on each and every face. "Habitat Four is done for. Just like she said. The main plexi is cracked and taking on water. Only a matter of time before it goes fully under. Those atlases would have to disengage and find a new home anyway, and now they'll have one on One and Two. We'll do the same for the atlases on Three when the time comes, so these resisters can make their stand. Again, if you take any kind of disliking to these details, feel free to cast off to the sea. No one's gonna stop you. And I'm not going to lie, your chances might be better off there. At some point, you're bound to run ashore. Maybe before you starve to death. There's a possibility you'll find food and drinkable water, but maybe you won't. Me, I plan to stay and fight. There's a chance that madman could turn his cannons on us, and if he does, I plan to put up a fight like my ancestors raised me." His voice rose to a high timbre, exciting the crowd. "My forebears taught me to defend my hard work, my family, my home, and my right to live freely!" A quiet cheer started on one side of the biosphere—quickly encompassing the masses, finishing in a deafening roar. Once the din died down, William continued, "To all of you who are with us, we need your assistance. Transferring those atlases must happen directly. It's going to take some good old-fashioned hard work. And one more thing," William all but shouted, stalling the people who had already began to move. "We need your artillery, no matter how small. I know you've got some stashed away, and now's not the time to hold on to it. You're no match for Bancroft by yourselves, but if we pool our resources, we can come up with something that just might fend that bastard off. Bring whatever you have to Station Room Seven. Everyone else meet on the walkway off Habitat Three. Before we cut Four loose, we need a group to go in and bring anything out of that sphere that's salvageable. Let's get this done!"

Ari scanned the crowd.

She could follow up with something of her own, but it clearly wasn't needed. The people were energized by William's words. She turned to the farmer. "Thank you," she said. "I appreciate it. And I'm grateful that you stand behind what we're doing. It makes things much easier. If you care to be, you can become the official voice if we need to do this again."

"It won't matter if I speak or not," William replied. "Once these people put their minds to something, they stick to it. You won't find much pushback now. In their heart of hearts, they want to survive, they want their children to survive, they want their homes back. They know their prospects are bleak, no matter how much they wish differently. There's nothing anyone can do now but plow on. I'm heading to my workshop to wait on those supplies. I'll talk to a few others and make sure most of the crates are transferred, along with some others, to Habitat Three right after we get those atlases hitched up and secured."

Ari nodded. "Sounds good. After we're done overseeing everything, I'll check in and see what you've come up with."

As the old man shuffled away, Jake took her hand. "You okay?"

"Yes," Ari replied. "I just wish I had something better to deliver to these people."

"You're giving them a solid chance at survival," Paris interjected. "That's more than anyone else is giving them."

"Come on," Brandon said. "Let's give them a hand with the atlases. Hector's already gone. He says the cables are ready to go."

The group filed out, making their way down the main stairway that connected the platforms. Once Ari reached the bottom, a woman caught the edge of her sleeve. Her face was lined with age, but her eyes were bright. Beside her, a girl of no more than twelve or thirteen clutched her arm.

"Our home is on Habitat Four," she said. "We share an atlas with three other families. We just wanted to let you know that we are thankful for what you're doing, Alaria Bancroft. We know how much you've sacrificed. My daughter, Genevieve, would like to offer her services to you. It's the least we can do. She's a hard worker and willing to do anything you need." The young girl looked terrified, but resolute.

Ari assessed her, and under the scrutiny, the girl's shoulders straightened and her head rose. "I appreciate that," Ari said. "But we have enough people already. Only a few will stand with us on Habitat Three." Herself and Jake, if she had anything to say about it. "The best help you can give will be taking anything you can salvage from the biosphere. Any seeds, plants, or tools. If William can get Habitat One fully working again in the future, he could use the extra supplies."

Genevieve gave her a sly grin. "Is it true you took hydro-skis across the ocean? At night?" Her voice barely contained her awe.

"Yes," Ari confirmed. "But it wasn't as hard as you think. With a little practice, you'd be able to do it, too."

The girl's mother looked horrified, but she masked it quickly. "Well, thank you. You have our support. We'll salvage whatever we can from the biosphere."

"Thank you," Ari said as they walked out.

Moving the atlases took more time than planned. It was full dark before the last of them was attached. Three to Habitat One, three to Habitat Two. Everyone was exhausted. But Ari was happy to see all the families situated and safe.

Hector bounded up to Jake and Ari, who were discussing schedules with some of the farmers. "Habitat Four is ready to be disengaged. How do you want to do it?"

"Turn on the props and let it go," Ari said. "Make sure it's heading against the current, directly behind us. It won't get very far, but that's all we've got."

"How long the propellers last is unknown," Hector replied. "But I think it should give us a big enough gap if they keep working. To further help the cause, I suggest we keep these three farms linked and turn on our own motors to propel us the opposite way. That'll place even more distance between us."

"That's a good plan," Ari said. "Let's do it."

"We can turn on the atlas motors as well," Hector said. "It'll take some coordination to get them cranked in the same direction, but I'll get it done."

Jake nodded. "The more distance between us and Ari's father, the better."

"Get to it," Ari told Hector and Paris. "Jake and I are meeting William to assess the artillery inventory. We'll meet you on Four to disengage when we're done."

"I certainly hope the farmers have delivered," Paris said. "Seeing a nice stack of firepower would do the heart good."

Jake and Ari made their way back to William's structure. A few men lingered outside. They quieted once Ari and Jake arrived. One of the men nodded, giving them a small smile. Then they moved away.

Jake knocked on the door.

"Enter," William said.

Ari went first, pulling up quickly. Her mouth dropped open, then shut with a click. "How did…how did these people manage to hide this much stuff?" Spread all around the room were storage boxes containing weapons. At least thirty guns lay on the steel table, the pots having been moved aside. But the most interesting thing, by far, was the cylindrical piece of steel, half a meter wide and a meter tall, sitting in front of William. It was matte black, worn with age, connected to a tiny cartridge Ari knew held liquid fuel.

"Is that a barrel laser?" She wanted it to be a barrel laser, but wasn't sure it was, because she'd seen one only from a distance, and it hadn't been black.

"This is indeed a barrel laser." William chuckled. "It's one of the old ones, built back before things got light and shiny. But it works great, same as the day it was crafted. Shooting concurrent bursts at megawatt power, you get just under three minutes of pulsing before it needs a refuel. They built them to last before everything got spangly and showy."

Ari wandered over to the table and picked up a few of the handhelds. These wouldn't do anything from a distance, but if the militia decided to board their habitat, they'd have a fighting chance. Tears pricked the corners of her eyes. "I can't thank you enough for making this happen, William. You've given us all a chance. We'll only need to keep a few, particularly the Gems. You guys take the rest. I don't want to leave you defenseless."

"We'll get it figured out with time to spare," William replied. "By my count, we've got plenty of firepower. That ship will have to get close to do any real damage. And when it does, you'll be ready to launch some real energy at them. Maybe even sink 'em."

The ship was massive compared to a single biosphere. It wouldn't have to get too close to fire a frequency missile. They were going to need a hell of a lot of luck to pull this off. But they had no other choice. This was it. The final showdown. The last round she and her father would ever take together.

"Let's hope we sink them," she said, "before they sink us."

Chapter 18

Ari sat at the edge of her bed. She was tired. They all were. They'd cut Habitat Four loose not even an hour ago. It was the wee hours of the morning. The medi-ship hadn't been spotted, so they were hopeful they'd be safe during the night. If her father decided to attack, there was a good probability he would go after the decoy first. Hector had managed to get the propellers running on all the biospheres and atlases, and even though the sea was angry, within fifteen minutes, the entire group had put some distance between them and Habitat Four.

Jake sat next to her, wrapping an arm around her waist, giving her comfort. After they got some rest, the plan was to transfer this atlas to Habitat Three and disconnect the ones there and rehome them on One and Two.

William had enlisted some farmers to help move their newly acquired arsenal to Three, and they would work into daybreak. Once that task was completed, Ari and Jake would have the hard decision of deciding who would go on Three and who would stay with the people.

"I think Brandon's right," Jake said. "He suggested we get the ten militia guards in holding to help us make our stand. They used to be our friends. If their lives are on the line, I think they'll help us. They don't owe an allegiance to Bancroft. They followed his orders because they were forced to. Twelve bodies would be more than enough to stand against the ship. We have three launchers and a barrel laser. Technically, we only need four people."

"You heard Paris. She and Hector are not letting us go without them," Ari said. "She's extremely stubborn. They won't budge." She leaned into Jake, resting her head on his shoulder. Now that she'd taken a breather, exhaustion coursed through her. Every cell in her body felt fatigued. "I don't trust the guards. They could easily turn their weapons on us, thinking they could hail my father and save themselves."

"True," Jake said. "But if we talked with them, I bet we could find a few who would rather fight on the right side."

"Do you remember our thirteenth birthdays?" Ari asked suddenly. She and Jake had been born less than a month apart, so they usually celebrated their special day together. "That was the day my father allowed us to climb to the very top of our floating city." Ari's father's private sanctuary was located far above the tallest residence. A spiral staircase led to a set of rooms and balconies fortified by the thickest steel and real glass—the ultimate luxury. "I remember it so well. How I felt as I gazed out at the sea. I remember feeling happy. Relief that our parents had managed to create a functioning world for us to occupy. For a moment, I even forgot about those struggling beneath us to survive." She closed her eyes. "The next day, he took us to the confinement areas. Another lesson for us to learn. The horror of seeing those poor people starving to death in those cells still haunts me. I've never allowed myself to feel that free again, like the day we spent on top. I've never let my guard down enough to feel thankful for anything. Until right now. Here with you." Her breath caught. "I just wanted you…to know that. There's been so much pain and sorrow, but I want you to understand that my time spent with you has been my greatest gift. I couldn't have done any of this without you by my side."

Jake brought her into his arms, his mouth against her hair. "I've been thankful for you every single day of my life. You are my sunshine, the air I breathe, the water I drink. My world is nothing without you." He eased her back, tilting his lips to meet hers.

The contact was electric. Then they were lost.

Her arms twined around his neck, tugging him closer. Ari needed him in a way she'd never needed anyone. This might be the last time they would ever be together as one. Emotion swirled in the forefront of her mind—fear, love, desperation, and hope. She clung to hope like it was a lifeline as Jake dragged her under, searing her with his ferocity, his love for her.

Green haze penetrated the room as they frantically undressed and reached for each other, their gestures wild and unstable, needy and possessive.

Jake was hers. And she was his.

Forever.

Pounding woke them. "Get up, get up," Paris yelled through the door. "The ship has been sighted!"

Ari was out of bed in an instant and dragging on pants. She tugged her shirt over her head and opened the door. Paris looked about as rested as Ari felt, which meant they both were still wiped. By Ari's estimation, she and Jake had been asleep less than two hours. "How far away?" she asked as she followed Paris up the stairs, Jake right behind them. "Damn, I was hoping we would have one more day to prepare."

Two farmers stood in their living area, apparently the ones who'd spotted the ship. Jake moved forward, addressing them. "What's the status?"

"We were using the macro-glasses, like you instructed," one of the men said, gesturing toward the other. "Lenny spotted something at first light. We weren't sure it was a ship at first, since it was just a smudge on the horizon, but then we figured it out pretty quick."

The other guy shook his head. "It's too early to tell

if it'll go after Four, but that sphere is hardly visible." The guy looked hopeful.

Ari asked, "Did William get the artillery moved to Three?"

One guy shrugged. "I think so, but I'm not sure. We never left our spot."

"Thanks," Jake said. "We'll take it from here. Head back to your atlases and alert the other families. We will be unhooking all the homes from Three as soon as possible."

Once they left, Ari addressed Paris. "Assemble all the resisters and meet at the lookout spot. We've got a lot of work to do in a very short amount of time." Without waiting for Paris to reply, Ari and Jake headed out of the atlas, quickly making their way along the walkway so they could get a better look at the ship in the distance.

Jake took Ari's hand to steady her. As they walked, they surveyed the new atlases, now secured by cables, gently rocking into the steel frame of the walkway. The inhabitants would have to be careful getting on and off, but it worked.

Once they arrived at the lookout platform, Ari held her breath. Habitat Four was several kilometers in the distance, the top of the sphere barely visible without glasses. Well beyond that was the outline of a large ship.

Jake donned a pair of macro-glasses and surveyed the scene. It was barely light enough to see, constant drizzle making it even harder. "It makes the most sense that he'd stop and deal with Four first. Logically, since it's right between us, they would sink it, which will take time."

"How many hours do you think we have?" Ari asked.

"At least five or six if he stops at Four," Jake said. "We know your father is worked up. When he's in that kind of hyper state, he'll act before any judgment sinks in. He's done trying to get you to repent. Once he sees that biosphere, he'll want to destroy it and survey the damage afterward. He'll need daylight to do that. I don't think anyone on that ship will go up against him."

"I have no doubt he'll get his way." Ari turned, walking toward the side where the farms were linked, holding on to the handrail as the ocean rolled. Jake followed closely. "I want to see the artillery."

A temporary connection bridge spanned the water between the two farms. It was made of a flexible, yet durable nano-fiber-infused polymer, complete with railings. Ari hurried across, making her way around the next habitat and crossing the next bridge to get to Three, which was now the last.

No one was outside, so she headed for the airlock. Once she and Jake were through, they heard quiet murmuring. A small group was gathered, standing next to a number of boxes stacked on a platform. William wasn't there, so Ari directed her comment to a farmer she knew as Murray. "I'm sorry to interrupt you," Ari called. "I'm assuming this is your farm. We're going to need to get your homes moved to Habitats One and Two as soon as possible. The medi-ship's been spotted, and we need to make this space ready for combat."

A woman stepped forward. "We've just been discussing that," she answered. "My name is Hattie. I've lived on this farm for thirty-three years, just after my family arrived with the Flotilla. I'm married to Murray, and we have two children. We will see to the efforts of moving our homes soon. We were skeptical yesterday that it would work at all, but we see the atlases have been secured. We also want to offer you our help." She gestured to the group. "Murray and Trevin and I would like to stay and help you fight. This is our home, and we want to defend it. Just like William said. We aren't quitters."

Ari cleared her throat. She didn't want to offend these people. "I understand wanting to defend your home," she started. "My heart breaks for New Eden and what will become of it. But we have enough people to stay and fight. The best thing you can do is stay together as a family."

The woman closed a hand over Ari's forearm and held on. "Just like you said, this isn't *your* home. You belong in New Eden," she intoned, stressing her meaning. "It's ours. And it's our job to protect it, not yours. How long have we really got here anyway? There's barely enough food as it is, so many hungry mouths to feed. If you think your father will let us all go after you're gone, you're mistaken. We'll stay here and fight for what's ours, and when the time comes, the sea will take us. We've made our peace with it."

Ari tried to swallow, but the lump in the back of her throat made it hard. She had to convince these people that this really wasn't their fight—it was hers. If she'd acted sooner, if she'd used her brain, she could have anticipated that her father would eventually lose his mind completely. She could've stopped him. She could've done something—*anything*.

Instead, she'd found her resistance too late, and that was her burden to bear. She knew she wasn't going to be able to convince this strong, confident woman, who was ready to die for her home, that it was Ari's battle alone. So she did the only thing she could. She exaggerated the situation. "When I was on the engineering ship, I enlisted help," Ari told her, loud enough for the entire group to hear. "I made contact with the dark city. There's more than a chance the remaining farms will survive if aid arrives in time. But the only way you live is to stay with your family, where it's safe, and leave the fighting to us."

Surprised, the woman dropped her grip from Ari's arm. "Are you certain they're coming?"

Ari nodded, not trusting her voice.

Jake stepped in. "It's true," he said. "There's also a resistance forming on the engineering ship. Help is on the way." Ari hoped Jake's added enthusiasm would be enough to sway them. "We hailed the dark city fifteen hours ago. They're slated to arrive soon." If only they knew that to be true.

The woman looked uncertain, glancing at her husband for support. Murray moved to his wife's side. "We understand what you're saying. But that help might not arrive in time to save this biosphere."

"That's true. It might not," Ari said. "But I'm the one my father's after. We have a long, complicated past together. If I wasn't here, he wouldn't bother to come at all, instead letting you die off on your own. I brought this danger down on all of us, and it's my greatest wish that you and your family do your best to survive. We believe help is on its way. There is a chance that we will make it through. To assist in that endeavor, we need you to move your atlas to a safer location as soon as possible."

A tear rolled freely down the woman's face as she clutched her husband's arm. "We can't thank you enough," she said. "We will share the news that aid is coming and rejoice. I never thought we'd live to see the day when we would be free of this place and that our children could have a chance to thrive and grow. May the giver of sustenance bless you and all your efforts."

Ari felt ashamed. She might have seeded false hope. But in doing so, she'd achieved her goal. These people would live for another day. It was all she could do.

Jake and Murray began discussing where to move the crates. Hattie gathered the other women, instructing them about what to do for their migration.

Walking up the incline in the middle of the sphere, Ari took in the space. Habitat Three had been in ruin for a long time. The stale stench of rotting bio matter permeated the air. The UV lights had broken, and everything had gone to waste in a matter of months. Her father could've had this fixed, but had chosen not to. She would have intervened had she known. Everyone had been too fearful to come forward, worried they'd be thrown into the sea for speaking the truth. The magnitude of disrepair had been overwhelming once Ari had come aboard. She'd launched a rebellion too late to pick up the pieces. They'd been forced to blow the connection between the farms and New Eden before they'd been able to gather needed supplies. So many things had gone wrong.

But the chance to stop him had finally arrived.

With the launchers and the barrel lasers, they had a real chance. If they could bring the ship down, they could get back to New Eden. They could quell the masses. They could make repairs and grow food again.

Jake walked up behind her. "What are you thinking about?"

She turned, gazing at her love, her rock, her world. "The future. Maybe what we told that woman wasn't an exaggeration. Maybe we do have the means to save them all."

"I believe it can be done," he said. "Your father is ruthless, but he's not infallible. Hector is coming up with a strategic attack plan on the medi-ship. He thinks if we strike the bow, close to the waterline, with a concentrated effort, we'll have a chance to do grave damage."

"A lot of ifs accompany that plan," Ari said. *If* her father came close enough, *if* they had enough light to see by, *if* the currents were on their side. "But I want to believe it can happen."

Both their minds whirred with the possibilities. "I believe in us," Jake said. "We can do this."

·HOLLY·

Chapter 19

An ear-piercing shrill hit the air. My hand shot out, palming a switch to silence the alarm. I stood in front of my weapons cabinet, strapping on extra firepower. It was eleven thirty. We'd managed to get a few hours of sleep, which had to be enough. We were due to take off in thirty, hoping to arrive in the sector Maisie deemed the likeliest location of our targets three hours after sunset. That time of night should give us ample cover, lowering the risk of being spotted in the sky.

That was the hope anyway.

Case rushed forward, his Pulse drawn. "Which alarm?" He knew I had a multitude of sensors set up, each with a different warning sound and signal.

"Roof," I said. "Somebody's landed."

"Do you know who it is?"

I snorted. "Last time I checked, I didn't have the ability to see through physical matter. I'm assuming it's

Lockland coming to say goodbye, but we're lucky we don't have to guess. Our military-grade status reader can tell us, no problem. Who's here?" I asked Maisie as she came to a stop behind Case. She made everything so much easier.

"One craft, two human signatures. One Lockland, one Claire," she replied.

"In the future," I instructed her, "announce any pertinent information immediately following a breach, including body count, weapons detected, or anything else you can think of."

"Noted," she affirmed.

Daze scampered down the hall from the waste room. "What's going on?" he asked.

"Claire and Lockland decided to stop by," I said. "I'm going out there alone. If this is a trap, and Claire drags me in, go without me." I nodded at Case. "Take Bender in my place. We can't waste any more time."

Case gave me a *yeah, right* look. "Nobody's taking you anywhere. Claire probably wants to make things right before you leave. Take Maisie. She'll be able to tell if there's anybody else is in the vicinity."

He was right.

If Claire was serious about stopping this mission, she would've landed a dozen crafts. "Maisie, you're with me." My eyes went between Daze and Case. "You two stay here until we know for sure it's safe."

"We'll give you three minutes," Case said. "The kid and I'll be right behind you."

"Fine." I slapped my hand on the heat sensor and

entered the hallway, Maisie close behind. Opening the hatch, I poked my head through to get a visual. "Do a weapons check," I ordered Maisie. "I want to know if there's anything out there I don't know about." It wouldn't hurt to be on the safe side for this interaction.

"Lockland has a Blaster holstered at his waist and a large serrated knife strapped to his left leg. Claire is unarmed. His craft contains twenty-three weapons, including hydro-grenades and bombs. Would you like me to list them?" If Lockland *hadn't* had a cache of weapons in his craft, it would mean there was a real emergency.

"No." I climbed out, leaving the hatch open so Maisie could follow, and walked across the expanse of my roof. I didn't draw my weapon, because that would be silly. But my arms were loose at my sides.

Claire stood three meters in front of the craft, one that Lockland had taken from down South and had yet to name. Lockland was positioned outside the pilot door. They hadn't made their way any farther, because they didn't want to risk tripping one of my wires, which was smart. I made eye contact with Lockland. He inclined his head, letting me know that there wasn't going to be any drama. I appreciated that.

"Hello," I called in greeting, my voice containing just enough sarcasm to get my point across. "I'm surprised to see you here. I know your schedule is incredibly busy these days."

"I deserve that," Claire replied briskly, her hands clasped in front of her. "But I want you to know that every decision I've made thus far has been in the best interest of the people of this city." She was dressed in standard-issue government clothing—a dark, nondescript shirt and pants. But she made the outfit look regal and less like the government was ready to enroll her in a specialized facility, like they did to so many others. Her black headgear deflected the drizzle, but I knew that underneath, her hair was ordered in her usual updo. She was thirty centimeters shorter than I was, but she seemed taller. Or maybe that was just the way I perceived her in my mind. Since the day we'd met, she'd always been the adult in the room.

There was no way I could stay mad, but I could pretend for a hot minute. "I'm not people, I'm family."

"I know." She fidgeted. Not like Claire at all. "I'd like a chance to explain myself, which is why I came. When Marty Bancroft's messages came through, it took everything I had to try and tamp down the rising panic. When he threatened to annihilate our city, news got out quickly. I made decisions that I felt were right." She took a short breath. "In those moments."

I wanted to cross my arms and slap a pissy expression on my face, but I couldn't bring myself to do it. "I'm assuming you're here because your decisions have changed in these moments."

"They have," she agreed.

"You locked Maisie up and threatened to put us in quarantine," I told her. "Those weren't choices based on fear of panic or uprising. There's more."

"There is," she said.

"I'm listening," I replied.

"I discovered something shocking when compiling information the Bureau of Truth had filed on the Flotilla," she started. "So shocking that I shared it with no one. Then when Bancroft's messages came, I knew his threat to annihilate us was real. It scared me, and I reacted appropriately."

"What shocking information?" Based on her expression and tone, I knew it was big.

"That madman has a nuclear armament," Claire said softly. "It was supposed to be a failsafe after the meteor. If they were dying, they could end it all at once. According to the notes, it's powerful enough to raze a two-hundred-kilometer area. If we deny him what he wants once he accesses our port, he would only need to push one button to end us all. He might do it anyway. I knew your instinct would be to help those people whether I approved it or not, and I was scared. I apologize that I kept this information from you, and Lockland, and Bender, people who I should've trusted to help me make very tough decisions. But in my heart, I had trouble balancing it all. I'm not going to keep you from your mission—I never was. It's noble, and if you succeed, the threat to this city disappears. I"—she wrung her hands—"just don't want to lose you. It was too hard to pick the citizens of this city over you, so I tried to choose both. It was silly. Everyone would suffer if you didn't go. But the risk is still great, and if you fail, we all lose. I feel it's too much pressure for so few to handle. I never wanted to settle it on your shoulders. I felt I shouldn't have to."

Case picked that moment to join us, followed quickly by Daze. Case read the look on my face and immediately steadied me. "What?" His arm looped around my waist. "What's going on?" He shot a look at Lockland when I didn't answer.

Lockland replied, "It seems your father has access to a nuclear weapon. We don't know where it is, but we're assuming it's mobile and that he's installed it on the ship he's using. It would explain his cockiness about wreaking destruction. If you'd gone in with the original plan to blow it up, the nuclear cloud would've annihilated everyone in a two-hundred-kilometer radius, including you."

I said to Lockland, "Did you know about this when we met last?" I didn't think so, but I had to be sure.

"Of course not," he snipped. "I told you, I had a *small* lapse in judgment. Claire just informed me about this an hour ago. I insisted we fly here immediately. If you'd already left, I would've followed. At some point, Maisie would've detected me. I wouldn't have let you go without this information."

"Do you think the girl knows?" I asked. "Ari? Do you think she knows her father can destroy all human life within proximity with one button?"

Case let go of me and wiped a gloved hand over his mouth. "That's unknown, but you'd think she would've mentioned it if it was a possibility. It's pretty pertinent information."

"And if she decides to use firepower on the ship?" I

asked. Ari was trying to save everyone, but she could inadvertently kill them instead. "We have to go. We've wasted so much time here already. If we're going to help them, we have to leave now."

Lockland placated me by saying, "Flying in blind would've been detrimental to the entire mission, especially since we didn't have this information. You did the right thing by staying."

Claire came to me and grasped my hands. "I'm so sorry. Your trust in me is damaged, I understand that. But I did what I did because I love you. I can't stop you from going, and it was silly of me to think I could. But you have to promise me you'll stay safe." Her voice broke. "You're the daughter of my heart. I know that without your efforts, all is lost. But losing you would hurt the most."

I embraced her. She held on. "You can't forget we have Maisie," I murmured to console her. "That gives us a decided advantage. Thank you for coming by today, instead of just sending Lockland. I knew there was a good reason behind your actions, and it was a valid one. Next time, if there ever is one, please tell me sooner so we can make these decisions together."

"I will," she promised.

I broke away gently, glancing at Lockland. "Did Darby fill you in on what kind of tech we believe is on that medi-ship?"

He nodded. "Yes. It would be amazing to have access to that technology, but however important it is, it's not worth trading your lives. Remember that."

Claire raised up on her tiptoes, planting a kiss on my cheek. "I wish you good luck and a safe and speedy return."

"If Maisie doesn't give us great odds," Case told them, "we plan to abort the mission and come back here and find a new way to defeat him." Case was theoretically correct, but in the depths of my soul, I knew that wasn't going to happen. We weren't turning back without first stopping Martin Bancroft Jr., whether the odds were in our favor or not. It was who we were. That didn't mean I wouldn't send Maisie and Daze back before we engaged the ship, especially in light of the new information, but Case and I would stay till the bitter end, no matter the odds.

Lockland gave us a salute and walked back to his craft, lofting his door, adding, "I'm sure we'll hear from you soon. There's no doubt in my mind. Once we do, we rendezvous. Good luck."

Claire grabbed my hand once more, her expression as emotional as I'd ever seen it. "I love you. Please be careful." Then she turned and headed to her waiting transportation. Lockland flew them out, leaving the four of us standing on the roof in the rain.

Case said, "We're all set to go. We can leave now."

I nodded, settling my hand on Daze's shoulder as we made our way toward Tilly. The kid angled his head to look at me, eyes inquiring. "Do you think we're going to survive?" His voice was so sincere it made my heart jump.

"I don't know," I replied honestly. "That's the truth. But I know here"—I placed a hand over my chest—"helping them is the right thing to do. And if it's right, it's worth the risk."

A grin broke out as he hopped along beside me. "I think so, too." He grabbed on to my forearm, swinging it back and forth as we walked the rest of the way. "I wonder what my aunt is like. She sounds nice. And tough. Like you."

I mussed the kid's hair. "I think she sounds smart like you. She was able to break away from her father to try to save the people. That takes guts *and* smarts."

"Yeah," Daze said as Maisie opened the passenger door. "I bet she's both." He climbed into the craft. "And if she's like Case, she isn't worried about anything."

"I have news for you," I said. "Case is definitely worried about something."

"What?" Daze asked.

"Losing you. So let's make triple sure that doesn't happen."

Chapter 20

"Are you sure we're in the right place?" I peered through the windshield, squinting hard into the darkness. I couldn't spot land—or anything—since the only light illuminating the sky came from Tilly. We'd been flying over the ocean for a few hours. I was at the helm. Case and I had switched on the last bit of land past Walt and Knox's old home. We hit water shortly after that. Their tribe really was the last bastion of people before the sea took its claim.

Daze had been resting in the back, but scrambled awake at my question. "Are we there?" he asked, wiping sleep from his eyes with the backs of his hands.

"Comparing the topography below to my database," Maisie replied. "We are forty kilometers northwest of the target destination. My lidar detects several landmasses, but they are more submerged than my pervious analysis presented. This area would not provide adequate protection from the open sea."

I glanced at Case. "Arriving at full dark is both an advantage and a disadvantage. We can't see anything, and not being able to assess what's going on out there makes me feel unsteady." Especially knowing that the only thing beneath us for kilometers upon kilometers was the ocean.

"We had no other choice," Case replied. "The only way to sneak up on them is to arrive at night."

"I know," I grumbled. "But it still sucks not being able to see. Are you picking up any radio frequencies?" I asked Maisie. "The sooner you can, the sooner we find them."

"I must be within a sixty-kilometer radius to detect radio output if I am not integrated into a tower." That had been her standard answer the last ten times I'd asked. One could never be too sure. Plus, what else was there to do except ask Maisie the same questions?

"If you're not picking anything up now, when we're supposedly forty kilometers within range," I said, "we're in the wrong place. So, which way am I going to veer? East or west?"

"What are the air and water currents doing?" Case asked Maisie. "That could be a deciding factor."

"My anemometric readings are corrupt," Maisie said. "There's too much turbulence for me to measure wind speed and direction." It was true. We were bouncing around quite a bit. The wind shear up over the craft was harrowing. I didn't dare get lower. I was white-knuckle flying as it was. "The water-current readings are also inaccurate, due to the wind speed across the waves, versus the temperature fluctuation beneath them."

"Well," I said, "we're going to make up our minds. We'll be over the original target in less than one minute."

"I think you should go east, toward the Caribbean Colonies," Daze said from the backseat. "That makes the most sense."

My eyebrows rose as I darted a glance over my shoulder. "Were you able to take some current readings back there?" I chuckled. "Okay, kid. We'll go east." I banked the craft left. "If we're wrong, we can loop south and sweep around westerly. That should cover all the points in this area." I was impatient for results. "I was kind of hoping bright lights would blink in the distance, like a beacon, once we got close enough," I mused. "Sort of like Ari was shouting, 'Here we are, come save us!'"

Case grunted. "Somehow, I don't think that's going to happen."

"I mean, it's a possibility. The supply sheet Darby had listed an abundance of solar panels powering tons of low-amp diodes and enough large-scale UV to grow food for thousands. They aren't short on illumination. Those ships were also stocked with tons of raw materials and special machinery to make any kind of component needed, for any purpose. Your grandfather thought of everything. I'm imagining a floating palace out here, like the ones our ancestors built that could easily accommodate twenty families, but this one accommodates thousands. Why wouldn't it be lit up?"

Case shrugged. "I don't know. I guess it might be. I hadn't given it much thought."

"We're looking for the farms, though," Daze said. "Those will look different."

"They might," I said. "But they have UV bulbs as big as your body sitting at the top. I think they'd always be on, but I'm not sure. They use them to grow vegetation, like Walt does, but on a huge scale." Walt had been busy gathering up all the UV he could find. He'd even commandeered another floor of the Emporium to start what he was calling his "seed and feed project."

"I can't wait to see a biosphere in person," Daze said. "It's going to be so cool. I can't believe after all this that the Flotilla really exists. I wish I could tell Rennie. She wouldn't believe it."

Daze had lost his pal Renata when Tandor had launched his battle against us. There was a chance the little girl was alive, hiding somewhere, but we had no idea how to find her. Claire had stepped up her street-kid program, but with everything else going on in the city right now, it would take time to round them all up. I wasn't going to say anything to Daze. The kid didn't need his hopes dashed.

"I'm picking up some interesting readings," Maisie announced.

"What do you mean by interesting?" I asked. When a status reader was unsure what she was getting, it couldn't be a good thing.

When she didn't answer, Case shifted his body. "Elaborate. What are you picking up?"

"I detect no human signatures, but I am receiving a low-frequency ping sixty kilometers south of this location."

"A low-frequency ping?" I asked. "Like a radio signal?"

"No," she replied. "According to the data I'm analyzing, the same frequency note was used for navigation in submarines over a hundred years ago. It's called active sonar. The frequency in my records is identical to the one I'm detecting."

"Active sonar, huh? I've never heard of it," I said. "Darby didn't have any data on that."

"There are no humans or bio matter in the same vicinity," she said. "It could be a lone device from the past, operated by wave energy. It's highly probable someone left it there for detection, although the purpose is unclear."

"Give me the coordinates," I said. "It's as good a place to start as any." Instead of verbally directing me, Maisie peeled back the tip of her finger, exposing a standard nine-pronged input connector. Leaning forward, she jabbed it directly into Tilly's dash.

The video screen flickered once as the flight navigation blinked on.

"Your lifecable has taken on a completely different look," I joked, referencing our last flight when she'd still been a status reader shaped like an egg and had had a cable hidden inside her—a cable that was now connecting her to Priscilla the LiveBot. "That looks so wrong," I muttered.

Once she was done, she popped her finger out, flicked the lifelike polymer skin back over the tip, and was back to normal.

Our crazy, mixed-up, surreal new normal.

Unlike Luce's, Tilly's flight navigation had an audio feature. A smooth male tone came out of integrated speakers, announcing, "If you would like to initiate autopilot to arrive at your destination, depress lever one." Lever one conveniently blinked a few times.

"Sorry, guy," I said. "No autopilot for us. We'd need a few hundred working satellites for that to happen." The program wasn't interactive, so the navigation guy couldn't hear me.

The computer voice intoned, "Bank your craft thirty-five degrees south and continue to follow the route indicated by the yellow line on the screen. You will reach your destination in seventeen minutes." A small graphic of an X craft followed along on a bright yellow ribbon.

In theory, the only thing I had to do was make sure the craft stayed on the line, and we would make it there. The same thing that autopilot could've done without me having to grip the levers. Our ancestors had had it easy.

Maisie's head suddenly cocked like she was listening to something. Maybe she was. "Another active sonar signature detected," she announced. "Sixty kilometers southeast. That makes two signals exactly sixty kilometers apart."

"That can't be a coincidence," I said. "What should we do? Do we continue toward this first beacon and see what it is? Or do I shift and follow the trail?"

"Maisie, do you detect any structures?" Case asked. "Anything attached to the signals themselves?"

"My lidar is picking up images of the sonar devices. They are secured to the sea floor by a heavy cable hooked to an iron anchor. The housing is no bigger than two cubic meters, made of an aluminum and titanium alloy to resist rust and corrosion."

"Is it powered by water current? Is that why it's still working after all these years?" Case asked. "My guess would be that the devices are fanned out in a large radius, directing would-be help to where the farms, and subsequently where New Eden, would be located. My grandfather could have deliberately deployed those beacons before the meteor struck, so others could find his family if something happened to the satellites."

"That's as good a theory as any," I agreed. "So which way should we head? Bank easterly to follow the next signal? Or continue on this path? We'll reach the first beacon in four minutes, according to the handy dash map."

"I think Case's right," Daze added. "I think our grandfather wanted people to find them so they could bring help. That means the city would be in the middle. Or a little past now, since they're drifting. Maisie can only detect sixty kilometers away, but now that she has two references, I bet she can figure out the

216

rest. Can't you, Maisie?" The kid was too smart for his own good.

"That is correct," Maisie replied. "According to the two points, the diameter of the circle is one hundred kilometers. The middle would be fifty-five kilometers northeast of our current location."

"Plug it in," I ordered Maisie. "If they're not there, then we're in the wrong location altogether, and we'll have to come up with a new area to search."

Maisie did as I asked, sticking her finger back into the dash. The computer voice alerted us to the change and repositioned the yellow line to the right trajectory. The computer finished with, "At cruising speed, you will reach your destination in sixteen minutes."

"Maisie should be able to pick up body signatures and radio frequencies in half that time," I said as I steered the craft to match the new line. Anxiety raced through me. This felt right. Finding the active sonar hadn't been a fluke. It was here so somebody could locate the survivors. We'd know soon enough.

Case rested his hand on my thigh, giving it a squeeze. He felt it, too. This was it. He was about to find his family, just like his grandfather had intended.

At the twelve-minute mark, I was about to ask Maisie if she detected anything, but a gasp from the kid derailed me. Daze had his face smashed up against the window, facing south. "I see something! I see something! It's really far away. There's fire. I can only see the light. It's right there!" He rapped his finger repeatedly against the glass.

A second later, Maisie intoned, "I detect hundreds of human signatures. Their locations are spread out. Most of the signatures are located southeast of here, a few more to the south, and at least two hundred in one location. We have just entered my lidar range. I will have more information momentarily."

I glanced at Case. "I'm following the light."

"Good idea," Case said, his jaw stiff. "If Maisie is detecting a vessel, it's most likely the medi-ship. We need to get there fast."

I banked us in an arc, getting an immediate visual out the front windshield of the fire Daze had spotted. I increased Tilly's speed. "What if we're too late? What if he just blew them up?" Fear wound itself through my belly. "Maisie, we need more information."

"I detect superheated metal and vaporized organic compounds indicating laser fire," she said. "Based on the chemical signature, I would surmise the target was a biosphere. It's damaged, but not fully submerged. I detect no human signatures in the vicinity of the blast. I'm picking up seventy-three signatures on a ship, which contains massive artillery, including a nuclear bomb, an abundance of technology, and an ample communications room emitting various radio frequencies."

As we soared nearer, I could make out flames licking the sky, but I couldn't discern the outline of the sphere itself or the ship, because it was too dark. "If there were no humans on board, why did the ship fire on it?" Relief and panic flooded through me at the same time, causing adrenaline to make my heart beat faster. Ari's people appeared to be safe, but for how long?

"My bet is that the people on the ship didn't know the farm was empty, or why shoot?" Case said. "Maisie, give me the status on any other farms in the area. They must account for the scattered human signatures you mentioned earlier."

Maisie confirmed, "There are three other habitats nearby. One biosphere is located thirty kilometers south. Two more are located approximately five kilometers beyond that, moving at five knots an hour. The closest farm holds nine individuals with heavy artillery, including bombs and a single barrel laser. The other biospheres contain a total of two hundred and nine individuals and a small amount of artillery. I'm detecting an independent radio frequency. It's weak, but accessible. It will take me a moment to connect." She went dark, knowing time was of the essence.

"I'm going to head toward that single biosphere," I said. "We can't fire on the ship, and we have to warn them not to either, that doing so would kill everyone in a nuclear firestorm."

I watched the flames die down as I turned Tilly south, the view of the wreckage transferring to my side window. We were far enough away, so I doubted anyone would detect us. "I bet Ari was trying to gain time," I concluded. "They cut that farm loose, hoping Marty would go after it. He did. They bought themselves exactly enough, and thank goodness they did. If they hadn't, we would've been too late, and they'd be dead down there."

Maisie snapped to attention behind me. "Connection achieved."

·ARI·

Chapter 21

Ari, Paris, and Hector stood side by side, staring off into the distance. Jake was inside the sphere. They could barely see the destruction happening to Habitat Four, but they could hear it. Ari's father had come for them in the middle of the night. He hadn't even waited until daybreak.

"There she goes," Hector said. "That bastard took her right down."

Paris said, "How long till he figures out we're not on there?"

Ari shook her head. "Hard to know. They used to have bio-sensing equipment, but it stopped working a long time ago. Once it gets light enough, he'll send some of his men on skis to investigate."

"They hit that sphere all night. If nothing is left by morning," Paris said, "he may think we went down with it. Maybe we'll be in the clear."

"There's a possibility," Ari said. "But my father's shrewd. He'll want proof of my death before he calls off this mission. He's acting on anger and emotion, not logic. The fact he hit the biosphere at night, and likely didn't try for any contact first, means he's deteriorated even further. There will be no reasoning with him."

"I think he didn't want to stand witness to having that much blood on his hands," Hector said. "Easier to do it in the dark like a specter."

Jake exited the airlock behind them. Ari immediately noticed his increased speed. "What is it? What's wrong?" she asked, meeting him halfway.

"Claude picked up a signal. He's trying to connect with it right now. We need you inside," Jake said.

Ari hurried after him, followed by Hector and Paris. This biosphere, like all the others, had one small area dedicated to communications. Before the meteor strikes, the farms had been set up with their own bandwidth, and that had stayed the same even after New Eden had been built. That way, essential communications about food and supplies could stay within the farms, not bothering anyone else. They'd been able to connect with the city if necessary. Something that couldn't happen now, because the distance was too great, and their short antennas weren't strong enough to relay signals more than ten kilometers.

"Either this is my father or another habitat." Ari took a deep breath. "I hope the other farms aren't in trouble. It can't be the city. We're out of range."

"Maybe the resistance took over the engineering ship," Paris offered, "and they're on their way." That would be a blessing.

Claude stood as Ari entered. The communications equipment was set up in a corner of the entranceway into the sphere. She nodded at him. They had given all the prisoners a choice: They could fight against her father and try to save their own lives, or be tossed into the sea. Five out of the ten had pledged their allegiance to Ari immediately, including Claude. She had believed them, and believed their willingness to fight for their lives, as she'd known most of them in her youth. Five of the others had tried to negotiate, but Ari hadn't had the heart to kill them in the end. They'd been detained on Habitat One.

Claude pulled off the headset he'd been wearing, which was connected to a small circuit board, and handed it to Ari. "A message just came through," he told her. "It's clear, no interference. But I don't know who it is. She said she won't identify herself until she hears your voice."

Ari set down the headset and flipped on the speaker so everyone could listen. Gripping the mic, she depressed the button as she sat. "This is Alaria Bancroft," she said into the small black mesh. "Come in." She took her finger off the button. Static buzzed for a few seconds before she heard a click.

"Alaria, my name is Holly," a female voice said. "We got your message and came as quickly as we could. We know you sent a decoy farm out and that your father just blew it up. No casualties that we can detect. We need a place to land so we can speak to you. It's imperative that you don't fire on the medi-ship in the meantime."

Someone had come. They'd received her plea.

Ari glanced at Jake and then Claude, Paris, and Hector, knowing everyone had just heard what she'd heard. She brought the mic off the table, bringing it to within centimeters of her lips, her hand shaking slightly. "You need a place to land? You're really here?"

"Yes, we're here," Holly asserted. "We're circling in a craft above you. Unless you're not in the farm with nine individuals and heavy artillery? Our sensors are picking up more people in two other farms approximately six kilometers away." Ari could hear someone speaking in the background, nothing more than a murmur on her end. "Scratch that, our technician says this communication is coming from this sphere. I repeat, we need a place to land."

"How can they set a craft down here?" Paris asked, her voice filled with excitement as well as fear. "There's no place big enough. Right? I don't know. I've never seen a dronecraft before. I've only heard about them. Are they big?"

"We have space," Hector said. "There's a pad underneath the walkway, but it has to be inflated or something like that. I heard a few farmers talking about it last week. Every farm has one, but I don't think they've ever been used before, except maybe before the meteor."

Ari had to tell the woman something. "I think we can find a way for you to land, but you're going to have to give us some time to figure it out." The mic was now touching her lips. "There are no farmers on board. We couldn't risk their lives. No one here knows how the landing system works." Then, after a second, she added, "Please don't leave." Emotion swirled inside her. Was this the beginning or their end?

"We're not going anywhere. Please don't worry about that," Holly answered promptly. "I'm handing you over to my…LiveBot. She has access to the data you'll need to release the landing pad and will guide you through the process."

"Ah…okay," Ari replied. She'd heard of the human-type robots called LiveBots, but had never seen one. Her father had complained many times that the dark city had eradicated them too quickly after the disaster. Ari sometimes had thought that he would've preferred bringing LiveBots to New Eden rather than humans.

A smooth, modulated, female voice came on the line. "To access the landing flotation, you must activate the source air valves. The switch is located inside the main utility panel directly inside the biosphere. According to my data, this panel is on the left."

"I know where it is. I'll do it," Jake called as he entered the sphere.

"Once the valves have been activated, you must manually free the buoys from where they're secured.

To do this, locate the recessed fitting, insert the provided tool, and rotate clockwise three full rotations. By my calculations, this will take forty kilos of pressure, possibly fifty, due to salt buildup and probable corrosion."

"Ask her where we find the tool," Hector instructed. "I've seen the divot in the walkway. I know what she's talking about. But I have no idea where the tool would be."

Jake came back. "The air valves are activated."

"We need some sort of wrench to crank the landing buoys out," Hector said. "Have you seen anything that would fit into a circular shallow recess around here?"

Jake shook his head as Ari spoke into the mic. "The valves are on. But we don't know what kind of tool we're looking for. Can you describe it?"

"It's a rod consisting of four ninety-degree angles, the entirety extending approximately one meter. The pictures indicate that the straight end is to be inserted into the recessed hole, and it shows two hands applying pressure on the ninety-degree bends."

"She's describing a manual crank," Hector said. "Now we just have to find it. Let's head inside and shake up those old storage rooms." He, Jake, and Paris rushed into the biosphere.

Ari glanced at Claude. "Go round up the other men to help. We need everyone on this." The guard nodded and exited onto the walkway. Ari bent over the mic once again. "Okay, we're searching for it now."

"This is Holly again. Our LiveBot is doing her own search as well. If she can detect where the tool is, we'll let you know."

"I don't know much about robots," Ari told her, "but if they can see things from afar, we could've used them a long time ago."

"She's not your typical LiveBot," Holly answered, chuckling. "She's actually a specialized military-grade status reader. It's…complicated." Ari thought she heard a snort. She liked this woman already.

A male voice came over the line next, sturdy and a little rough around the edges. "This is Case," he said. "In the event we can't land because the tool is missing, you cannot fire on the ship."

"Why not?" Ari asked. "It's the only hope we have of defeating him. Well, until you guys arrived."

"Your father has a nuclear bomb on board. If you destroy the ship, everyone within two hundred kilometers dies."

Ari reeled from the news. It settled deep inside her gut, like an anchor hitting the seafloor. She'd known nothing about nuclear armament. "Are you sure?" she asked weakly, even though she knew what the man said was true. This was exactly the kind of thing her father would keep from her—likely from most.

"One hundred percent," he confirmed. "Please don't despair. We will find a way to stop him."

"This is Holly again," the woman said. "Our LiveBot can't locate the tool. So, we're thinking it's not on board. But we think we might have a solution."

There was murmuring in the background. Ari thought she heard a child's voice, but she couldn't be sure. "That sounds crazy. Okay, fine," Holly uttered in a sure tone. "Sorry about that. Everybody is talking at once. We have a titanium prop wrench about the right length. With enough force, it can be manipulated into the shape and size you need. The only one strong enough to do that is our LiveBot. So, we're going to drop her and the tool down on your walkway. Are you okay with us doing that?"

"Sure?" Ari said, not intending to make it sound like a question. "I mean, yes, of course. Whatever it takes." They were about to have an encounter with an actual robot.

"In order to do this," Holly continued, "we have to fool our craft into thinking we're making a landing, or the doors won't open. It's a standard protection our ancestors built into these drones, but something we haven't overridden in this particular craft. The closest position for us to do that is on top of your sphere. Once the craft is within a meter of something solid, the locking mechanisms will give. Then we'll send Maisie, our LiveBot, out. She assures us the fall won't harm her. In order to lessen the chances of anything happening, she has to do some damage to the outside shell of the biosphere so she can regulate her speed. Are you okay with that?"

"Yes, yes, of course. Whatever it takes," Ari repeated. "Honestly, without your help, our lives are forfeit anyway. We appreciate everything you're doing."

Jake and Hector entered, shaking their heads. "We can't find it," Jake said. "We searched everywhere. There's barely anything left."

"It's okay," Ari said. "Our rescuers have a solution. They're sending their LiveBot down with a similar tool. They're going to be landing on top of the biosphere any minute."

"Cool," Hector crooned. "I don't want to miss this." He ducked outside.

Holly's voice came over the speaker. "We're within twenty seconds of our pseudo landing. The props are going to be loud and windy. Once the LiveBot is out of the craft, I can't communicate with you. If this doesn't work, we'll figure something else out. We hope to see you soon." She signed off.

Ari stood and followed Jake and Paris out onto the walkway.

Watching the craft descend out of the sky, its propellers creating gale-force winds, was awe-inspiring. The dronecraft was bigger than she'd thought it would be. At least five meters in length, three meters wide. It was black. The soft glow of the biosphere was the only thing illuminating it against the dark sky. It resembled a monster, something that would bring harm rather than hope.

Then one of the doors opened vertically, and a woman dressed head to toe in syn-leather, with long flowing hair the color of a ripened apple, jumped out. She gripped two things in her hands. She plunged one into the plexi as she slid down the side, a loud grating sound reverberating around them. She descended fast, like a ghost out of the sky, landing easily with her knees bent, straightening to face them.

"My name is Maisie. I'm here to help."

·HOLLY·

Chapter 22

"Shut the door fast," I ordered. The wind was whipping everything around. "I can't see anything. Is she down yet?" I couldn't believe Maisie had just launched herself out the door. "This was an insane idea. What if she hits too hard and malfunctions? Or ends up in the water?" But our plan of spoofing a landing had worked perfectly, just as Maisie said it would, though I'd had to get closer to the biosphere than I'd wanted.

Case closed the door, and I eased Tilly up, angling her underbelly toward the sphere, before redirecting her to maintain and hover just off the walkway over the water.

"I'm certain the superheated knife she used to puncture the shell kept her momentum down. She's fine. And there was no other way to do this," Case reminded me. "They never would've gotten the landing pad open on their own. Maisie put her odds of success at ninety-three percent."

"I see her!" Daze shouted. "At least, I think that's her." He jabbed his skinny arm between us, gesturing out the windshield. "She's behind the people. Yes, there she is!"

I snapped on Tilly's headlights, so we could all understand what was happening. "You're right. She made it." I nodded toward the small crowd that had gathered. "They look a little nervous. I think that means Marty didn't bring any LiveBots with him." We watched as the group collectively took a few steps back as Maisie moved forward. "She's intimidating, but don't get used to it." Maisie stood, feet apart and braced on the walkway, which was rocking beneath them to a shocking degree. She looked completely unruffled. It was as if she'd spent her entire existence on an aquatic farm. The rest of the group huddled together. "I don't know how they live on that thing," I muttered. "It doesn't look safe. Yeah, there's railings, but they're just basically handholds. An adult male could fit under, no problem. You're knocked off balance, and you're a goner."

Finally, one guy and a girl broke away from the rest. They both stepped forward in sync, each wearing what looked to be synthetic-leather outfits, but none like I'd ever seen before. The material seemed almost pliable, glistening as they moved, beads of water from rain glimmering in Tilly's lights. They resembled pictures of wetsuits on Darby's pico, which made sense because they lived on the water.

The guy was half a meter taller than the girl, broad-chested, hair lighter than most and close-cropped. He seemed sturdy. The girl, whom I took to be Ari, had an athletic build, with light brown, chin-length hair tucked behind her ears. She wore a determined look on her face, had high, sculpted cheekbones and a nose strikingly similar to Case's, which meant it was strong and perfectly aligned. She held a natural air of authority. You could see it in the way she stood—at ease, yet ready to strike. She addressed another guy, who nodded and stepped forward. He was shorter than the other men in the group, with a round face and a head full of dark, curly hair. He made a motion with his arm, and he and Maisie began to walk around the outside of the sphere, everyone else trailing behind.

"I'm following them." I eased Tilly back, doing my best to keep the prop wash directed away from the people as I maneuvered into a new position, angling the headlights so everybody could get a clear view of their surroundings. It wasn't necessary for the LiveBot, who took in images with her lidar, but for everybody else it was a bonus, as there wasn't much light to be had on this farm. The few safety bulbs positioned every ten meters barely gave off enough to see your feet on the platform. The UV didn't seem to be very bright on the inside, or everything would've been more lit up.

"Look!" Daze crooned directly in my ear from his position at my shoulder. "She's bending the titanium!

Just like she said she could. She's gonna make it work. I knew it!"

Maisie was, in fact, bending and retrofitting the prop wrench with her bare hands. "If she decides to make a few cuts with her new eyeball lasers, I'm not sure how that group is going to react. I hope nobody faints and tumbles into the sea. In retrospect, we probably should've eased them into this more slowly. I can't imagine what they're thinking right now."

We watched as Maisie crafted her tool, thankfully without the need to shoot hot lasers out of her orbs. She had one end in the hole with no time to waste and was cranking it with what looked to be minimal effort. I leaned forward. "It's working. I can see some sort of a platform moving underneath." A large mass was extending from under the walkway, bobbing in the water. "It doesn't look large enough." Or sturdy enough, for that matter.

"Maisie told us it comes in four parts. It has to be inflated first," Case said. "Just give it a minute." Case was as restless as I was.

"I'm prepared to give them all the minutes they need," I retorted. "That's not the issue. The ocean is rolling, and everything's unsteady. To an insane degree. It's making me queasy just watching it. Even if the inflated landing pad is strong enough to support a craft of this size, and we manage to set down on it, how are we possibly going to secure it? I'm not risking Tilly. She's the only thing standing between us and certain death. Not to mention, she's our only way out of here."

"Maisie mentioned securing brackets," he said, distracted as he watched the LiveBot work. "I'm sure it will be fine."

"They might be rusted out after all these years." I arched an eyebrow at him. Case shot me a look, part impatience, part frustration. I held my hand up. "Okay, fine, I'll stop talking." After a short few seconds, not being able to help myself, I continued, "You know, I'm not saying we should abort this mission, but we can't risk the craft. It's our only way home. Without Tilly, we die."

Daze chimed in, "Look, it's opening. It's huge!"

As we watched, four panels expanded, layers of metal unfolding and forming an interlocking grid as air inflated the structure below. The thing was so large that, once it finished assembling, two crafts would be able to land there safely.

"Do you see any cables?" I asked, leaning forward. "Or securing points?"

"I see some indent bars for locking, but no cables," Case answered. "Once you land, I'll get out and assess." He turned, giving me a slow grin. "I agree with you, by the way. We don't risk this craft."

"By the way, are you going to tell Ari right away who you are?" Case and I hadn't discussed the personal stuff. Up until this very moment, we hadn't known for sure that we were going to make contact, so why discuss things that might not happen?

But here we were.

Case ran a hand around the back of his neck. A restless movement. His helmet was off, his face stark. It'd been a long journey. It was hard to believe we'd actually made it—and that all this really existed. The Flotilla, and all it encompassed, had been a myth to us until recently. "I don't know," he replied. "I only learned Marty was my father a short time ago. This entire thing doesn't feel real. I don't want to freak her out. I think I'll take it slow."

"Good idea," I said.

The landing pad was fully engaged. The people on the walkway were busy connecting it to the farm using the end of one of the metal panels. They appeared to be struggling a little. "It's clear nobody has done this before. I see Maisie's lips moving. She's giving them directions. Thank goodness Darby had her upload all the blueprints from the pico into her database."

A few minutes later, everything seemed to be secured.

Maisie lifted her arm, gesturing for us to land. I held my breath as I whisked us up, aligning Tilly directly above the very center of the structure, reducing power, and approaching as slowly as I could. We landed with a soft bounce, but it didn't feel like a landing, because we were still moving—because we were on a freaking raft in the middle of the sea.

I couldn't let go of the levers. "Case," I mumbled, "get out and see what's going on. Daze, you stay here." When the kid began to push back, I said through my clenched jaw, "Don't argue with me. You're staying here until we make sure it's safe." The kid got the picture. Case lofted his door.

The overpowering smell of salt burst through the confines of the craft, assaulting us with its briny thickness. I'd smelled the ocean, but not like this. It was as if it'd been shot directly into my bloodstream. Dizziness came next. Before Case could fully exit, I reached out, grabbing hold of his arm, preventing him from moving another muscle. He must've registered the panic in my eyes, because his expression softened.

I hadn't expected there would be anything more harrowing than flying in the clouds. But an extended trip over the ocean and then landing with the sea nearly lapping at our ankles was right up there. My mind had relinquished all decisions, allowing my body to take over, and apparently keeping the people I cared about in one piece was at the top of my body's to-do list.

Case covered my hand with his. "I'm not going to let go of the craft," he told me softly. "I promise. I don't want to drown. If Maisie can't secure this thing to my liking, you two take off."

"Look, Maisie's coming," Daze announced, gesturing in front of us.

We both turned.

The LiveBot briskly rounded the side of the craft and approached Case's open door. She didn't look at all off balance, even with the sea undulating beneath us. Oh, to have the stomach of a droid—or no stomach, as it were. She told us, "I have located cables of sufficient strength to hold down the craft. I sent two men to retrieve them. They will connect to four D-rings built into the pad. Once they're attached, the craft will be fully secured."

"Are you totally, completely sure?" I asked, gazing up at her through the open door. "What's the probability?"

"Ninety-seven-point-six percent," she asserted. "The only way this craft could be dislodged from this location is by the impact of a wave larger than forty meters high traveling at fifty knots and hitting the landing pad from a southwesterly direction."

Okay, forty meters was crazy high. If a rogue wave like that hit, it would probably take out the entire farm.

I released my grip on Case's arm centimeter by centimeter, my muscles stiff, but I ignored the discomfort like a champ. We didn't have to wait long for the cables to arrive. The short man with the curly hair and the tall one with the broad shoulders carried two apiece. They waltzed out onto the platform with no fear. I guessed that was what living on the water did to you—it made you immune to the absurdity of it all. At Maisie's direction, they clipped in the cables and tethered Tilly in under three minutes.

When the LiveBot motioned for Case and me to exit, I glanced at Daze, who was more than eager to hop out onto the rolling deathtrap. "You're not going anywhere without Maisie," I told him. "No arguments." The kid kept his lip zipped. Case exited his side as I opened my door. The fear I felt about leaving Tilly was oppressive, the salty smell still overpowering, but I dealt with it. I'd purposely left Tilly's running lights on so we could navigate with the aid of the illumination. As an added bonus, the glow highlighted the white foam breaking at the tops of the dark waves, making it look like cans of polyfoam were exploding with every swirling motion.

Suddenly, Maisie was in front of me, and I'd never been more grateful to see anyone in my life.

I motioned for Daze to crawl over my lap. "Get him to safety first," I ordered. "Then come back for me." Maisie took Daze into her arms, and the kid shouted with glee as she hauled him off the platform, chattering about how awesome it was to see the ocean this close.

Nothing inside me shared even a sliver of the kid's enthusiasm for our current situation.

Instead, I carefully placed my legs outside the security of Tilly and proceeded to bend over, placing my head between my knees. "I can do this," I muttered, taking slow breaths in and out, trying to bypass the thick, foreign air clogging my throat. I had to make sure enough oxygen was entering my lungs. My head felt tingly, like it was full of argon. "We won't be here long," I began my mantra. "It's mind over matter. I'm not going to spill my guts. I'm going to keep them inside where they belong."

A low chuckle had me glancing up. Case stood outside my door, one hand reaching toward me, his other arm braced on Tilly's roof, his legs splayed. "It's not that bad. I promise."

"The scale of badness is a matter of perception," I said, reluctantly grabbing on to his hand, allowing him to pull me up on shaky legs. Once upright, I fought for balance, knocking into Case. He wrapped his arm tightly around my middle, stabilizing me. I leaned into him, thankful he was there. "Living on the sea must be coded somewhere in your DNA," I muttered. "To me, this feels all wrong. My body is boldly rejecting the notion of getting out of the safety of the craft. I hope we don't stay here long. I don't think my psyche can take it."

"I hope so, too," he whispered in my ear. "Would it help if I tell you I'm faking it and I'm just as terrified?"

"Yes," I said. "It helps." My stomach heaved as we wobbled our way toward the walkway, me grasping on to Case, Case holding on to the craft. Then Maisie was magically back by my side. I reached out blindly, taking her hand in mine.

"Your vitals are elevated," she stated as we weaved our way toward relative safety. "I recommend a dose of the antinausea medication Walt included. Your neurotransmitters are stress-firing, your heart rate is high, blood pressure is low, your stomach can't stabilize—"

"*Enough*," I croaked just before losing my stomach contents over the side of the railing.

Chapter 23

Ari handed me a cup filled with water. I took it gratefully. Walt's dart for antinausea had already been drained into my thigh, my body immediately thankful for the reprieve. Walt had thought of everything. I was going to kiss that old man on the lips when we got home.

We were situated inside the biosphere after a long, slippery walk, the rocking gentler, but still constant. The place itself was enormous and beyond all reckoning. The pictures I'd conjured in my mind, based on the graphics Darby had shown us, hadn't come close. The vegetation in this farm had died some time ago, the smell of wet earth and rotted compost lingering. But the imprint of what it had been was still very much alive.

Large pots of all different sizes and colors, along with specialized raised boxes made of some sort of polycarbonate, likely to keep the water in, were packed with rich, fertile dirt. Every centimeter of the space had been utilized in an orderly and precise fashion. The focal point of the biosphere was a large hill, at least ninety meters high, that was covered with what had once been healthy trees and bushes and made to look how I would imagine a park would have looked in the days of my ancestors.

A path wound its way upward, meandering back and forth, creating terraces so those tending plants had easy access, and the trees had room to grow. There were also places to sit and enjoy the spectacle of it all. I imagined people from New Eden would have come and enjoyed their time here, receiving their UV from a faux sun positioned above rather than from a sleeping pod. In the biosphere's prime, I imagined the scents of fresh leaves, growing fruit, and blooming flowers would have been wondrous.

A spiral platform made of thin, sturdy steel ranged around the outside of the hill. Workstations were dotted at regular intervals. Barrels and crates leaned against the railings, every tool a farmer would need for pruning and planting. A sprinkler system laced across the entire space, with efficiently styled nozzles aimed in multiple directions to provide daily water, likely recycled from the condensation the low-pressure environment created. A perfect, sustainable cycle.

I glanced up, trying to contain some of my awe, but not succeeding. Several tall trees stood—none that I recognized—but all likely to have provided some kind of edible fruit or nuts. One tree in particular contained numerous branches, stubborn yellow leaves clinging on for dear life. I'd never seen a real leaf before that wasn't black and crumbling. Every trunk in sight was still a rich brown color, unlike the ones back on land, which were twisted, dead for at least sixty years, weathered and hardened by the constant iron-infused rain that spewed from the sky.

These trees had been alive a short time ago, and seeing them, even in this state, was magnificent.

I took a sip of water, feeling overwhelmed, as were Daze and Case. None of us had said much since we'd entered. The water tasted clean and fresh, no hint of iron or salt. I raised my eyebrows. "How do you do this?" I asked, lifting my cup. "We have filtration systems at home, but our water is still tinged with iron. You can't get away from it." Daze came to sit next to me on the edge of a raised garden bed. Withered vines, twisted and brown, lay on top of black soil. He reached a hand in to touch them.

Ari stood a few meters away, her hands clasped in front of her, allowing us to take the time we needed, evaluating us as we took in our environment. "Our filtration systems are very good," she replied. "They were made to eliminate everything. Saline-infused water would be very bad, not only for the vegetation, but for us as well." Ari spoke clearly, but I detected some nervousness. "It's a miracle this system is still working. The other farms are having trouble with theirs. But it's not something that can be transferred between spheres. The water-management system is integrated." She took a step forward, suddenly appearing a little flustered. "I'm sorry. I'm having trouble believing that you're actually here. We didn't know you existed until a short time ago. Now you've arrived, with your"—she made a small gesture toward Maisie—"robot. I fear somebody will wake me up and tell me it's all a dream."

I gave her a smile as I nodded. "I totally understand. I feel exactly the same way. As much as I'd like to, it would take too much time to trade stories about both of our histories now, but I'm certain we'll manage soon enough. By the way, I'm Holly." I addressed the entire group. "My surname is Danger, but I don't use it much. This is Daze." I patted the kid's shoulder, handing him the rest of my water, which he gulped down greedily. "That's Case." I gestured to where Case stood under the small canopy of branches of a nearby tree that had no remaining foliage. "And you met Maisie. She's actually a military-grade status reader stuffed inside the body of a retail bot. It's a long tale, but she's the reason we're here. Really, the only reason. Before her, we didn't have the kind of tech it would've taken to locate you. It was all destroyed more than sixty years ago. Finding her has been our miracle. Now it's yours."

The tall, broad-shouldered boy stepped forward. I said *boy*, because up close, we could see that they were practically children, barely in their twenties, if that. "I'm Jake," he said. "That's Hector and Paris." He gestured around. "That's Claude, Dean, Agee, Geo, and Dom."

The antinausea dart had worked its magic, and I was feeling much better—refreshed, even. I wouldn't have put it past Walt to have added an adrenaline boost. I stood, thankful the ground was fairly solid beneath my feet. I studied the group Jake had just introduced. Five of the nine wore militia uniforms of some kind. Outfits like that were unmistakable, even though these were extremely faded.

"You have the militia on your side?" I asked. My voice held my suspicions. If the rebellion truly had the support of the militia, this should've gone a much different way.

"Not exactly," Jake hedged. "These guys were sent by Ari's father, Martin Bancroft Jr., to take us into custody. But we took them prisoner instead. Then, when Bancroft came after us, we gave them a choice." He appeared uncomfortable. "We all kind of...grew up together. So we didn't want to..." He trailed off.

I put him out of his misery. "I get it," I said. "This seems like a sticky situation at best. Has it always been like this? With your leader going after his own people?"

Ari chose to answer, "Yes and no. My father's behavior has been erratic for as long as I can remember. But only recently, in the last month or so, has it gotten to an extreme point, where lives were put in immediate danger and we felt we had to launch a rebellion." She glanced down at her feet, then back up. This girl carried grief along with guilt, clearly a heavy burden. "I think something triggered him. My best guess is he received information from your city that made him snap. After that, there was no reasoning with him. He began raiding the farms and taking innocent people prisoner. It was chaos. We had no choice except to act fast."

I settled my hands on my hips, my eyes still roaming the interior of the sphere. It truly was incredible. "That timeline adds up, since we recently defeated his allies and commandeered resources they'd been hoarding for years. Your father had some sort of an agreement with them. He was supposed to bring the Flotilla back to repopulate the city with his disciples. Or something like that. The details are murky, mostly because they never made sense to begin with. The plan to build your floating city was hatched by your grandfather before the meteor struck as a failsafe if land was no longer habitable. It turned into something much darker throughout the years. And here we are."

Ari nodded. "My father always talked about going back to the city—craved it, obsessed over it. I got the impression he wasn't allowed to and that he was waiting for something or some command from them. Unfortunately, when it came, it launched him over the edge."

Case said, "Your father's allies could have succeeded, but we discovered them before they could enact their plans. We'll share everything we know, once the threat is eliminated. We must move quickly. In order for that to happen, we're going to need all the information you have. As I told you already, the ship your father's taken charge of has a nuclear bomb on board, so taking him unaware is a necessity. If he knows we're coming, he may decide to flip the switch. At first light, he'll most likely figure out there was no one on that farm he destroyed. Then he'll turn his sights on this sphere. We have to get to him before he does either."

Ari paled. The others looked uncomfortable. "I didn't know anything about the nuclear weapon, I swear." Ari gazed at the men wearing the militia outfits. "Did any of you know?"

One of the guys replied, "There were murmurs here and there that Bancroft had something powerful, but not what it was." There was genuine fear in his eyes. "He likes to keep secrets."

Jake addressed Case. "Did you only bring one craft? How are we going to defeat him with only one?"

"Yes," Paris added, "and how are we going to get to the city once this is over? We all won't fit in that thing."

"We aren't using crafts to get you back to the city," I answered. "Even if we could, we don't have access to as many as it would take. You'll have to go back on the working ships. By your estimate, how many people live here? On the farms and New Eden combined?"

Ari bit her lip. "I'm not sure. My father kept an accurate count a long time ago, but people have been starving, and the conditions in most of New Eden have become abhorrent. By my guess, less than a thousand." She shrugged. "A few years ago, it was up two thousand. But, honestly, it's hard to know, especially since my father kept the classes segregated. The elite didn't mix with the commoners or the hulls. I've never seen everyone all in one place."

That was somewhat surprising. "That's a much lower number than I was expecting," I told her. "When people in my city talk about the Flotilla, the story is that at least thirty ships full of people and supplies left the harbor. I was thinking that meant at least ten thousand souls."

"According to the history we've been told, there were over twelve thousand when they first arrived. Around a thousand already lived on the farms. But during the years-long construction of New Eden, many people perished, consumed by the sea. My father is a hard man, and he was unrelenting in his focus to get the city built. Things calmed down once it was finished, so I was told. Then there were a couple of outbreaks of sudden illnesses. Other than that, I'm not really sure. By the time I was born, less than half of the original population existed. That was over nineteen years ago."

"The farms used to be twenty habitats strong," Jake added. "As of right now, there are only three, including this one. And only one has a semiworking biosphere. It's been a slow decline of our people. If you hadn't arrived, their fate would've been sealed. The biospheres are designed to generate food. There are bio-printers in New Eden, but they're useless without organic matter."

I read the look on Case's face. From what these guys were telling us, his father was directly responsible for thousands of deaths. Case appeared stoic on the outside, but I knew better. Emotion was beating just under the surface. "Well, we have a secret weapon," I told them. "Something your father won't anticipate. With Maisie, we don't need an army of crafts. We can isolate where the weapon is located, ascertain where everyone is on the ship, and figure out a successful plan. With an accurate description, she might even be able to figure out where your father is specifically." I glanced at the militiamen. "Are you guys required to carry weapons on you at all times?"

They shook their heads in unison. The same guy who'd spoken before said, "There aren't enough weapons to go around. Lots of them stopped working years ago. You know how lasers are." He indicated the Gem on my belt. "They can be finicky." Yes, they could.

I walked up to him, full of curiosity. "What's your name?"

"Claude," he answered, straightening his shoulders as I took his measure. "Are you in charge of keeping these guys on task?" I casually glanced at the other men standing in a row.

He shrugged, skirting a look at Ari. "I guess so."

So he considered Ari in charge. That was good. As long as he kept that mentality, things should go fine. "Why don't you take these men outside and keep an eye on the horizon? We want to know exactly when that ship comes into view." Once again, Claude glanced at Ari for confirmation. She nodded, and they filed out. Once the door was shut, I turned. "I'm sorry for stepping on your toes, Ari. But we need to talk to you alone. We know a lot about militias and how they run, how they think, and who they listen to. Even though I believe Claude sees you as their commander, we don't want to include them in our plans. You have working communication that I'm assuming has the capability to hail that ship. We can't take the chance that they'll try to do that."

"It's okay," she said. "I agree with you. I would've dismissed them anyway. But, honestly, after watching your LiveBot come down the side of the biosphere and bend titanium with her bare hands, I think their greatest fear is of you and her."

I chuckled. "That may be true, but we can't take any chances." I glanced at Case, giving him a nod.

Before he could start talking about how we were going to make this mission work, Daze jumped off the planter where he'd been sitting and announced, "I know how we can disarm the bomb."

Chapter 24

I stared at the kid, my mouth open. Then I closed it. I should be used to him announcing such things, but it was still surprising. "What are you talking about?" I asked. "How do we shut it off?" Making sure Bancroft didn't flip the switch to activate the bomb was imperative. It would keep us all breathing for another day. A madman pressed into a corner was going to be tricky to handle.

"It's easy," Daze said. "We just kill the power." I arched an eyebrow. He continued, "In order to start a nuclear reaction, something has to trigger it. He probably has an electric fuse hooked up," he explained. "Without power, no fuse. That means there can't be an explosion." He'd stated it all matter-of-factly, like it was a shame we hadn't thought of the obvious by ourselves.

I crossed my arms. "And how do we kill power on a ship that utilizes solar?" As far as I knew, there wasn't a main switch for that kind of a setup. Usually, grids were tied to different components, making everything complicated and intertwined.

"Darby showed me pictures." Daze stuck his chin out, pushing back against my doubts. "The medi-ship runs different than other ships. All the cables go into one battery room, kinda like at the barracks. Then those battery groups link to different quadrants. There are eight. Darby said they did it that way because they have a lot of high-powered stuff that needed to be split up. If the cables are disabled in the exact place the bomb is in, the guy can't blow it."

It sounded almost too good to be true. My head bobbed toward Case. "What are the chances? It sounds too easy."

Case grinned, his mouth arching up on one side. "I've yet to question the kid's intelligence."

"If we can shut down the electricity," I said, "and board the ship at the same time, we'd have a solid chance of taking everyone unaware. We can't disregard a remote-controlled detonator." I addressed Maisie. "If Marty has a distance switch, would a power outage be enough to disarm the bomb? Is there any possibility the bomb has a dedicated off-grid battery? Or is the kid right that all we have to do is cut the power?"

"Daze is correct in theory," she replied. "Even if there are multiple detonation devices, without power located at the connection interface, a charge cannot be created."

"In theory?" I asked impatiently. "Make the data spin a little faster, please."

"At this distance," she replied, "I cannot ascertain if there is a backup power source. Throughout history, a valuable asset used in war would have multiple power sources in the event one failed. Probability is in favor of this. But if the device was recently transferred from another location, the probability dips considerably."

I glanced at Ari. "Do you know if it was moved?"

She shook her head. "I didn't know it existed until you told us. But it's unlikely my dad had it stored on the medi-ship before now. He probably had it protected in an isolation unit. That would be the best place to have it guarded and go unnoticed."

"Okay, well." I scratched my head. "We'll have to do a flyover before we engage. We need that information." I addressed Maisie. "We should've had you do a thorough scan of the ship when we were in the vicinity the first time. That was a mistake."

"A complete scan would have required two-point-six hours," she said. "The ship is full of specialized technology, medical equipment, inoculations—"

"Got it," I stopped her. "But once you do the flyover, you'll be able to zero in on the right quadrant to receive adequate data within a few minutes, correct?"

"Yes," she replied.

"Good," I said. "Let's do it."

"We have to do it now, before it gets light," Case said. "We can't risk detection."

"How many hours until daybreak?" I asked the group. I'd lost all track of time.

"Approximately three," Jake answered. "I could... you know...go with you?" He'd formulated his request as a question. "I'm familiar with the medi-ship," he hurried, "and can provide useful information."

I refrained from grinning. This kid looked like he enjoyed action—possibly lived for it. His first ride in a dronecraft would be memorable. "I'm sure you'll be an asset, Jake," I told him. "Why don't you, Case, and Maisie do the run? Collect all the information we need to make this mission successful. We need an accurate head count of all on board, where they're located, best entry point, weapons check, everything possible in fifteen minutes. Maisie knows the drill." I addressed the LiveBot again. "This is an analysis mission. When you have the info you need, calculate our best odds and come up with a success ratio above eighty percent. Take into account everything we have access to here as well." As a military operative, Maisie was designed to compute ratios and calculate odds of success. If she had access to a complete list of all of our resources, she could extrapolate a best-case scenario relatively easily.

"I've been scanning since we arrived," she announced. "Should I include the two hydro-skis in my calculations?"

"Hydro-*whats*?" My gaze darted to Ari for confirmation.

Hector replied instead, his voice jovial. "She's talking about our skis. We just used them to get to the engineering ship, so we could pick up supplies. They worked like a charm."

"I don't know what skis are," I admitted. "The first time I flew over the ocean was a couple months ago. We know next to nothing about it."

"They're mini water vehicles," Hector explained. "You pilot them kind of like a personal helidrone, except they're made to ride the surface of the water instead of fly. No props, only an impeller."

I slung my hand out toward the sea. "You ride on something as small as a helidrone on top of those waves?" That did not compute. Helidrones were basically single-operator transportation, though sometimes they were made for two. They were economical and deadly. You basically strapped yourself into a bubble with no airframe and with a lone propeller stuck on top. I'd seen only one in my entire life, and it had been in pieces. Why? Because they were dangerous as hell and usually crashed. "You can't be serious."

Hector tipped his head back and hooted. "I like you," he said. "Direct and to the point. My kind of people. Yes, you ride them in the ocean. But I didn't grow up with them." He indicated Jake and Ari. "They did. Hella good pilots, too. Taking the skis will be the only way onto that ship without landing your craft right on its deck."

Daze began to jump up and down. I held up my hand, palm toward his face. "You are *not* getting on a hydro-ski, so save it." Visions of Daze being hurled like a rocket off one of the skis and floundering in the ocean set my heart racing. "If you guys choose to do such a thing, we can't stop you. We"—I bobbed my hand between the four of us—"don't ride."

"From my initial assessments," Maisie piped in, "the likely point of entry is at water level. The skis are an asset."

I glared at her. "Don't you have someplace to be? And while you're making future assessments, I'd be more likely to strap on Darby's jet pack than get on the back of a hydro-ski. Keep that in mind."

Maisie appeared unfazed, as usual. "Utilizing the jet pack would increase—"

I jabbed my finger toward the door. "Out. We're not having this discussion until you get back. If several plans have similar odds, we pick one that does *not* include gratuitous bodily harm and probable death by drowning. If there's only one way to do this, we discuss it when you get back. Not before." Case was grinning so hard I thought his face might break. "What?" I demanded. "You think this is funny? Are you planning on riding on the back of something that skims those waves?"

He shrugged, still smiling. "I wouldn't say that, but picturing you on the back of one is better than eating one of Walt's cupcakes."

I narrowed my gaze. "Is that so?" I replied. "It's good the cupcakes are already gone. We'll see you back in a half hour. If anything happens, have Maisie send a message. We will have someone manning the board." After they left, I turned to Ari. "Is it okay if the kid and

I explore for a bit? This place is amazing. Nothing like what we have at home." Daze was already scampering up the hill, his brain thankfully veering to something other than riding a hydro-ski.

Ari nodded. "Of course." She addressed Paris and Hector. "Paris, you listen in for communications. Hector, go help them undo the cables and bring them in for safekeeping."

I followed Daze up a small slope. Fairly quickly, it turned back on itself as it wound its way up. Ari came behind.

Daze shrieked, "Can I climb one of these trees?" He already had his arms around a trunk, reaching for the lowest branches.

"Go ahead," Ari answered. I slowed so we could walk together. "I climbed them myself as a child."

"Did you come here a lot?" I asked. The UV bulb in the center cast generous light. It was much brighter inside than out, but it didn't feel particularly warm. My guess was that it was a regular light.

"Yes and no," she said. "I wasn't allowed out of my area until I was eight years old. After that, my mother would bring me down sporadically. As I got older and had a little more freedom, Jake and I would visit whichever farm was docked as often as we could. They rotated habitats weekly, so people could access the resources, but not so much as to overwhelm or deplete the vegetation. It's hard not to want to pick a flower or a piece of fruit. As Jake said before, when we were children, there were twenty farms in rotation."

"It must've been something when this place was full of people and activity. All that greenery and fresh air. I bet it was warm, too." I tried not to sound envious. I didn't think she blamed me. After growing up in a world filled with drizzle and darkness, this was a revelation. "The only real green thing I've ever seen were small plants under UV on a table. I can't imagine being surrounded by it anytime you wished."

"Habitat One is still green," she said as we continued to walk. "But things are dying there. The water-filtration system is damaged, and the UV light has lost some power. But if we make it back to your city, I'm confident our farmers and engineers can fix it. They can probably fix this one as well." She gestured upward. "The UV bulbs up there have been replaced. Once they're repaired, you'll see for yourself."

"We have a few scientists in the city who would die for a chance to learn from your farmers and scientists. Altogether, they could reboot our entire population. It would change so many lives for the better." It was staggering to think about. The resources we'd come to possess in the last few months were completely life-altering.

"What's your city like?" she asked. "My father never said much, only that he missed it. I don't think he ever liked living at sea. He tried to create his own nirvana, but it never really worked."

I kept an eye on Daze, who had climbed to the very top of the tree and was waving. I waved back as Ari and I came around another curve. This area had a bunch of skinny trees with withered brown leaves stuck to their branches. "It's nothing like this," I told her. "There's very little order. The meteor, and aftereffects of the hits, damaged everything. Decimated buildings, tore apart structures, blew out every piece of glass for miles. It was basically like the whole world was scooped up into the sky and smashed back to earth. Nothing really got put back together again, because we lacked so many resources. I'm a salvager by necessity, and because I'm good at it. If you're talented enough, you can carve out a decent life for yourself. But it takes work." I scanned the view from the top of the hill. "This sphere is amazing. What does New Eden look like?"

"It doesn't resemble this. Unlike your city, everything is structured from the top down." Ari paused. "My father valued the air and sky above all else. The higher, the better. Anyone who lived on the top decks had a pretty good life. Our homes were built with steel panels and windows made with real glass. Neat and tidy. Walkways connect the residences, as well as the school I attended and recreational places, like our training facility and a small supply shop." She hedged for a moment. "But I learned quickly, after the first time my mother took me out, that not everyone enjoyed the life I'd been granted. The lower you went, things got tougher, more crowded, everything there built with inferior resources. Two cruise ships are the city's east and west anchors and are considered the commoners' areas. At one time, I think they were adequate—at least nice enough, though small. But they have degraded to a great degree over the years. Then there are the hulls, the empty expanses of the military cargo ships that brought most of the supplies. Individuals unlucky enough to end up living down there were given meager supplies and denied vaccines and medical care. That's where Paris and Hector come from." Her voice held sadness. I couldn't blame her.

"It's not your fault things happened the way they have," I told her. "Your father is a despot, and you were a child with no sway."

She nodded. "The first time I was led out of the sky, out of my protective enclosure, I knew something was terribly wrong. But I was scolded by my mother, made to feel ungrateful for questioning my birthright. I was forbidden from trying to help people until my early teens. That's when I began rebelling and my father began punishing me. When my mother took her own life by jumping into the sea, life changed dramatically for both me and my father. Her death altered something inside me. I just wish I would've found the strength I needed to take him on before we got to this point." She spread her arms to encompass the dead vegetation. "So many lives were needlessly lost. If only I'd—"

"Seen into the future like a magician?" I interrupted. "I understand your sentiment, but blaming yourself for something you had no control over is like banging your head with a titanium rod—it does nothing but damage your skull."

She made a face. "A magician?"

"You know, magic?"

She shook her head.

"Our ancestors apparently loved doing something called magic tricks. I don't really get it either. But magicians performed feats that looked impossible and fooled the audience. They also had something called fortune-telling that used a clear ball to foresee future events. It was all just a show. Nobody has time for magic these days. We're too busy trying to survive."

She replied, "I think I understand. We had someone here who loved performing feats that seemed impossible. But we didn't call him a magician. We called him Hank."

I smiled. "I don't know any Hanks. But what I meant was that you couldn't possibly see into the future. There was no way to predict what your father would or wouldn't do."

"That's where you're wrong," Ari said, coming to a stop. "I knew he was crazy. I saw it in his eyes from a very young age. I paid attention. I recognized that he was slipping further and further into his madness. I could've done something."

"You did," I said. "You acted out, and he punished you."

"Yes, that's true. I started smuggling food and supplies to the people in the hulls. I stole inoculations and vaccines from the sky centers and brought them under. I started a rebellion network to carry on in my absence."

"I'm impressed," I said. "How old were you the first time you got caught?"

"Fourteen," she answered.

"What did he do to you?" I asked.

"He locked me in my room for a week," she said.

"And next?"

Her eyes flicked away. "He beat me and locked me in a cell for two weeks."

"Did that stop you?"

"No." She sighed. "I just learned to manipulate him. We had a reliable cycle. I would break the laws, he would catch me, he would punish me, I would apologize, do my penance, and wait for the next opportunity."

I crossed my arms as I watched Daze scamper back down the tree. "It doesn't sound to me like you could've done much more."

Her eyes narrowed. "Oh, yes, I could have. I could've killed him."

Chapter 25

"I'm not getting on that thing." I was trying to argue, but my words came out more as a sad plea. Maisie and Case stood on either side of where I clung to the rail with both hands, the waves rolling in a steady rhythm beneath us. "Hydro-skis are not the solution we need right now." I tried to make my voice firm. Maisie had made her calculations, and the highest ratio of success included using the death machines.

"You don't have to join us," Case said. "But if we're going to take Bancroft down, we have to get Maisie on that ship. There is no place to land a craft, and even if we could, it would make too much noise. We can't open the door and drop her down either. That only leaves one solution—we take the skis and climb up the ladders, just like they did to get on the engineering ship."

I felt an urge to cross my arms in a huff, but I couldn't because they were occupied saving my sorry life. "I have to go with you. According to Maisie, it'll take all four of us, plus her, for this to work." The plan was for her to get on board the ship and cut the power and for us to follow, each heading to a different part of the ship to tamp down any resistance. Ari insisted that three of us could fit on one ski, but I had my doubts. And they were huge. "There's barely enough room for two people on that thing. I don't see how a third is going to fit."

"You could always use Darby's jet pack," Case said.

"That's funny," I countered. "It's still dark, and we can't even reliably spot the ship. If it falters, that's the end."

"What if Maisie uses the jet pack?" Daze asked. The kid was out here against my better judgment. I'd gotten my way, though, in that he was hooked to Hector by a short tether.

"If we lose Maisie," I said, "the entire mission is over. The risk is too great."

"Darby promised the jet pack is safe," Daze said. "And it's really powerful."

"Let's talk about this inside," I said. We'd come out here so Case and I could get a visual on the skis. The visual confirmed the fact that the skis were a terrible, awful idea for anyone interested in remaining alive.

We found our way back inside without slipping to our deaths. I was going to need another of Walt's antinausea darts sooner rather than later. Once inside, I addressed Maisie. "You need four bodies and yourself to get to the ship. You board first, cut the power, and we each take a different area to contain the people on board. What's the success ratio if we take the craft in instead of the skis?" I needed to hear it again.

"The statistical success of the mission declines by thirty-three-point-seven percentage points if we employ the use of a craft," Maisie replied. "It drops from eighty-seven-point-two percent, to fifty-three-point-five. We lose the element of surprise, which would mean higher loss of life and a reduction in the statistical probability of me shutting down the power before a massive explosion could be triggered. I detected no backup power source, so if I can get in unseen, the chances of completing the mission are much greater."

I ran both hands over my face. "The jet pack is loud," I said, dropping my arms and shaking them out. I was having trouble getting my head around all this. "It doesn't make sense to use it."

"No, it's not," Daze insisted. "Darby made a bunch of improvements. He even showed me. It's quiet."

I gave him a look. "When did he show you?"

"A few days ago," Daze said. "On the roof."

"Do not tell me he strapped you into that thing and you took a ride." Darby was going to be in serious trouble if he'd let the kid do that.

"No." Daze's face took on a sullen expression as he kicked his foot out. "Darby wouldn't let me. But he did it. It was almost soundless. I swear. He only flew a few feet up in the air, but it was amazing."

"I bet it was," I groused. "Why didn't you tell me

about this before? And why does Darby have such a big interest in jet packs?"

The kid shrugged. "He said it's because he hates using the cable swings. But, really, he thought you might need it over the water. He was worried about you."

"I'm worried about me, too," I said. "That's why using those skis is not an option. There has to be another way." I began to pace, trying not to follow the path uphill to lose myself in the trees. I wasn't used to being out of my element. Nearly everything I'd ever done so far had been on or over land. This water stuff was throwing me.

"There is one other solution that has the same statistically probable outcome," Maisie said, interrupting my inner struggle.

"What?" I asked. I took one look at the human emotion on her face and frowned. "I don't really want to know, do I?"

Maisie had actually produced a grimace, sensing I wasn't going to like whatever she would suggest. "I'm detecting sarcasm," she said, "so based on that, I will assume that you do, in fact, want me to relay the information. The plan includes using the emergency deployment in the X craft."

It took me a moment to register what she'd said. "You're not talking about sacrificing Tilly, are you? The only way to use the emergency sequence is to bail out. Once engaged, the craft will eject its passengers. The seats shoot you out like an old-fashioned weapon."

Emergency bailout had been integrated in P class crafts and later. "I'm not sure what you're getting at. If we don't have Tilly, how do we get home?"

"We would take the ship back to the city," Maisie answered.

"Yeah, but only if the plan works," I said. "If it doesn't, we'd be trapped here. Then we all die."

"Statistically, if we enacted the emergency sequence at a specific time, high enough in the sky so there's no detection, the odds of success would be eighty-five-point-four percent. The X class would eject us cleanly, and the seats have gel capsules along with kite landings. We would arrive safely on the deck of the ship and complete the mission."

I gaped at her. "You can't be serious. We can't sacrifice the craft. It's not like we have tons more at home. It's a crazy idea."

"How long would it take to sail one of the ships home?" Case asked.

My head whipped toward him. "You can't really be considering this plan."

Case gave me a look. "We're running out of time. Once it's daybreak and Marty figures out he didn't do the damage he wanted to last night, he turns his weapons this way. We have to get to him before that. That means we use the skis, the jet pack, or the craft. Whatever it takes."

"The skis are safe," Ari said. "I understand your distrust of them, having not grown up around water. But we can get you there alive. I swear it."

Paris rushed through the doorway. "Ari, your father is on the line. He's demanding to speak with you."

We all raced into the communications area. Ari immediately sat at the table, flicking on the speaker. Before she could announce herself, a harsh voice echoed out of the speaker. "I know you're there, girl. I'm coming for you. You're not getting away from me this time!"

She was about to reply when I settled my hand on her shoulder. "Don't answer," I told her. "Not yet. From the tone of his voice, he's frustrated and confused. He doesn't know for sure if you're gone. It's still dark. Answering him would confirm you're still alive. It's better to keep him wondering."

Bancroft's voice cracked again. "You think you can protect those folks, but you can't. You never could. Once I finish with you, I'm going to the dark city, and they're going to receive the same fate." Manic laughter issued out. "Nothing's going to be left standing when I'm done. That will teach them to ignore me for all these years. That city was my right! They kept it from me! Made me stay out on the sea until the continuous rocking bashed my brain around in my skull. I won't stay here a second longer. I deserve my right!"

"He sounds incredibly unstable," I commented. "His voice keeps breaking between statements. Do we have something to throw him off, something that would confuse him and make him second-guess himself? We'd gain an advantage. What if we tell him that the city has already been blown up, or that Tillman has a message for him? Something to stun him, make him rethink what he knows to be the truth."

Case gestured for Ari to stand, and she complied. He depressed the button on the mic, his mouth hovering close to the mesh. "Hey, Marty, remember me? We go back a very long time. When you left, I wasn't more than a couple of years old."

"Who is this?" Marty roared. "Where's my daughter? Put her on. I know she's there!"

"Alaria's not here, but I am." Case was eerily calm. "You should be interested in me, not her. After all, you left me behind all those years ago, but I found ways to survive. So many ways. But I've always wondered why you didn't take me with you." No emotion wavered in his voice. "Maybe it was because my mother fled from you. Knew what you were, knew the kind of harm you would bring to the world. You know, she died from the plague a few years after you took off, which wasn't surprising since you took all the vaccines. Did you ever wonder what happened to me? If I survived? Did they tell you I was alive? Tillman knew. Dixon knew. You remember Dixon. He was part of the Bureau of Truth."

"Who is this?" Marty was still angry, but his intensity was rapidly deflating. I detected fear and something else. Possibly yearning. "This can't be you. Where's my daughter?"

Beside me, Ari stilled, Jake's arm running protectively across her shoulders. I was certain this wasn't the way Case had wanted to inform her that they were siblings, but Case's instinct was correct.

Announcing himself could be the something that could change Marty's direction—the direction of this entire endeavor. If hearing from his long-lost son wouldn't make him rethink things, nothing would. Hopefully, he'd feel less like flipping that pesky nuclear switch.

"You know it's me," Case said. "You recognize my voice. It sounds a lot like your own. I think it's time we meet. How about a quick visit before you blow everyone up?"

"I'm gonna punish that girl," Marty said, his voice tentative. "She's playing a joke on me. You can't be alive. My son died a long time ago. They told me! He's dead!"

My eyebrows rose. It surprised me that Tillman or anyone else had taken the time to tell Marty that Case was dead, especially when they knew he wasn't. They could've used him as a bargaining chip to try to reel in this madman. Like we were doing.

"I survived," Case stated firmly. "Dixon found me. Tillman was angry, but we took care of that. We uncovered your father's computer. He left his story. My grandfather arranged all this so everyone could live, not die. You're not abiding by his wishes."

"No, he did it for me!" Marty shouted. "It was all for me."

"What about for Robert?" Case asked. "Did your brother deserve anything? I guess you think he didn't, because you killed him." Daze's hand snuck into mine. I gripped it. Daze knew the gist of what had happened to his father, but I was certain it was hard to hear Case discussing it so openly. "He was trying to save your mother, and you killed him for it."

"That's not true!" Marty's words quavered, ending on a cry of desperation. "They told me he was sick. That he wouldn't survive. They did what they had to do."

"He had a son," Case said quietly.

Static came across the line.

I wasn't sure Marty was going to come back. Ari hadn't said a word. Finally, Bancroft responded, "Robert had no family." The man finally sounded defeated, which could be good for us. "I would've known."

"He did. The boy is with me," Case said. "He looks just like your brother. Let us come on board. We just want to talk. After that, you can do what you want." Before Marty could form a rebuttal, Case continued, "Do it for your wife. She would've wanted you to see your son one last time. I have a craft. I can be there in twenty."

"I don't think he's going to fall for it," I said. "Maybe try to redirect—"

"Bring the boy," Marty said, surprising us all. "I have a bomb that will bring you to your knees if you try to manipulate me." The anger came zinging back. "I won't hesitate to harm you or the child! Come without weapons! I mean it."

"I'll be there. No guns," Case affirmed, shutting off the power. I took a step back, tugging the kid with me. Jake reluctantly let go of Ari. Case stood and faced his sister. He bowed his head. "I'm sorry I didn't tell you who I was when we first arrived. I found out that Bancroft is my father only a few weeks ago. If I'd known earlier that you were here, I would've come much sooner. I swear I would've—"

Alaria reached out and grabbed Case, gripping him in a hug like her life depended on it, tears streaming down her cheeks. "He told me about you," she said. "You were his one regret. The one thing in his life he wished he had done differently. I'm so glad you're here. You, and you alone, might have a chance to stop him. I heard it in his voice. He thought you were dead. I thought you were dead. Having you here, like this, will work in our favor. He's caught off guard, enough so we can make a move. Thank you."

My throat was full. Beside me, Daze made a little mewling noise. "Just because Bancroft wants you on board that ship, doesn't mean we're letting you go alone," I said.

"We can't risk taking more people than he's expecting. It might set him off," Case said. "I go alone. As much as Ari thinks I have a chance to sway his decisions, I don't feel that confident. My mother fled from him when I wasn't even a year old. He came to visit me once that I can remember, likely to say goodbye. He may feel emotional in this very moment learning that I'm alive, but that will go only so far. We don't know each other. We all heard the madness in his voice. I can't take Daze with me, it's too risky. I'm going to use the kid as a bargaining chip instead. I'll make a deal with Bancroft, telling him I'll let him see

Daze if he gives me the detonator. Once everything is under control, I'll contact you."

"We're going to need to retool that plan," I said to Case. "If Marty doesn't see Daze get off that craft, there might be trouble, especially since he demanded that you bring him. We get one chance. You've given us a powerful distraction, and we're not going to waste it. While you're flying over, we'll be shutting down the power. That way, everybody stays safe."

"And how's that going to happen?" Case crossed his arms, ready to argue.

"We use the damn skis."

Chapter 26

"I must've been out of my fucking mind!" I screamed at the top of my lungs. My arms were clutched tightly around Jake, hard enough to compress his ribs and make it hard for him to breathe. Nobody, other than Jake, could possibly hear me, as my voice was lost among the perilous waves crashing all around us. I could feel Jake chuckle at my distress, his chest vibrating beneath my iron grip. "Stop laughing and just focus on keeping us alive!"

Four meters to our right, Ari was piloting her own ski with Maisie on the back. Both Ari and Jake, combined with Maisie's distance computing, had assured me that the ride would be quick, no longer than eight or nine minutes. It felt like a lifetime had already passed, but we'd been on the stupid skis for only a few moments. The plan was for us to arrive slightly before Case landed on the deck of the ship.

Case would take his time setting down while we slipped on board.

If we lived through the ordeal.

At this rate, it didn't seem likely. Seawater sprayed in my face, a coating of salt had already forming on my skin. The constant rising and falling of the ski as it skimmed the waves was brutal, my body bouncing around like a lifeless bot, even though I'd been instructed to try to follow Jake's movements.

"Almost there!" Jake shouted. We weren't linked by a mic, so shouting had to suffice. I was hooked in with Case, and Jake was linked to Ari.

"Bullshit," I murmured harshly. *Almost* wasn't good enough. I had one thing to be thankful for in this mess—Walt's darts. I'd used the last two in the box before I'd agreed to get on this thing.

It was still dark, but light was filtering through the clouds on the horizon. We had only a few moments at best to keep our cover once we arrived. "Nine minutes is a lifetime!" I yelled to nobody in particular. Despite being so distressed, I appreciated the fact that Jake and Ari were effortlessly guiding these machines over the crests of the waves, bounding down and back up again, like a pair of dancers from the past intertwined in a complicated, beautiful rhythm.

But I couldn't appreciate it for long. There was too much distress in the way.

It was awful being this close to the sea. I was wet, cold, and out of my mind with worry. Not only for myself, but for Case and Daze heading into such a treacherous situation. Worrying about them was the only thing keeping my mind from being completely focused on the threat of being swallowed by the water.

Everyone had assured me that once we arrived at the ship, there would be some sort of ladder, and we could connect the skis to the hull with a magnetic anchoring system. But no one was sure if the ship was moving. It hadn't been when we'd left—Maisie had checked—but it could be now. If the ship was in motion, we'd have to abandon the plan to climb the nice, stable ladder in favor of a more complicated maneuver that involved flying.

Which was why I had a jet pack strapped to my back.

Trying to figure out how I'd fallen so quickly into this mess was not an option. There was no helping it, I was in it, so it served my purposes to try to keep my head relatively clear. Daze had briefly shown me how to operate the pack before we bounded into the sea like thrill-seekers from the past. I had to hope the pack would work like he'd promised it would. I'd used one in my early teens, so I wasn't exactly a novice. Just the next best thing. The jetty I'd used then had been loud and cumbersome. This one felt light, strapped tightly over the inflatable they'd given me.

"There it is," Jake yelled. "Over there." His arm shot out, motioning. "She looks like she's moving. That means you and Maisie are on your own." I couldn't tell if I'd heard relief in his voice or not. I knew he was worried about Ari going up against her father, so it very well could've been relief. I didn't blame him. I just wanted off this thing.

I spotted the ship a second later. White foam spewed around the sides, making it too dangerous to get as close as we'd need to find a ladder. Maisie wore the other jet pack. In a way, I was relieved these kids weren't going into harm's way. They had orders to go back to the habitat and start motoring toward the other farms. If we ultimately failed, at least they'd have a chance to get farther away. Not that that would help if Marty detonated the nuke.

Ari had argued vehemently with that part of the plan, but she'd been overruled.

"I'm going to get you as close as I can," Jake called. "When we see Case overhead, that's the signal." Maisie would go first, then I would follow. Easy as making a bio-printed cupcake.

Or so not.

Ari pulled ahead. I lost sight of them as the low light around the skis faded.

Case's voice dinged in my ear a second later. "Almost there. What's the status?" I was happy the amplifiers were working. That meant he was close.

"The ship is on the move," I told him. "Maisie should arrive on deck in the next minute or two. I'm going to follow with this damn jet pack."

"Have I told you recently that I think you're amazing?" Case said.

"Save it." I snorted. "I'm doing this for the kid."

"Yeah, right. You're doing it for a thousand innocent lives," Case replied. "They will thank you once this is over."

"I hope that's incredibly soon."

"I'm going to take my time landing. Hover a minute or two," he said. "That'll give you more time. Maisie should have no problem disconnecting the power. Let me know when it's done."

"I will." I was accompanying her, because we figured most of the crew would be waiting to meet Case's craft on Marty's orders. There was no way Bancroft was going to face off with his son alone.

"And no more screaming." He chuckled. "My eardrums are blown out."

"That's what you get for putting me on a ski," I grumbled. "Nothing but a flimsy aluminum frame separates me from death. Screaming seems appropriate."

Jake made a sudden turn. I gripped him harder, trying not to gasp. From this angle, I watched Maisie take off into the sky, light shooting out of the bottom of her pack as she rose effortlessly off the ski and was out of sight over the railing a few moments later. She probably had a special program for how to operate a jet pack in her database. We'd agreed she would assess the best place to land, opposite of where they were clearing things for Case to set down. I marked the location in my mind. It was fairly easy, since it was near the end of the ship.

"Showoff," I muttered. "Maisie's on board," I told

Case. "I'm about to follow." With effort, I unclenched one of my arms from around Jake's waist, patting my side for the control pod that would activate the jetty's power. I felt Jake loosen the safety belt securing us.

"Holly," Case said.

"Yeah?"

"Don't die on me."

"I'll try not to. Same goes for you. We're going to take this bastard down."

"I'll see you when I see you."

"Almost there," Jake yelled. "I'm going to spin you as close as I can." He took off toward the treacherous white water spraying up from the ship. Ari passed us coming from the other way, giving us a salute. He turned in a circle. "Now!"

I pegged the throttle on the jet pack and held on to the straps for dear life.

The pack shot me upward, pretty much in a straight line.

It was programmed to react to subtle body movements. It took me a moment to ease my shoulders forward, my other hand busy with the throttle.

Daze had been right—it was quiet. It was intuitively agile as well, reacting to my movements much more smoothly than the one I'd used as a teen. Maybe Darby was on to something, but he wasn't going to hear it from me.

The edge of the railing rapidly approached. I leaned back a bit, which directed me away from the ship enough that I wouldn't brain myself against the cold steel. As I flew over the deck, relief flooded me when I spotted Maisie's shadow. I overshot, soaring over her head before I remembered to punch the controlled-descent button, which immediately lofted me straight up five meters before the thrusters billowed and began to lower me. I landed with a thud, thankfully remembering to compress my legs. I caught myself just before landing on my backside.

After steadying myself, I unhooked while making my way toward Maisie. We had no time to linger. "Where did you put your stuff?" I asked.

She gestured to a small crate filled with supplies. I handed her my pack, then my inflatable. She tucked them away. I drew out my Gem and my taser. "Where to? Is it clear?"

"There are human signatures throughout the ship, but most are congregating at the bow. Marty has engaged workers to move crates out of the way, so Case can land the craft. It will take time. This way."

We rushed toward the middle of the ship, stepping lightly. Halfway down, she ducked to the side. She had a taser out as well. "On your orders, we will use half-tase to bring down anyone we encounter."

I nodded. "We don't kill unless absolutely necessary. All we need to do is keep them down until the power's out."

She ducked into the stairwell. I followed.

We descended two flights before we encountered our first civilian. Maisie incapacitated him before he even realized we were there. He crumpled quickly. She grasped him under the armpits, dragging him out of the way in less than two seconds.

We kept moving.

We entered a short hallway next. "There are only three human signatures on this floor," she whispered. "This is a maintenance level. It might be beneficial to bring down all three, so they do not discover us and alert anyone else. Two of them are equipped with shortwave communication devices."

"Let's do it," I agreed.

Maisie stopped at the next door, pivoted her hips, and gave it a solid kick directly under the handle. It popped open, and she shot two civilians. We left them where they fell. Behind me, there was a shout.

I turned, tasing a solid-looking man squarely in the chest. He let out one protest before he crumpled, the communicator in his hand spinning toward me. I placed my boot out to stop it, bending to pick it up. It resembled a tech phone, but there was only one channel. I placed it in my pocket. "We're almost there," I murmured to Case.

"Landing in two," he said. "They're still clearing a place for me below."

I couldn't hear Tilly's props, but I knew they'd be loud overhead. I doubted anyone standing under them would be able to hear a message coming through on a communicator, but it was better to be safe. "Let's hit the power room now," I told Maisie.

She tugged the man out of the way, confidently moving forward. She holstered her taser, stopping in front of another door. She didn't try to kick this one open. I watched, horror mixed with fascination, as red light shot out of her eyes, efficiently melting the locking mechanism above the handle. It was pretty incredible, I had to admit, but it also looked so very wrong. Maisie resembled a human in most aspects. Humans couldn't shoot lasers out of their eyes. It was as monstrous as it was engrossing.

The door cracked open a second later. We entered quickly. I shut the door, pressing my back against it to keep it closed. The room was dark. I fumbled for a light switch along one wall. Maisie was already in front of the complicated wall grid. She didn't need light to see, which was another thing humans couldn't do.

"Some of these wires have been rerouted to other quadrants," she said. "Without doing a full scan, I'm uncertain which wire feeds the unit we're looking for. It will take time for me to track each individual cable."

I shook my head. "We don't have that kind of time. Case is landing soon. Shut it all down."

She gave me a curious look. "If I cut all power on the ship, they will be alerted to our presence. They will send someone here to fix it."

"It doesn't matter. All we care about in this moment is preventing Bancroft from killing a thousand people. Shut it down."

With lightning speed, her hands meticulously began unhooking connections faster than I could track. We'd decided not to risk damaging the panel by using a weapon. If everything went the way we intended, we would commandeer this ship, and we'd need the power to make it home. She continued to work. The room went abruptly dark. I tapped on a shoulder light and watched her finish the remaining panel. There were eight in all.

Once it was done, she turned to me. I told Case, "Power's down. All of it."

"Landing now. Thirty seconds from contact," he said. "Daze says hi."

"Tell him hi back." My heart skipped as I grabbed Maisie's arm. "We have to back them up. Let's go."

On the way back up to the main deck, we encountered no one, so that was a plus. I had my Gem and taser out. "Find someplace we can hide," I told Maisie. "We're approaching the area," I told Case. "I heard you shut down the props. I can hear voices, but don't have a visual yet. Well, I don't. Maisie can see just fine. Sounds like a large group has gathered. I'm clicking off the mic so we don't get any feedback. Good luck."

"On my way out," Case told me. "Opening the door now,"

Maisie led us through an area thick with supplies. We were a few rows back from the main walkway. "We have to get eyes on Marty," I whispered. "If he looks like he's going to fire on Case or Daze, we have to take him out." A group of people passed us a few meters away, all talking fast, not bothering to look at where we were hiding among the stacked crates. There was a definite energy in the air, but nobody seemed to be disturbed about the power outage.

Maisie said nothing as we wound closer. She stopped, crouching low. I peeked between two stacks and spotted Case and Daze from behind. The kid was holding on to Case's hand, his shoulders stiff. They moved forward together. Through the space between their bodies, I caught a glimpse of a man facing me. He held a large weapon in one hand and a tiny box in the other.

He looked exactly like Case.

Chapter 27

"Stop right there!" Marty commanded them. Case and Daze obeyed. Bodies began to fill in around them, and soon I had only a glimpse of the top of Case's head. But I had a clear view of Marty. I raised my Gem.

"Damn, I can't get a good shot," I muttered. Too many heads were blocking my sightline. If I fired my weapon, there would definitely be other casualties, possibly even Case himself. I couldn't risk it. "Do you have one?" I asked Maisie.

"I don't have a clean target," she intoned. "The number of humans in a compact space exceeds my allowable risk parameters."

"We have to fix that," I said. "We need a new location."

"There is no more cover," she replied. "We are as close as we can get without exposing ourselves."

I swore under my breath as Marty began to speak. "If you try to harm me in any way, all I have to do is press this button." He held up the box. "And then we all die. Each and every one of us."

"Why isn't anyone telling him the power's out?" I whispered to Maisie. Then I realized that Case had left Tilly's running lights on. The entire deck of the bow was lit up. Maybe they hadn't noticed.

"That would require me to read human minds, which is impossible," Maisie said. "But I do detect elevated heart rates, increased blood pressures, the scent of fear coupled with excitement. By extrapolation, I assume that these people are hoping for a resolution that's not in favor of their leader. But that is just a hypothesis based on emotion and not absolute facts."

"Sarcasm plus a human guess," I said. "I like it. I'm impressed. But it's not enough. We can't just hope these people are against Marty. I wouldn't bet Case's and Daze's lives on it. We need a better position."

Case's voice rose in the air. "What exactly am I going to do? I haven't seen you in over thirty years. This is supposed to be a reunion, not a massacre."

I angled my head while standing on my toes. Marty looked skeptical at this distance, but I couldn't be sure.

"It's not a coincidence you came for me now, after all these years," Marty argued, his attention seemingly scattered as his gaze bounced around. "The Bureau of Truth sent out an SOS. Then they stopped communicating altogether. I know what's going on. They're after me. They want what I have. They want New Eden, my resources. But they're not going to get any of it!"

"Who are you referring to?" Case asked calmly.

Marty seemed baffled at first, then regained his composure. "The government. The other government! They've been after me for years. They want what I have. They won't get it. I'll blow everything up first."

"Nobody needs what you have," Case said. "We've recovered the resources Tillman was hoarding. Did you know how much they kept for themselves? Did they tell you that before you left? Or did you think you'd taken it all?"

"What...what are you talking about?" Marty sputtered. "I have it all. It's *mine*. It was rightfully mine. I was supposed to come back before this. They lied to me. They kept me out here. They want to steal my things." Marty's head kept bopping around like a short-circuiting droid. The man wasn't well, clearly delusional. There was no dealing with someone who was out of their mind.

I leaned over to Maisie. "Scan Marty. Give me his vitals. What's wrong with him?"

"His brain synapses are overfiring," Maisie said after a moment. "His pulse is dangerously high. I detect a large mass protruding into his front temporal lobe. According to my data, a mass in that location can affect logic, speech, and reasoning."

"He's sick," I murmured. "I wonder why he didn't use a medi-pod. Surely they have stuff on board that could fix him. They even have a gene-splicer thingy."

"Again, answering that would require me to read minds—"

"No need to answer a rhetorical question," I snapped. "That's an order until the end of time. There's no way Case can reason with him. Marty's brain won't allow it. We're going to have to take him out. Or let Case know somehow." I contemplated turning my mic back on, but we were close enough to generate feedback. The whistling would be detected.

What to do?

Daze spoke. "Are you my uncle? Was Robert your brother?" The kid was trying to pull Marty's attention in a different direction. Daze could probably tell there was something physically wrong with his uncle. "I'm happy to meet you. I wish I could've met my dad. He was a scientist. Everybody said he was really smart."

My heart broke in a whole new way.

This had to be tough on the urchin. Daze was one of the strongest people I knew. I watched Marty's face change rapidly, his expression morphing from anger, to fear, to shock, and finally to something that resembled compassion in less than a single second. Compassion was good. Bancroft's illness had affected all the people I cared about in grave ways. It was hard to know how to feel about that. Then I remembered that Case's mother had fled from him over thirty years ago. There was no way he'd had this illness that long. It would've killed him by now. He'd always been a despot. Now he was just a sick one.

"Robert...Robert was my brother," Marty stammered. "I didn't kill him. They had to do what was right. He was dying. He couldn't save my mother. He tried...he couldn't do it."

"It's okay," the kid said. "My dad lived. He moved down South. His work was important to him. I'm sad he had to leave me behind, but I'm glad he got to live for a while. He only died recently. He had a disease that they couldn't cure. But maybe they can cure you." Right on the nose. The kid had something that couldn't be taught—intuition coupled with pure intellect.

Marty's face transformed into wretched anger, spittle arcing out in front of him as he snarled, "They'll never get me into that pod! I know what they do to you once you're inside. They reprogram you! They suck the life from you. You're nothing but an empty shell when you emerge. They won't get me in there. I don't care what they say. I'm not sick!"

"Data suggests that the form of abnormality in his brain can also cause paranoia," Maisie announced, iterating what was abundantly clear. "Jake and Ari have just boarded the ship. Their estimated time of arrival here is less than one minute."

I gasped. "What do you mean they're here? The ship's moving. It's impossible to get through churning white water."

"When I cut the power," Maisie answered, "the engines shut down and the ship slowed to a stop. They turned back."

"*Damn*," I muttered. "If Marty sees her, he may snap." He was on the verge of snapping without seeing her. Who knew what he would do if he did? "He feels she betrayed him. We have to stop her." I began picking my way back the way we'd come to try to cut them off.

I could still hear Daze as I backtracked. "The medipods you have here are super cool. They won't hurt you. I wish my dad could've gone in one. I bet he would've. He would've taken the chance. He would've wanted to get better. If you want, I can stand guard while you use one. I'd make sure no one tries to hurt you." The kid had a heart of gold.

I scooted behind another crate, craning my neck to get a view just in time to see Marty swing his weapon wildly, aiming it straight at Daze. Air left my body as I watched Case lift his arm.

"We have to get out there," I said urgently. "Marty has a gun on Daze."

"Ari and Jake are almost here," Maisie said. "Follow me." Maisie darted down a narrow path. Not even three seconds later, Ari and Jake came hustling around the corner.

They looked surprised to see us. "What are you doing here?" I whispered. "If your father sees you, he's going to break."

"I couldn't let you handle this alone," Ari replied. "These are my people. I belong here. I'll stay out of sight, but as soon as you have my father down, they're going to need me."

"Did you know he's sick?" I asked. "Maisie says he has a mass in his brain."

Ari shook her head. "There've been rumors for years that he was unwell, but I attributed that to increasing mental dysfunction—he's always been off. There was no talk of a physical ailment."

"I'm sure he had a mental dysfunction his entire life," I said. "But this mass has exacerbated it. Maisie said it affects logic and makes him paranoid. I'm not excusing his past behavior, by any means. I'm just explaining what we see now. Or why he may have been more off-balance recently." I turned. "We have to get back there. The kid is trying to reason with him, and he pulled his weapon. Maisie needs a clear shot."

A voice erupted behind us. "Hey, who are—"

Maisie tased him before he could complete his sentence, pulling him effortlessly behind a crate. "I was remiss in not registering another bio signature," she said. "I was scanning for a way to get us closer without being detected. It is not possible for me to do both at once."

"Don't worry about it," I said. "You're at capacity with this mission. We'll look out for anyone else. Just get us there."

She took off, and we followed.

A blast erupted from the direction of the bow.

A weapon had discharged, but it wasn't Case's Pulse. A cry escaped. *Please, please don't be the kid.* I ran, my Gem out. Maisie was ahead of me, Ari and Jake just behind.

I spotted Case. He was in motion. Then he was down. There were shouts throughout the crowd. I couldn't see what was happening. With incredible relief, I spotted Daze. His head bobbed next to Case's. As I rushed forward, I spotted Marty on his back. Case had the detonator in one hand, his other on his father's chest. Blood spilled out like a river of death beneath it.

A moment later, Ari's voice rose, firm and stable. "This is Alaria Bancroft. These people are here to help from the dark city. My father has been shot. If you attempt to retaliate, this LiveBot will respond with force. I repeat, do not attempt to retaliate. Help has finally arrived." The murmurs reached a fever pitch.

I finally reached them, crouching next to Case. "I'm sorry it had to be this way," Case told Marty. "But I couldn't let you harm Robert's child. Or anyone else." The small weapon he'd concealed under his sleeve was on the ground. His sister's mini Blaster. Small enough to fit almost anywhere unseen.

Marty was trying to speak, his face crumpled in pain. "You…you're here. You…came here."

Case nodded. "I did."

"I didn't think I'd ever get to see you again." Marty coughed, blood trickling from the corners of his lips.

Ari moved in, settling to her knees on the other side of her father. Her face was resolute. Jake joined her, his arm protectively around her waist. "You can't be saved," she told her father. "The fragments inside the Blaster were combined with a death serum." She'd used one of Walt's darts. Then she'd given the weapon to her brother. I couldn't blame her, but I was surprised she'd managed to perform something like that without us noticing. "I had to make sure this came to a final end. I did it for the people—*our* people." Her voice broke. "Enough lives have been lost, enough torture doled out, enough fear instilled. It ends now. For the good of the people. They will survive. I will make certain of it."

Anger etched Marty's features. "You could've been a good leader," he snarled. "You're like me. But your mother was weak. She ruined you. Made you soft."

"No," Ari replied with absolute certainty. "She *saved* me. It was her inability to fight back, struck down again and again by your hand, that made me who I am today—a compassionate leader who cares about innocent lives."

Marty's eyes darted to Case, then to Daze. The kid had tears streaming down his face. Death was hard, even though this man had killed many and threatened our lives and the dark city. Marty addressed the kid. "Your father...he was better than me. He should've lived. I welcome death. My only regret in this world was not"—his gaze landed on Case—"bringing you with me. If you had been here, things would've gone differently. You could've saved me from myself."

That would've been a tall order.

"Maybe," Case said. "But now we'll never know."

"No," Marty said softly. "We never will." He took his last breath as the blood continued to leak from his wounds. Walt had been right. His death because of the serum had taken less than three minutes.

Ari wept softly as Jake comforted her. For her, it was likely equal parts sadness and relief. She'd been in the direct path of Marty's rage for most of her life. It was a blessing it was over.

Case wrapped his arm around Daze's shoulders, drawing him close. "There was no other way for him to go," Case told the kid. "Marty knew it. He pulled his weapon on you, knowing I would stop him. It was his choice, his way to go. This is what he wanted."

People had gathered behind us. Everybody was waiting to see what would happen next. No one looked even a little inclined to react in a negative way.

Ari finally stood, stepping forward, ready to address them and calm their nerves, soothe their anxieties.

Before she could do that, Maisie announced, "A ship has entered the area. It's moving at twelve knots an hour. It will rendezvous with us in sixteen minutes."

"That must be the engineering ship," Jake said with a grin. "That means Justin is at the helm. They're coming to help us."

Yet another relief. "Will the efforts of these two ships be enough to transport everyone back to New Eden?" I asked.

Ari and Jake shared a look. "Yes," Ari said. "But we'll have to tow the farms with cables attached to the stern."

"We'll accompany you," I told her. "We're not leaving until this is finished. We'll radio in more help as well. Is there a place to land multiple crafts in New Eden?"

"I think so," Ari said. "There are areas with abundant space throughout. Jake and I will go first. The people must hear the news from me that my father's gone, as well as an assertion that you only mean to help. We'll summon you once we've told them. If you want to contact your people, there's a communications room with a strong signal on this ship."

"Good. We'll do that," I said. "Right after Maisie reconnects the power."

Ari turned to face the anxious people, her expression set. "As I've just told you," she started, "help has finally arrived. I'm going to need each and every one of you to play a role in our new mission, which is to rescue the people of New Eden, your friends and family, then ultimately sail to the dark city, where each of us can begin a new life. They are waiting for us. The city has food and water, enough for everyone. Are you with us?"

A chorus of *yays* rent the air.

Case pulled me close, whispering in my ear, "I still can't believe you got on the back of a hydro-ski." He grinned a single second before his lips landed on my neck. "The things you do for us."

"I did it for the kid," I murmured, shivering at his touch.

"Keep telling yourself that."

Epilogue

"I can't believe they're choosing to stay out there," I complained, my hand shielding my eyes from the drizzle. "There are plenty of permanent residences on firm ground right here in the city." We stood on the roof of a building near the edge of the canals. Three farms bobbed in the distance, atlases ringed around the outside. "I guess it's safe enough. I mean, no one from the city is going to venture out there."

"The water has always been their home," Claire replied easily. "It makes sense they would choose to stay with what they know."

"You wouldn't catch me out there," Bender grumbled. "Seems stupid when firm land is right here."

Inside the harbor, where the waves rolled steadily but with nothing like the force of the open ocean, four ships were anchored along with the three full habitats. Darby and Walt had just landed a craft on one of the farms. A dozen or so engineers were already out there, helping to make needed repairs. The farmers had insisted on staying in their homes, as had Ari and Jake. Repairs had also started on the two cruise ships. It'd taken us four days to separate those ships from New Eden, using people power along with several localized explosions. It'd been messy, with large chunks of the internal structure of the city lost to the sea. But it had worked.

Bender, Lockland, Knox, Julian, and Darby had flown out to help us with the dismantling of New Eden. Only once the ships had been freed, new UV lights installed, and the entire Flotilla was heading back the way it had originally come, had we all flown back. The ships, towing the farms, had arrived last week after a two-week journey.

"How they constructed New Eden was amazing," Lockland said wistfully. "I was sorry to see it go. The concept was brilliant. All those passageways and connection points. It was efficient. They had commerce as well." He was right that they'd utilized coin. Everything had had a value and a cost. "And schools and training facilities. They can teach us a lot. It's too bad Marty let the bottom tiers go to hell. It was wretched down there."

The people in the hulls had lived in squalor, most of them sick from living without UV and with very little food. We had insisted that those people float back on the medi-ship, taking turns being healed in the medi-pods. Their care, now that they were back, was being overseen by Nareen, who had trained as a doctor in her youth. The upgraded health care the city would receive from that ship was going to be life-altering. People would again be inoculated against various diseases. The equipment could grow organs if needed. Nareen was implementing a new program to train doctors. It was all happening so fast, and everyone was thankful.

"Yeah, the bottom dwellers were in bad shape," Bender said. "The hulls. He might've just as well called them what they were—death chambers."

"The people in the actual prisons got out before we arrived," I said. "Hector and Paris had given them laser keys. Many of them would've died before we got there if they hadn't."

"The only people to give us any problems were the people up top," Case said. "Figures."

We'd been forced to engage with at least forty people who considered themselves "the elite." Fearful of losing their luxuries, they'd fought back. But they hadn't been hard to overcome. Along with everyone else, they'd been without food for long enough to make them weak.

"Darby and Walt landed safely," Claire said. "Let's head inside. This is one of the buildings we're rehabilitating with the new resources from the engineering ship. It's going to be a landing point for them as they travel back and forth from water to land. Eventually, the medi-ship will be docked here, so people in the city can utilize it, too. We'll be moving all the stuff we've commandeered from down South, along with what we have here, and installing it on the ship. We will christen it the new floating Medi Center."

We followed Claire inside. Work on the city had begun in earnest. Unsurprisingly, the best workers were the retail bots. Claire had them toiling day and night to get things done.

Daze and Knox were waiting on the ground floor, along with a couple of Claire's aides. Daze and Knox were flying over to the farms next, once they got the okay from Darby. Daze cradled a bunch of packets in his arms.

"Walt trusted me with the seeds," the kid announced proudly. "Once all the lights are fixed, they're going to plant them! We're going to have lots of green food again. He said I'll get to taste a real strawberry! Walt said they're sweet, like a cupcake, but juicy."

I chuckled, ruffling his hair. "I can't wait to take a bite."

The farmers had an abundance of seeds as well. They'd kept good care of their harvests. All the trees could be planted again. I couldn't wait to see them in full bloom. Just thinking about it made me happy.

"The new bio-printers from the South are almost ready for big-scale production," Claire said. "I'm heading to check on them now. We'll see you guys back at the office tomorrow morning." She gave me a quick hug. "I have something to show you when you get there. Interesting documents have surfaced. Have you heard of a woman named Mina Kane?"

My head cocked as I walked with her back to her craft. "The surname sounds familiar, but not the first name." Kane was definitely familiar to me. No one really went by a surname around here, but our ancestors had used them.

"We've uncovered a lot of information about her in the Bureau of Truth's sealed files. Darby broke the code while you were gone. Apparently, she was one of the key individuals who figured out Plush was turning pleasure seekers into Seekers. She was about to blow the top off of Bliss Corp when the meteor struck. She was part of a secret government protection agency, some program only a handful knew about. We've decided, in honor of her achievements, to name the new seeker rehabilitation facility after her. There's even a rumor going around that she might still be alive."

"Was she a spy?" I asked, my curiosity piqued. Since our ancestors' government had been basically run by oligarchies and multitrillion-dollar companies with plenty of money to throw around, spy networks had been vast. Some had been good, some bad.

It was all muddled and very intriguing.

"I'm not sure if we'll ever know for sure," Claire said. "From what I'm gathering, it's very complex. This particular group infiltrated businesses as workers to gain information. They were considered the good guys of the people." Claire headed across the road, followed by a young man and a woman, each carrying etch boards, to where her craft was parked. This area had been specifically cleared of all debris for landings.

We were going to see more of that, which was weird. Our city might even become clean at some point. "It's my understanding," Claire went on, "that she put a few years in at the Pleasure Emporium right here in the canals. You can read the documents yourself tomorrow. It's interesting stuff. Think about the name Kane. See if you can remember anything." She gave me a wink and a salute as she got in, taking off to finish her business, which, it seemed, was never ending.

Case came up behind me, grabbing my hand, leading me toward the end of the street, which butted into the harbor. "What was that about?" he asked.

I shook my head, feeling a little overwhelmed. "Claire uncovered a bunch of documents. She wants me to take a look at them tomorrow. Seems like she thinks I should recognize the name Kane. Right now, I have no recollection. Maybe I said something to her as a child?" I shrugged. "I guess I'll know more later when I look over the files. Maybe it will trigger something."

We came to a stop next to Lockland and Bender, who were waiting with Daze and Knox. "They're coming across on skis now." Lockland gestured toward the water.

Sure enough, I spotted Ari and Jake piloting, Paris and Hector behind them.

Excited to see his aunt, Daze began to bounce, one of the seed packets he held shaking loose. Case snatched it before it hit the wet ground. I knew Walt had given Daze extras, but we couldn't risk losing even a single one.

The kid looked embarrassed as Case handed him the packet. "Sorry," he squeaked. "I'll be more careful. I promise!"

"Don't worry about it," I told him. "Walt sprayed those packets with sealer so they wouldn't get wet."

Ari and Jake efficiently directed their skis to shore, hooking their anchor cables to the two platforms that had been modified for this very purpose. Paris and Hector got off first, helping to facilitate the securing of the death machines. Once everything was settled, the four of them made their way up a short incline to greet us, albeit a little wobbly. It always took them a little time to shake out their sea legs.

Hector's eyes went wide as he scanned the tops of the buildings next to us. "Man, I'll never get tired of seeing this. Paris wants to stay on the atlas, but I think we might get a place here, too. So much to explore."

Paris grinned. "After years of living in a cramped space below the sea, nothing really beats the openness of this city. I might actually be talked into living here…eventually."

"After you see my residence, you'll definitely want one of your own." I chuckled.

Once Ari had a firm footing on land, Daze went in for a hug. She obliged, giving him a kiss on either cheek, careful not to upset his seed packages.

The kid blushed to the roots of his hair. "I'm going to the farm to help Walt plant stuff," Daze said. "Knox is taking me. I won't be here for the tour, but Holly will show you everything. This is her city. She knows it the best." The urchin was right. It was my city, and it seemed I was finally ready to share it.

The plan was for Case and me to take the four of them around and show them every nook and cranny of importance, including our residence, Bender's shop, the government buildings, the places to get food and clothing, the Emporium, and finally the barracks. It was going to be a full day.

Knox held his hand out to Jake. "It's nice to see you again," Knox told him. "Holly said you're interested in joining the new security task force." Knox gave a nod in Lockland's direction. "We're definitely looking for well-trained men and women. It seems you fit that criteria. Welcome to the group."

Lockland and Jake had forged a bond while on New Eden. It seemed Jake had been more than well trained. Jake's father had also passed on vital tactical measures as the head of security. We could learn from Jake.

"The security group is coming along nicely," Lockland agreed. "We're still trying to get Holly on board, but she's insisting that scavenging is the only way to survive in this place."

"Damn right," I said. "We still need supplies, and honestly, having a few of us on the *outside* of the government will provide much-needed perspective. Wouldn't you agree, Lockland?"

Bender grunted his approval, crossing his arms.

Lockland grinned. "If you say so. But I think taking Ari along with you is going too far. She's as well trained as Jake is—an asset to the group. She also has direct influence with the militiamen from New Eden we're training." He turned to Ari. "I hope you'll consider at least stopping by once in a while to give us some needed instruction."

"I will." Ari smiled. "But scavenging, at least for now, sounds fun. I'd never done it before yesterday, but Holly swears I'm a natural."

I shrugged. "You found a pixie motor on your first try. That's saying something. I haven't found one in years."

"I'm heading back to the shop," Bender announced. "I'll see you there in a couple hours. I'm calling a meeting in The Middle. We're going to start changing the way we do things, whether they like it or not. Claire is trying to open up residences, and things have gotten physical. They need the space, and we have it."

My eyebrows rose. "Good luck with that. Your neighbors aren't exactly *flexible*." A huge understatement. "You want some backup? We can change our plans around and be there in thirty."

Bender shot me a look, half exasperation, half amusement. He shook his head as he headed toward his craft. "The day I need backup in my own neighborhood is the day I fucking die. I'll handle it. See you in a few." He shot Hector a glance. "I'll expect you tomorrow morning. Early. If you're going to be working in my shop, you better show up with your expertise front and center. I don't teach. I do."

Hector grinned. If Lockland and Jake had struck up

an unlikely friendship, so had Hector and Bender. The boy was beyond talented when it came to fixing stuff. He was a natural. Bender had never offered to work with anyone. So it was kind of like Earth had stopped rotating on its axis. "I'll be there, old man. You don't got to show me nothing. I bring the knowledge *you* need," Hector challenged good-naturedly.

Bender grunted, but I spotted the ghost of a smile as he closed his door and took off. Or maybe that was a stain from aminos. Hard to know.

Knox rested a hand on Daze's shoulder. "We should get going. Staying most of the day. I'm bringing Walt and Darby back with us."

I nodded. "We'll meet back at the Emporium at dusk. Daze wants to join us at the barracks. The seven of us will likely stay there for the night."

"Celia is expecting you," Ari told Knox. "We have landing pads linked in a row on Habitat One. People will be there ready to secure the craft once you land. New handrails have been installed." She shot me a look along with a smirk. "You'll also receive a flotation device. Keep it on at all times."

"Hey, blame me for installing better safety," I groused. "Those things you live on are accidents waiting to kill. I can't believe you're choosing to stay out there when land is finally within your reach."

"Once we manage to get you inside an atlas, you'll see why," Ari said. "There's serenity there. No rain. No sound. Just pure contentment."

"I'm pretty solid staying right here," I said. "But I'm

betting once we get you into a sleeping pod, you'll change your mind."

"See you later." Knox gave us a nod.

Daze looked as though he might want to give everybody a parting hug, but his arms were full. Instead, he stuck his chin out in his way, managing to gather three fingers at his forehead to give us a salute. It was adorable. "I'll see you when I see you," he said, his smile showing teeth.

Case replied, "Not if we see you first."

We watched Knox and the kid get in the craft and take off. Then we began to walk toward our rides. I headed for Tilly, and Case headed for Seven. I shook my head. "Not again. We can't have this argument every time." Exasperation seeped out, so did a half giggle.

Instead of putting up a fight, Case settled a hand on Jake's shoulder. "Take care of her. She's yours now." He made a sweeping gesture to encompass Seven as Jake's mouth fell open, along with my own. Case had been giving Jake flying lessons since they'd arrived last week.

"Are you serious?" Jake asked. "I can have this?"

"Of course," Case replied, walking backward toward me and Tilly. "How else are you and my sister going to get around the city?" He reached into his pocket and tossed Ari a tech phone. She snatched it out of the air with zero effort. "We're on channel seven. Use our real names. Try to keep up. Holly is a less-talented pilot than I am, so don't blame me if you get lost."

I snorted. "The actual term is *better* pilot. It's a good thing Maisie's not here," I muttered as I popped Tilly's door, "or I'd have her repeat it for everyone."

Maisie was coordinating efforts on the cruise ships and helping to keep the people under control. They were completely in awe of her, and we'd found fairly quickly that nobody could quell the masses like she could. Surprisingly, Mary had elected to join her, handing some of her seeker-rehabilitation responsibilities to Ned.

Mary and Maisie made a good team.

"Hundredths of degrees don't count," Case argued as he got into the passenger seat as I fired the craft up. Before I could tell him how wrong he was, his lips were on mine. The kiss was searing, his hand sliding behind my neck, bringing our foreheads close together. "Did you plant that pixie motor for my sister to find?"

I kissed him again, enjoying his taste. "I may have. Do you have a problem with that? She has a gift. I can see it in her eyes. You know, eyes tell a lot about a person. They give us a glimpse into the soul. Or something like that. Cozzi used to spout stuff like that all the time. All I know is your sister is smart, and she's got a keen eye. She'll do well for herself here. But you don't have to worry. She won't be scavenging for long."

"Why not?" Case asked, letting go reluctantly and settling back in his seat as I lofted us into the air.

"My guess is Claire will take her under her wing sooner rather than later," I told him. "Groom her for a future in politics. Ari's a leader, not a follower."

"That she is," he agreed. "She has a lot to learn, but she'll do it quickly."

"Yes, she will," I said. I checked to make sure that Jake was following us.

Case noticed my brows were knit. "What's up?"

"Something is scratching at the back of my brain about the name Kane, but I can't pinpoint the memory," I said as I cleared the building next to us, heading west. First stop was my residence. If that couldn't persuade Ari and her friends to leave their atlases, I didn't know what would. It felt weird exposing myself after so many years of staying hidden, but we were entering a whole new era. One with fewer secrets and more resources, better health, sustained longevity, and hope right there for the taking. Based on what we'd discovered in New Eden, there was solid evidence that we could begin to function as a real commerce again. Resources could be produced, coin reinstated. It was a wonderful thing, and in response to all this, Claire had decided to christen this time in our world as the ReGenEra. *Regenerating our losses, to rebuild New Atlantic.* That was the slogan for this new era, and New Atlantic was our city's newly christened name.

"I'm pretty sure my mother told me a story about a woman with the name Kane who's related to us. It's right there, making a face at me."

"Do you think it's the same Kane Claire is talking about?" Case asked, his hand comfortably settled on my thigh. His warmth permeated me, making me happy. "Surnames were common back then. It could be a coincidence."

My gaze met his. Eyes really did tell the whole story. His were full of love, commitment, and something I couldn't name at first. Fierce loyalty coupled with a kind of permanency I'd never felt before. He was my partner in all things. I could count on this man, whatever happened. He was my family and I loved him. "It could be a coincidence, but somehow I think not. If the memory is there, I'll retrieve it at some point. Claire said this woman might be alive. If that's true, we'll have to track her down and make sure." I banked Tilly, easing back on the throttle, coming in for a landing on my roof—*our* roof. "Finding her suddenly feels very important."

"If you share a surname, then she could be your—"

"Grandmother," I finished.

His hand tightened on my thigh. "We'll do our best to locate her."

"I know. But right now, we have more important things to do, like showing your sister and her partner and their friends what it means to be residents of New Atlantic." Saying that felt strange. I set Tilly down. "Can we talk for a second about you giving Seven away? You didn't have to do that. Lockland has access to crafts that were left behind down South. We could've given Jake one of those. You love that craft."

Case shook his head, reaching for me. His lips brushed mine. "No way. I've finally succumbed to the mercy of the superior pilot. No more craft wars. Wherever you go, I go."

"Are you sure about that?"

"Absolutely."

Sneak Peek of

AN

AGENT KANE

NOVEL

THE NEXT INSTALLMENT IN THE
DANGER WORLD
HITS RETAILERS FALL 2019.

AMANDA CARLSON

Chapter 1

"Hello, and welcome to The Spire, the tallest, most integrated megascraper in the city." The woman cradled a clear, voice-activated superboard, no bigger than an antiquated piece of paper, in the crook of her arm. "My name is Suzanne. And you must be"—she squinted down at her device as if her luminous eyes had suddenly decided to play tricks on her—"Wilhelmina KandyKane?" A small snort escaped her otherwise unruffled façade. Her hair was an elegant twist of platinum, silver streaked to give it a subtle sparkle under the ultra lights that were spaced evenly across a lobby large enough to house an entire sport arena. Her irises were refracted a mystic purple, too dark for mauve, too light to be amethyst. Her cheeks shapers were almost undetectable, save for the fact that the upper portion of her face stayed firmly in place each time she smiled. "Wasn't that the name of the children's screencast back in the day? Wilhelmina Hover & The Candy Cane Adventurers? It was a quest

313

program, wasn't it? They hid items in hologram episodes and kids had to find them. It was before my time, but I know it was popular."

Extremely popular.

Mina already had her identity chip out, passing it to the woman between two fingers, nails glossed, not dyed. Mina wasn't an anti-enhancer, but she wasn't full tilt either. Expectations for modified appearances were fueled by public opinion. Mina sat firmly in the middling range of acceptability for her income bracket, but wasn't remotely close to diamond status like this rep. "Yes, it was the number one screencast twenty-two years ago." She should know. "I was unnamed my first three years to avoid accumulating interest. When the time was up, my parents allowed me to choose." Wilhelmina Hoover had been a heroine to an inquisitive young girl like Mina. A woman who could solve any riddle, defeat any obstacle, secure every prize without ever breaking a sweat. She was just the kind of person Mina's childlike self wanted to emulate. So why not become her? At age three it made perfect sense. Now, not so much. "I go by Mina Kane. The identity chip reflects that. Please change it in your system."

"Will do," Suzanne replied, her plum-colored lips curving as she tapped the two centimeter square against the edge of her board before handing it back. Mina slid it back into her wrist cuff. "I've come across a few like you before, but none with such an unusual moniker. You were certainly lucky to avoid accruing that interest. I'm sure if I'd had the chance, I'd be named something like TinFoot Tooty." She tinkled with laughter, her perfectly aligned, micro-enameled teeth flashing.

Assigning debt to a fetus in utero was commonplace in their world.

Having a child was expensive. Cost accrued immediately. But if the baby didn't have a name, it couldn't be assigned a debt number. A loophole that'd been immediately expunged by the high banks almost as soon as it was discovered. The window of opportunity for self-naming closed quickly, but that hadn't stopped thousands of parents from leaving birthing centers all over the country with nameless children the month of May, 2076.

Most of those children, however, had parents with enough sense to guide their three-year-old into making a sensible decision. Instead, Mina's parents had thought her choice brilliant and inspired. She was their perfect little Wilhelmina KandyKane, the spelling altered to avoid any intellectual property infringement. Mina loved her parents, but would never understand their indulgence. Now she was stuck forever explaining her toddler-inspired choice to anyone who had access to her identity.

When Mina didn't join Suzanne's chiming, teeth flashing giggles, the mega-rep gathered her composure, resetting herself back into professional mode with a capital P. "It says here you're"—her precisely drawn brows, no more than three millimeters wide at any given point, furrowed—"a tri-linguist?"

She glanced up at Mina for confirmation. "That sounds…interesting." The entire world had taken English as its first commerce language more than sixty years ago, but second languages had been deemed culturally important, but remained mostly overlooked.

"It is," Mina replied comfortably. "I specialize in second languages, teaching holo courses for those in the process of completing their advanced degree cycle." Mina did no such thing, but it was her standard assigned back story. Mina had been exposed to second languages all her life, due to her parents' lifelong mission to retain diversity in the world. Fluent enough to teach? Not exactly. In any event, Mina was well-versed if Suzanne decided to quiz her on her specialty. But she assumed the rep would choose to espouse the megascraper's many selling points, rather than probe her on the finer points of linguistics. "Does this structure come equipped with virtual offices, hologram integrated?" Mina asked helping her along.

"Oh yes." Suzanne flourished a hand, her nails contoured to perfect ovals, decorated in a purple hyperglo that blinked intermittently as she swished. The color was an exact match to her eyes, as well as her restrictive business shirt and top, made of something shiny and obviously expensive. "The Holo Centers occupy the four corners of the structure. We have no less than eight hundred and forty cubicles, all individually programmable, holo 4-D compatible. The cubes come with integrated wave-melds, so you can link to outside holocams without a cable. Some of the bigger offices can accommodate twenty hologuests at a time." She took a breathy pause, then leaned in. "Honestly, you can't get any better without going private. You can book a cube day to day or reserve regularly. The fee is fifty world standard currency for a two hour window and can be easily attached to your monthly borrow. It only takes a DNA swipe to unlock."

"Good to know," Mina said. Virtually *anything* could be attached to your borrow—a soft term banks had established in place of the word debt a few years after mass outcry. The average person carried nearly five million dollars across their lifetime, never hoping to clear it. Instead of outlawing the corrupt system, the banks had opted instead to change the term, and offer minor compensations to next of kin as reparation, allowing them to dissolve their lost loved one's *borrow* over a two year period. A small The "fix" had been like caulking a gash the size of a canyon with PlexiFill. Completely implausible. But people lived at the mercy of the oligarchs and banks. That's the way this world ran.

Which was why Mina was in the business she was in.

Someone had to stop it. Or at least give it a damn try.

Mina glanced at her wrist, tapping her cuff a few times. If they stood here much longer, Mina's schedule would be thrown. Taking a day off in the middle of a case was tricky, but there'd been no way to circumvent it. Residents in her last building had become alarmed when an armed criminal had kicked her door in. A tail she should've noticed, but hadn't. It'd been a complete rookie mistake, not to mention completely embarrassing. Mina had never lost control of the situation and the wretch was now rotting in a box, but because of it, she had to be here instead of doing her job.

What this mega-rep didn't know was that Mina had movers scheduled to arrive at her new unit within the next hour.

Suzanne noted the data check Mina had performed, and suggested, "Let's get going, shall we? Time to visit the upper floors." The rep turned on a blade thin heel, defying the laws of standard physics, and briskly clacked toward the nearest hub of levitation tubes, designed to zip the rider up to dizzying heights in a matter of minutes. The tubes ran on zero-fric magnets, same as the mag-lev trains, which crisscrossed the city beneath them.

As they made their way across the expansive lobby, Mina's trained eye raked over the interior. It was her first time getting a real, physical look at the scraper, instead of studying virtuals. The large water feature, located in the middle, routed pedestrian traffic and commerce efficiently around it. It was the size of a small lake, with not one, but two cascading waterfalls tumbling off clear polymer sheets, three stories high. Natural light streamed in from angled skylights trailing up the sides of the triangular base. Layered balconies jutted out at varying intervals, hinting at more to offer the shopper or resident just out of eyesight.

It was a busy, bustling mini-mecca with thousands of people scurrying to and fro. Just what Mina needed to keep a low profile and blend, especially if another perp came knocking, or kicking, as it were.

The floor beneath them gleamed white, marble infused with soft ribbons of gray, no doubt the real thing. Printing would've been considered basic, not luxury. Lush greenery, provided by a multitude of dense trees and flowery vines, spilled out of raised beds set at intervals to effectively mimic outdoor space. Specialty shops coalesced at pedestrian junctions, enclosed by glass walls, staffed with retail bots ready to serve your every whim with a smile and a pleasant offer of satisfaction. Food printing stations with crisp green awnings offered hard-to-find trace element options, like ginseng tea, oysters, and exotic nuts.

This scraper was the fifth to be built in the city, three more were currently underway, and housed twenty graduated stories of commerce, along with two-thousand eight-hundred and thirty-eight residential units, starting from its pyramid base and narrowing up to a two kilometer high spire. These kinds of buildings were originally called tower scrapers, because their shape resembled the famed Effiel. But they were so vast and fully integrated, the term mega had stuck.

"The Spire is a fully enclosed system," Suzanne offered over her shoulder. "Everything is ground and recycled by atomic weight to twenty-second century standards." She didn't so much as blink as she rattled off the rest. "Our Zine rating is a two. The lowest of any other building this size in the city. We have mingling stations, enhancement centers, integrated spas, large-scale 3-D shops specializing in expertly designed, custom printed items. We even have a real gemstone jeweler. She's the only licensed dealer in the entire city." She tapped a hyperglo nail to her earlobe, highlighting what appeared to be a real amethyst, producing a single blink. Her salary must be excellent to afford real stones. Gems were the epitome of luxury, something that hadn't changed one iota throughout history. "There are ten holotheaters, twelve VR domes, each containing seventy-five rooms, where you can relax and take a virtual vaycay or have an adventure of your choosing. You name it, The Spire has it. We're even lucky enough to employ two authenticated print-free restaurants with *actual* chefs." Her voice bubbled over with giddiness. A real meal would cost triple a printed one. The ultimate way to borrow. "It's such a treat to have real food after such a long era of print-on-the-go, don't you think?" She gave Mina a wink and dipped into a conspiratorial tone. "We even have an entire level devoted to pleasure. Those suites book out in advance, and come complete with sensory nodes, floor to ceiling wallscreens, and access to Plush if you have a prescription. Be sure to use your residential calendar to schedule those dates as soon as possible." When they finally reached the bank of tubes, Suzanne's custom poly-sling backs, likely printed from home, tapped to a stop as the pad of her finger lightly brushed over her superboard. "It says here you're preapproved for anything in the gold sector, which spans floors two hundred to three-twenty. I have seventeen units available in that sector. Are you interested in an integrated home health pod? It comes with a small monthly borrow, but overall it'll save you time and money. I have one, and adore it. Twelve units have personal soakers. Three have family-style holocams, so you can achieve that interactive time in the comfort of your own living room." Her eyes sparkled. She was clearly suited to her job of delivering happiness in the form of borrowed dreams to her clients. "All the units have premier shower rooms with two-person sprayers and dryers as standard."

Suzanne didn't have to keep her spiel going.

Mina knew which one was hers. "I'm actually interested in a specific unit. Three-twenty-eight," Mina said. "No need to see any others."

The rep didn't mask her surprise, her frosty purple-hued eyes narrowing as they fluttered back to her board. "Have you been here before? If you have, you're required to sign on with the same rep at all times. It protects all of our interests and saves time and repetition." Her finger worked double time. "Hmm...it doesn't look like you've been assigned to anyone else. Not under your legal debt name or your identity. That's odd."

Mina faked a good-natured chuckle as she swept her long brown hair, free of any sparkle, behind her shoulders. "This is my first time visiting, don't worry."

She couldn't admit to this rep that she had access to sealed sites. That in perusing the detailed virtual schematics of The Spire, it'd been a snap for Mina to make her decision. A corner unit with everything she needed, and then some. "I've been perusing your holosite. The realtime graphics are superb."

"The graphics are good," Suzanne agreed, "but nothing compared to seeing the units in person. Show me unit three-hundred and twenty-eight," Suzanne ordered her board. She'd been making good use of her fingers, but they must need a break. The hyperglo was already starting to lag. Talking to your tech was considered rude in professional settings, but Mina couldn't care less. Anything to make this process go faster. A moment later, a low, satisfied sound came from the back of Suzanne's throat. Her commission would be hefty, which changed everything. "Three-twenty-eight is an excellent choice. It's fully loaded, upgraded this week. It's one of the only units with floor to ceiling wallscreens in every room, surface charging throughout, state-of-the-art meal printer, and a new spacious platinum sleeper. This unit also comes with that home health pod we talked about"—Suzanne blinked rapidly, suddenly flustered—"but it states here that it's a X600." A hand snaked up her chest. "That's strange. As far as I know 600s are military grade. I've never seen one in a scraper before." She frowned, her cheeks unmoving, finger back to tapping over the board as quickly as she could. "Yes, it looks like this is the only one. It also has a soaker and several custom printers, which are speced larger than usual. Because of that, your monthly elemental utility borrow will be higher." Suzanne met Mina's gaze, nipping the edge of a dyed lip, flashing a blink of extra white. "And with the recent reno and upgrades it's not on our holosite yet, and it's actually over your preapproval range because of the X600. If you want it, I'll have to get upper-level permission." Then she surprised Mina with a chuckle and another wink. "But, who knows. After those three years of interest savings, maybe you can afford it after all."

"I'm sure it won't be a problem," Mina responded smoothly. "Contact your supervisor."

She knew it wouldn't be an issue.

After all, the upgrades had been designed especially for her.

This book is not up for pre-order. Sign-up for my Book Alert newsletter to receive the release info in your inbox so you don't miss a thing!

www.amandacarlson.com

NOTHING IS CREATED WITHOUT A GREAT TEAM.

My thanks to:

Awesome Cover design: Damonza.com

Digital and print formatting: Author E.M.S

Copyedits/proofs: Joyce Lamb

Final proof: Marlene Engel

ABOUT THE AUTHOR

Amanda Carlson is a graduate of the University of Minnesota, with a BA in both Speech and Hearing Science & Child Development. She went on to get an A.A.S in Sign Language Interpreting and worked as an interpreter until her first child was born. She's the author of the high octane Jessica McClain urban fantasy series published by Orbit, the Sin City Collectors paranormal romance series, the contemporary fantasy Phoebe Meadows series, and the futuristic/dystopian Holly Danger series. Look for these books in stores everywhere. She lives in Minneapolis with her husband and three kids.

Find her all over social media

Website: amandacarlson.com
Facebook: facebook.com/authoramandacarlson
Twitter: @amandaccarlson
Instagram: @author_amanda

CPSIA information can be obtained
at www.ICGtesting.com
Printed in the USA
LVHW111653190220
647495LV00005B/931